The Illuminated

Kingdom

The Voyages of the Legend, Book 4

By Alina Sayre

Other books in The Voyages of the Legend series:
Book 1: The Illuminator's Gift
Book 2: The Illuminator's Test
Book 3: The Illuminator Rising

The Illuminated Kingdom

Text copyright © 2017 by Alina Sayre

Cover design copyright 2017 by Jenny Zemanek at Seedlings Design Studio

Map created by Brian Garabrant

This is a work of fiction. Names, characters, places, and incidents are either the product of the author's imagination or are used fictitiously.

ISBN: 1979020442
ISBN 13: 978-1979020442

Praise for The Illuminated Kingdom

"...[an] astounding, imaginative world...a perfect combination of surreal imagery and realistic detail."

- *Readers' Favorite*

"*The Illuminated Kingdom* ends the story in a most satisfactory way...This is, simply put, a great adventure story...I could not put it down."

- Lloyd Russell, book reviewer at *The Book Sage*

Praise for the award-winning first novel
The Illuminator's Gift

"...magical...the book is a real page turner."

- *Readers' Favorite*, 5-star review

"...dramatic, steadily building adventures set in a vividly imagined world."

- The BookLife Prize in Fiction

"Sayre has brought us characters that are interesting and feel real. The writing is spot on. The reader will be brought into the story and care about what happens to Ellie and her friends."

-Writer's Digest Self-Published Book Awards

"I...was captivated by a world of coral archipelagos, airborne islands, and flying ships...Sayre paints an enchanting world with a deft brush and lovely prose."
- Rabia Gale, author of *The Sunless World* series

"...written with an imagination and poetic elegance reminiscent of C.S. Lewis's *Chronicles of Narnia* and Tolkien's *Lord of the Rings*."
- Angela Wallace, award-winning author of the *Elemental Magic* series

"I got blindsided.... I was cheering, crying, gasping, crying, shaking, and, you guessed it, crying. It's rare that a book does that to me.... Alina gets high marks for the 1st 2/3 and off-the-chart marks for the last 1/3."
- Lloyd Russell, book reviewer at *The Book Sage*

"[*The Illuminator's Gift*] is a fabulous read that had me turning the pages...I predict you'll soon be hearing a lot more about this talented author."
- A. R. Silverberry, award-winning author of *Wyndano's Cloak*

"A strong first novel...refreshing."
- *The Wooden Horse: Toys for Growing*

Dedication

For Nova

and for all the children who give me hope

that the Kingdom is coming

and it is already here.

Contents

The Known Map of Aletheia

The Numed Archipelago

Jura
Nakuru
Haffiu
Kwarlod
Kisumu
Markala
Kefindi
Rhincha
Ajmer

Arjun Mador

Arrhenius
Sikar
Oahye
Suor
Dhuma
Sukka
Suranga
Amalpura
Dhar
Rhynlyr

Newdonia

Anadyr
Mundarva
Freith
Twyrild
Bramborough
Gwafior

Syft

The Orkent Isles

Eglhwyr
Dwyren
Innish

The Ellarra Cluster

Damsuit
Horin

Chapter 1
Retaking Rhynlyr

Ellie shivered. A dusting of snow swirled in the freezing wind. Spring was just around the corner, but it still felt like winter on the flying island of Dhar. Ellie huddled deeper into her nautical coat, gazing at the distant shape of Rhynlyr.

Rhynlyr. Retaking the flying island had been the Vestigia Roi's only goal since the fleet had arrived here three months ago. The Council had spent every day planning a campaign to oust Draaken's evil Lagorite forces from the island, and Ellie was helping them with her Sight. In her official role as Ellianea Reid, Vestigian seer, she knew that Rhynlyr's recovery was supposed to be her first priority. Yet when she was alone, when she was just Ellie, she could admit there was something she wanted even more. Not a day passed when she didn't think of her twin brother Connor, who was still a prisoner in the Enemy's clutches—if he was even still alive. In the three months since Ellie's last vision of him, there had been only silence, and their fourteenth birthday had passed just a few days ago. Ellie's crewmates from the *Legend* had tried to help her celebrate, but she just couldn't muster any enthusiasm. The Council insisted that Ellie's visions were useful, but she was frustrated that she couldn't do more to help her brother. She'd be on a rescue ship to find him in a second—if she only knew where to start looking.

A heavy door opened behind Ellie, and a tall girl in nautical uniform joined her on the balcony. Meggie Radburne had once been a shallow and selfish councilman's daughter, but over the last few months she had proven herself to be not only a resourceful leader, but a good friend. She laid a hand on Ellie's arm.

"Ellie? The fleet commanders are ready to continue the meeting. Are you all right?"

Ellie glanced back at Rhynlyr. Fog now hid most of the island. "Just thinking."

Meggie's brown eyes were genuinely compassionate. "It's Connor, isn't it?"

Ellie nodded. She couldn't deny it. "I keep trying for a vision of him, but there's still nothing. I'd give anything to know he's all right."

"Of course you would." Meggie's father had been missing since the attack on Rhynlyr, so Ellie knew she understood. Although if Connor had been a traitor like Consul Radburne, Ellie wasn't sure if she'd miss him so much.

"As soon as you find out where he is, I'm sure the Council will send a rescue party," Meggie assured her. "But for now, the best way you can help Connor is to fight the Enemy. The Council needs your visions. Ready to go back inside?"

With a last glance over her shoulder at Rhynlyr, Ellie followed Meggie inside.

The Vestigian fortress of Vellir was almost as cold inside as it was outside. Ellie and Meggie walked down a solid stone passage burrowing straight into the side of Saklos Mountain. The vast underground base had been built to protect large numbers of Vestigians in times of emergency, and so far it had served its purpose. Well defended and well supplied, Vellir had resisted several attacks by the Enemy's small fleet of flying ships. But the underground refuge was as cheerless as it was safe. Ellie looked forward to the day when she could walk the open streets and lawns of Rhynlyr once more.

Meggie shoved open another door leading to a low stone room. Around a wooden table, the new councilmembers were resuming their seats. When the Vestigia Roi had arrived on Dhar, the previous acting councilmembers had voted to step down, making way for leaders with more military experience. It hadn't been too big of a sacrifice for most: Serle and Phylla were both older and glad of the chance to retire, while Meggie's prissy sister Katha had never really enjoyed governing anyway. Only Meggie, who had recently discovered her talent for leadership, had been truly disappointed to give up the Council. But all of them had agreed that Vestigian survival was the first priority. For herself, Ellie had been glad to leave behind the pressures of the Council. However, when the new members had asked her to return as their seer-advisor, she casually mentioned that Meggie was smart and had excellent handwriting, qualities which would make her an ideal Council recorder. So although Meggie could no longer participate in the debates, at least she still got to attend the meetings.

As she resumed her seat at the table, Ellie scanned the room. All in all, she liked the new councilmembers. Trull, the former vice admiral who'd led the Nakuru mission, was now fleet admiral and leader of the Council. He could be stubborn at times, but nothing could douse his bravery or zeal for the Vestigian cause. The other four members were fleet commanders representing each of Aletheia's archipelagos. Calida, a lean and muscular woman with a piercing gaze, represented Newdonia and specialized in airborne navigation and explosives. Omondi, representing the Numed Archipelago, had come recommended as an excellent climber and an expert in stealth and camouflage. Ahearn had been chieftain of the island of Innish in the Orkents, and he had tried to execute Ellie upon their first meeting. But now that he sailed under Ishua, he was using all his wiles and ferocity to give the Vestigians an advantage in battle. Finally, Ellie looked with fondness at Kai, who had once been her bodyguard and now represented his native archipelago of Arjun Mador. When he'd lost his eye in battle years ago, he'd been declared unfit for fleet service. But his heroics on the island of Nakuru had proven otherwise. Ellie wasn't a military strategist, but she had absolute faith in Kai's intelligence, bravery, and loyalty.

Besides the Council, there were two other people in the room. Ellie's friend Alyce, a gifted singer, had returned to help as Ellie's accompanist. Finally there was Lady Lilia, a winged Alirya of Ishua, who watched the Council with calm dark eyes and a long katana strapped to her back. She and her two brethren, Kiaran and Hoyan, were not permitted to interfere with Council decisions directly, but could offer advice stemming from their greater knowledge of Ishua. The three of them divided their labors: while one Alirya assisted the Council, the other two served as scouts and guards around the base.

Tomorrow had been set as the date of the first strike on Rhynlyr. After months of planning, nearly everything was ready, and the Vellir kitchens were already buzzing with preparations for a celebratory feast tonight. As the Council began to discuss the final details of the attack, Alyce started to sing softly from the Song. At the sound of the music, Ellie's vision made its familiar transformation. She watched auras of color form around each person in the room—blue, green, pink, yellow, lilac, beige, orange, red. Some of the hands resting on the table even had glass-clear fingertips. Lady Lilia was like a pillar of glass and gold. Ellie exhaled, relieved not to see any dark smudges, as she had on Consul Radburne so long ago. At least this Council didn't have to worry about treachery coming from within.

After a few minutes, the Council door cracked open again, admitting a little girl with a black falcon on her shoulder. Alyce's little sister Aimee wore a nautical uniform like all Council messengers and held a sealed envelope.

"Message, Your Honors," said Aimee.

"Thank you, Messenger," said Admiral Trull. Aimee dutifully handed over the envelope and stood waiting by the wall in case she needed to carry a reply. Her forehead puckered with concentration as she tried to do her job just right. Ellie smiled. From the outside, no one would know that this little messenger could also communicate with animals, a gift of Rua that the Council occasionally found very useful.

Admiral Trull broke the seal on the message and read it. His bushy brows contracted sharply.

"Messenger, send for Translator Sterlen, please. Then go ask the sentries for the current reading on Rhynlyr's altitude."

Aimee dashed out of the chamber, forgetting to bow on her way out.

"Our codebreakers have intercepted intelligence that the Lagorites plan to raise Rhynlyr far above its normal altitude," Trull said, tossing the message onto the table.

"Flying islands can move?" said Omondi, raising his eyebrows. His command of the Common Tongue had greatly improved during his time on Dhar.

"Yes, although they rarely do," said Trull. "If this message is true, it means that the Enemy's forces have not only located the Atrium—the control center housing the island's *lumenai*—but know its purpose. It would mean they can control Rhynlyr's motion."

"So if all flying islands can move, why don't we just sail Dhar over there and ram into those urken blighters?" said Ahearn, cracking his knuckles. "Seems simple."

"It's not, unfortunately," said Kai. "Motion drains islands' lumena power, and vertical motion carries the highest energy cost. A single drained lumena can require hours or days in a cool salt water bath to recharge, and most flying islands have at least half a dozen lumenai. If its power is drained too far without recharging, an island can forfeit its ability to move, or at worst, lose its lift and drop out of the sky entirely. That's why we don't move Dhar, and the urken wouldn't be moving Rhynlyr if they had any sense."

"Why are they doing it, then?" said Ahearn.

Kai shrugged. "A foolish display of force, perhaps. Maybe they're trying to frighten us into attacking before we're ready."

"Or to force us closer to the ground when we do," Calida frowned. "All lumena-powered devices have altitude limitations, and that includes flying ships. If Rhynlyr is elevated, we'll have to fly low over the island, exposing us to ground fire."

There was a knock on the door, and in stepped Vivian Sterlen, now using her linguistic skills to translate enemy messages. Though

Vivian stood to attention in her nautical uniform, Ellie noticed how tired she looked. With three-month-old baby Tal keeping her up at night and an important translating job during the day, Vivian didn't have much time for rest.

"You sent for me, Your Honors?"

"Yes." Admiral Trull held up the envelope. "We've just been informed of the Lagorites' plan to raise Rhynlyr. We need a full briefing from your department."

"Right. Early this morning, the Alirya Kiaran was running a scouting mission along with Aimee's falcon, Zira. The falcon brought down a flying enemy messenger—apparently some sort of bat—and delivered its paper cargo to Kiaran, who brought both the message and the bird back to us. The message was in the urken's language, but I was able to translate it. It described the plan to raise the island's altitude."

"And the—" Trull cleared his throat, still acclimating to the surprising gifts of Rua—"the falcon? Did it…say where the bat was headed?"

"Aimee did question it, yes. Zira said the bat was heading southeast."

"Toward Newdonia?" said Calida, frowning.

"Or toward the flying prison of Ilorin," said Kai, crossing his arms. "Doubtless the Vestigian traitors there are only too supportive of the Enemy's cause."

Another knock on the door brought in another uniformed Vestigian with Aimee trotting at his heels.

"Right. Watchman Keene, what is the current report on Rhynlyr's altitude?" Trull's piercing gaze made the watchman stand up straighter.

"Y—Your Honors, the island is—is *rising*. It's not quick, but it's steady. It's already gone up by several degrees."

Trull frowned. "Thank you, Watchman, Translator. You may both go."

Aimee followed them out the door, offering a tiny wave to Alyce and Ellie.

"So it's true, then," said Ahearn.

"We need to change our battle plan," said Calida, her expression tense. "We'll have to cancel tomorrow's attack and rework everything completely."

"Not completely," said Kai. "With some modifications, our plan can still go forward. Even if we're forced to fly low, our ships are still our biggest advantage. Soldier to soldier, the urken far outnumber us."

"What urken cannot see, they cannot shoot," suggested Omondi. "If we fly at night, darkness will protect us."

As the Council debated the idea of a night attack, Ellie watched the map of Rhynlyr. With Alyce singing softly in the background, tiny swirls of gold started to flicker around the island. Ellie knew that gold lines usually revealed the direction the One Kingdom was moving. Ellie pictured a microscope, and the vision magnified. She saw a gold arrow plunging toward the Inner City, the center of Vestigian civilization on Rhynlyr. Picking up a pencil, Ellie traced over the golden lines. The debate around the table quieted as all eyes focused on her sketch.

"The Inner City," said Trull. "It makes sense. Strike at the heart. Drop explosives from the air and break up the enemies' headquarters."

"Then work out from there to clean up the rest," agreed Ahearn.

From that point of agreement, the Council decided to go ahead with tomorrow's attack, but delay their departure until darkness offered them some cover. They worked to adjust their plans for timing, positions, and weaponry. Ellie offered one or two observations from her visions, but mostly sat silent until the Council finally adjourned. Ellie headed for the dining hall, feeling anything but ready for a celebration feast. Alyce fell into step beside her.

"Hungry?"

Ellie shrugged. "Not very."

"I know, these meetings can be so boring some days."

"It's not just that." Ellie pushed her hands into her pockets. "I just feel so…frustrated. Here I am sketching a line on a map once every few hours when I could be doing something actually useful."

"Like rescuing Connor?"

Ellie grimaced. "Is it that obvious?"

"Maybe not to everybody. But if Aimee were missing, I know I'd never stop thinking about her."

As if on cue, Aimee came down the hallway, dragging her feet slowly.

"Why so glum?" Alyce asked her little sister.

"I'm so…tired…" Aimee panted melodramatically. "So…much…running."

Alyce laughed, putting an arm around Aimee's shoulders. "You *have* done a lot of running for the Council today. I think it's time for a rest."

"Can Sunny sit with us at dinner, Liss?" Aimee begged.

"I don't know. You'll have to ask Owen."

"Yippee! Come on, let's go ask!" Aimee whooped, suddenly energetic again. She dragged Alyce down the hallway behind her.

Ellie watched the sisters, feeling a hollow place open up inside her. She'd give anything to run down these hallways with Connor or share dinner with him tonight. Yet she didn't even know if he was alive or dead. Feeling glum, Ellie continued on to the dining hall and scanned the huge room filled with long tables and benches. The cooks were setting up huge pots in a serving line along one wall. Ellie spotted Laralyn, the friend who'd helped deliver Vivian's baby, arranging a thick bundle of utensils. Among the tables, a comical group was trying to set up pinecone centerpieces. A gaggle of children too young to run errands, including Laralyn's daughter Gresha, kept dropping pinecones and trying to throw them at each other. In charge of this small army was Katha, carrying baby Tal. She was surprisingly calm amidst the chaos, instructing the children where to put the pinecones and redirecting them from their arguments. *She's good at this*, Ellie thought. At the orphanages where Ellie had lived, taking care of younger children had been one of her least favorite chores, yet Katha seemed to fill the role comfortably. And it was good to see Katha, no longer a councilmember or a councilmember's daughter, finding a useful purpose.

A few steps away from the group stood Hoyan, the red-winged Alirya, carrying a large basket of pinecones and looking uncomfortable.

His real purpose, Ellie knew, was to guard Tal. The baby's gift for healing coral made him the Vestigia Roi's treasure and hope, to be protected at all costs. But Hoyan's guard duties seemed to have thrown him into an unfortunate role as table decorator. The odd tableau was so funny that Ellie smiled in spite of herself.

"Well, look at that! A smile." Someone jostled Ellie's shoulder, and she looked up into a pair of friendly gray eyes. Finn had finally been issued a nautical uniform, and Ellie noticed how handsome her tall Innish friend looked in his sharp collar and leather boots. He carried his harp, Tangwystl, in the crook of one arm. Behind him, a wave of uniformed sailors began to pour into the dining hall, and Ellie and Finn stepped out of the way.

"Any visions of Connor today?" Finn asked hopefully.

Ellie shook her head, her expression clouding over. Finn's free hand fidgeted, and he stuck it in his pocket. "Sorry. I shouldn't have asked."

"It's all right. It means you haven't forgotten about him. I just wish I had something to report."

"We won't give up on Connor. In fact, I composed something about him today. I thought maybe it'd cheer you up. Want to hear it?"

Ellie shrugged. "Sure."

Finn shifted his harp and accompanied himself as he sang softly:

Connor Reid, the captain of the seas
None could match the prowess or the ease
With which he'd conquer enemies
His eyes bright, ready for a...

"Sneeze," sang a voice from Ellie's other side. Jariel, Ellie's best friend, slipped an arm around her waist.

"Well, it was going to be *breeze*," said Finn. "But I think I like *sneeze* better."

"Maybe I should switch from being a lookout and become a *shanachai* like you," Jariel teased. "Come on, let's go eat. Combat drills make me hungry."

The dining hall was buzzing with excitement as sailors anticipated tomorrow's attack. If all went well, they might finally be able to go home after months of exile. The room's décor matched the mood, between Katha's festive centerpieces and Ellie's large illumination of a volcano on the wall. Its hopeful message, RISE UP, still shone in flamelike golden letters. A band of musicians, organized by Meggie to represent all four archipelagos, played spirited tunes. Once most of the sailors were sitting down, Admiral Trull gave a short, morale-boosting speech. Several choir members, led by Alyce, sang from Canto Thirteen of the Song.

Normally all sailors over twelve years old sat with their crews at supper, but for tonight's celebration that custom was overlooked, and the sailors of the *Legend* gathered together at one table. Jariel had been stationed as lookout aboard Kai's ship, the *Defiance*, while Finn, native to the island of Innish, was posted aboard Commander Ahearn's ship. Owen soon arrived, rolling a metal ball around in his palm and trailed by his dog, Sunny. He set his tiny tortoise, Pinta, on the table while his bluestripe ribbon snake, Moby, curled up his arm. Since he was only ten, Owen would normally have been assigned to do chores or run messages with the younger kids. However, Commander Calida had found out that Owen had a knack for explosives and came from her home island, Twyrild. She'd taken Owen under her wing and had him assigned to her ship as ballistics support.

Deniev, Laralyn's husband and now Kai's chief gunner, joined the crew with his family. Gresha idolized Jariel and insisted on sitting next to her. Alyce and Aimee followed once the choir finished singing. Aimee gave Sunny a gleeful hug and scratch behind the ears, and he thumped his furry tail on the floor. They were joined by Vivian, Jude, and Tal, with Hoyan trailing not far behind. Tal, now three months old, smiled and gurgled when he saw the children. Jariel stretched out her arms for him.

"C'mere, Tal! Come to Auntie Jariel!"

Vivian handed the baby over, and the children competed to make him smile. Jariel made funny faces, and Finn strummed chords on his harp. Owen eventually won, though, handing the baby the apple-sized metal ball he held. It rattled when he shook it, and Tal cooed and waved his arms.

"Please tell me that's not dangerous," said Vivian as Owen put the rattle into the baby's hands.

"Not really. It's just bits of scrap metal inside a capsule I fused shut," Owen explained.

"Good, because now it's dinner. When this boy isn't supernaturally healing coral, he's putting everything he can reach into his mouth," Jude smiled as Tal began to suck on the rattle. Jude had been appointed surgeon of Omondi's ship. The two had become friends after Jude had saved the Nakuran prince from a dangerous illness. The position kept Jude busy, though, and it was obvious that he enjoyed every moment with his family.

"My turn." Ellie reached for Tal. Though Ellie had never enjoyed the screaming babies at the orphanages where she'd lived, Tal was special. When Vivian had almost died of the underground fever before Tal's birth, Ellie had been the one to argue for the cure that saved both their lives. Ellie had also been one of the first people to meet Tal after he was born. After a long day of frustrating meetings and worrying about Connor, Ellie found comfort in holding this tiny, trusting person.

Kai joined the crew at the table, followed by Korrina, captain of the *Venture*. Both had removed their nautical coats and were slick with sweat.

"What happened to you two?" Vivian asked.

"One more sparring practice," Kai grunted, practically diving into his bowl. "There won't be time tomorrow."

"Isn't the plan to attack from the air?" said Alyce.

"Yes, but sailors should always be prepared for hand-to-hand combat," said Kai. "I wanted to show Korrina a few last attacks."

"She already gives a pretty good black eye," Jariel winked at Korrina. The tale of how she'd punched Kai on Nakuru had long since become legendary.

Kai's ears reddened, and he focused on his dinner.

"So tomorrow's finally the day," said Finn. "I've never seen Rhynlyr before. What's it like?"

"Beautiful," said Alyce. "Or at least it was, before the urken attacked. There were green lawns and old buildings, wide-open squares and a sparkling river. But now that the Dome and the Kingdom Bridge and *stellaria* tree are gone, I have no idea what it looks like."

"The tree is a real loss," said Jude, taking Tal as Ellie handed him back. "It was ancient and beautiful. But once we retake Rhynlyr, buildings can be rebuilt and gardens replanted. Perhaps we can even transplant a stellaria sapling from one of the Havens, assuming any still survive. In any case, I'm sure the Vestigia Roi will make Rhynlyr a lovely place to live again."

"And I'm sure you'll be a part of that," Vivian said. "I can already see you picking out plants in your mind."

Jude patted Tal's back with a smile. "It's true. When Rhynlyr is won, I'd like to build us a little house with a back garden. Then I'd never ask for anything else in the world."

"As long as there was a library, of course," Vivian added.

"Of course," Jude agreed. "I've seen enough fighting to last me a lifetime. I'd like to settle down and let Tal grow up in peace."

"Strange that we fight in order to win peace," Kai reflected. "Keep thinking about that back garden tomorrow, Jude. It's important to remember why we're doing this."

"And stay safe," said Vivian, fixing Jude with a stern look.

"I'll be careful," Jude assured her. "If all goes as planned, we'll be in and out before they even know we're coming. Who knows? We could be moving back onto our island in just a few weeks."

Tal suddenly made a noise and spit up all over the shoulder of Jude's nautical coat.

"Oh no! Your uniform," said Vivian, trying to clean it with a napkin.

Jude glanced at the stain and smiled. "It's all right. It's a badge I'll wear with honor tomorrow."

"Speaking of which," said Kai, "we'd better get some sleep. Tomorrow's a big day."

Ellie yawned. It was absurd how tired one could get from sitting in meetings. ed pooled on the palette like a lake of blood. A drop of yellow splashed in, intense as the hot core of a bonfire. Swirled together, they created a brilliant orange like a sunrise at sea.

Chapter 2
Connor

C onnor was lying on the floor of an empty room. A giant black snake with yellow eyes loomed over him, its body as thick around as a tree trunk. Connor's face was bruised all over, and his eyes were sunken in purple shadows.

"I will asssk you once again, boy," the snake said in a voice as smooth and deadly as poisoned honey. "Where is your sssister? I wish to ssspeak with her."

Connor's expression was stony, his eyes focused on the far wall. "I've already told you. I don't know where she is. Even if I did, I wouldn't tell you."

The serpent struck Connor across the face with the tip of its tail. "Insssolence! I will get the answers I ssseek. But you will pay for your lack of cooperation."

Ellie had a vague awareness that she was dreaming. *At last! A dream of Connor!* She had to test whether it was true. In the dream she began to hum softly from the Song.

Ellie's vision shifted, and a haglike creature covered with scales appeared beside Draaken, holding a basin of water. *Nikira.* Ellie had seen Draaken's evil commander in her true form once before. Whatever Nikira's form, Ellie could never forgive her for leading the attack on Rhynlyr, trying to kill Vivian, or kidnapping Connor.

Now Nikira forced Connor up from the floor, his arms still tied behind his back. His knees buckled with weakness, but he did not cry out.

"Thisss is your last chance, boy," Draaken hissed. 'Tell me what I want to know, or I will enter your mind and force it from you."

Connor glanced at the water basin out of the corner of his eye, then looked back at Draaken with fierce, cold eyes. He opened his mouth, and as Draaken leaned in to hear his confession, Connor spat in the snake's face. Enraged, Nikira plunged Connor's head into the water, holding his face down while the rest of his body flailed. After some twenty seconds, she yanked him back out by the hair, just long enough for him to gasp in a breath, then pushed him down again.

To Ellie's dismay, her perspective suddenly shifted to a window in the torture chamber, then fled through it. Outside, she saw dingy buildings, a harbor, an open-air market. Her home island of Freith? What was that doing in her dreams tonight? Still singing, Ellie caught one more glimpse of Connor, his face red-purple as he came up for air. Suddenly she recognized the room Connor was in. The rough floorboards, the brick fireplace—it was the back room of the Sketpoole Home for Boys and Girls. Connor was being held at her old orphanage! The dream flashed away to a glimpse of Freith's island core. The coral was gray and shattered, the once-healthy branch severed from its tree. Ellie glimpsed Miss Sylvia's face, heard people screaming as the island drifted toward the Edge...

The dream was suddenly cut off by the clanging of the morning bell. Ellie's eyes snapped open. So Connor *was* alive, and he was on Freith! She'd even tested it with her vision, so she was sure it was true. But he was being tortured! She had to act quickly.

Ellie grabbed her sketchbook and quickly set down the images from her dream. When she finished, she scrutinized them carefully. Yes, this was certainly Miss Sylvia's orphanage. But if the island's coral was broken, what had happened to Sylvia, its Vestigian caretaker? Could her supply of *caris* powder have run out when the Rhynlyr tree was destroyed? In any case, there wasn't much time. Throwing on her uniform, Ellie bolted for the Council chamber. *Hold on, Connor. I'm coming for you.*

Admiral Trull was alone in the Council chamber, drawing up a final map of the battle plans.

"Admiral! Where are the others?" Ellie panted, too excited to bother with formalities.

"With their ships, preparing to set sail tonight," said the admiral, not looking up from his drawing pencil and compass. "I'd be going with them, if it were up to me. But they insist someone has to stay behind and coordinate."

"Because I had a dream last night," Ellie blurted out. "I found out Freith—my home island—is falling. And that's where my brother Connor is being held. They're...the Enemy is torturing him. We have to send a rescue mission right away. And I'd like to go with it. Please."

Trull set down his pencil and looked at her, his eyes piercing in his square face. "Slow down. You *dreamed* of a falling island and now you want to run off after it?"

Flushing, Ellie opened her sketchbook and pushed it toward him. "Sir, part of my gift is that I sometimes dream true dreams. If I test them by singing, I can be sure they're real. And I tested this one. I *know* Freith is falling. And I *know* my brother is on it. These are pictures of what I saw."

The admiral looked at the sketches. Though Ellie had drawn them in a hurry, she knew the details were too realistic to be invented.

"Well," he said after looking. "I know your gift gives you clear vision. If you're sure Freith is falling, then we must bring this before the Council."

"So you'll send a rescue mission?" Ellie asked hopefully.

"I will talk to the other commanders when they return, but yes, I do think we must send a ship. It is our duty as Vestigians."

Ellie's heart soared. "Can I go with the mission, then?"

Trull frowned. "Of course not! Don't you know how important you are to the Vestigia Roi? Your visions guide our strategy. And the Vestigians look to you as a symbol of Ishua's coming victory. There is no way you can go on a rescue mission, to Freith or anywhere else."

Tears stung Ellie's eyes. "But…sir. It's my brother. I've been watching for a sign of him for months. Shouldn't I be the one to go rescue him? Aren't I a Vestigian too?"

The admiral's craggy face softened slightly. "I understand, Ellie. I'd give my right arm to be sailing out to battle with the others now, doing something active to retake Rhynlyr. And I could, if I were an ordinary sailor. But because I am the admiral, the Vestigia Roi needs me to stay here and direct others. So it is with you. Sometimes our duty lies away from the main action. Don't worry—the rescue mission to Freith will be notified about your brother. I'm sure they will search for him after the mission's top priority of healing the coral is accomplished."

Ellie struggled to contain her emotions. *After the mission's top priority? What if they can't save the coral and the island falls? Who will rescue Connor then?* "But…but can't we at least wait until the other commanders are back to decide if I can go? Can I ask them for a general vote?"

The admiral shrugged. "You can ask. But they'll only repeat what I've said."

That's what you think, Ellie thought. Outwardly she said, "Thank you, sir. I'll go fetch Meggie and Alyce so we can help you today."

As she pulled the Council door shut behind her, Ellie's mind was whirring. Surely Kai would vote in her favor. He knew Connor and how much he meant to Ellie. And Lady Lilia—she was an Alirya advisor. She'd see that Ellie's knowledge of Freith would make her a valuable addition to the rescue mission. There were the three other councilmembers, true, but with the Alirya's support, it seemed likely that they'd take Ellie's side. She felt her steps growing lighter.

But—suppose the Council voted against her? Ellie stopped for a moment. She imagined a ship leaving for Freith, ready to repair the coral or rescue the islanders. She imagined herself standing in the ship hangar, waving as it took off, wondering if they'd find Connor. If they'd even look for him. *After the mission's top priority,* the admiral had said. Her heart burned. That wasn't good enough. Connor was top priority to her. Only she cared enough to make sure he was found, and only she knew exactly where he was. If he was to be saved, she *had* to be on that mission.

But what would happen if she went against the Council's orders? Would they shame her in public? Strip her of her role as Council advisor? She wouldn't care if she never had to sit through another meeting. But what if they threw her out of the Vestigia Roi entirely? All her friends belonged to the fleet. Even Connor did. Would she be cut off from them? Where would she go? What would become of her, alone and outcast?

Ellie walked slowly down the corridor, the fortress's chill seeping into her. But what would become of her if she did obey the

Council? What if she stayed in the fleet and lost Connor? If he went over the Edge or was tortured to death because he wasn't somebody's top priority, because Ellie wasn't there to rescue him—that thought was too much to bear. She would risk anything, *anything*, to bring him back safely. Even if she failed, at least she would have tried. It would be better than wondering forever, living with the guilt of knowing she could have saved him and didn't.

That settles it, she told herself quietly. *I'd like to have the Council's permission, but with or without it, I'm going on the mission. If they punish me, I'll bear it. I have to try to save Connor.*

Chapter 3
Night Attack

Kai felt a new vigor as he strode up and down the deck of the *Defiance*, quietly delivering orders to his crew. The Vestigian fleet had waited until full dark to leave the Dhar hangar, spilling out into the night like leaves on a gust, their lamps extinguished. In the two hours it would take for them to reach Rhynlyr, the plan was to raise their altitude gradually, conserving lumena power as much as possible. Battles could be unpredictable, and Kai liked to keep a range of options open. He had long since memorized the battle plans and now mentally reviewed them to make sure they were still sharp. The Vestigians planned to approach Rhynlyr from the northeast, avoiding the small enemy fleet docked in the harbor and sheltering behind the Melkyr mountain range. They would then split into a pincer movement, Kai and Omondi's divisions approaching the Inner City from the west and Calida and Ahearn's from the east. Lady Lilia traveled with Ahearn's division to watch for supernatural threats like *helkath*, which were invisible to humans. If all went well, the four commanders would be able to pick off the strongest urken fortifications from the air, then let down footsoldiers to secure the Inner City before the enemy fleet could swoop in.

Kai also stole one more glance at the dark smudge that was the *Venture*. Part of him was glad Korrina was in his half of the fleet. Though she had little formal training, she was fearless and her combat instincts were excellent. She was never more coolheaded than in the crush of battle. In that respect, Kai could relate. Fighting for a good cause had always brought him focus and peace, offering some relief from the troubled memories of his past. But though he enjoyed his sparring sessions with Korrina and was glad to have such a capable warrior at his back, Kai also felt less peaceful when he was fighting beside her. She reminded him of someone whose memory still whispered in the night's quiet hours. Could the past repeat itself? He hoped not.

After nearly two hours, Jariel gave a soft *land ho* from the lookout's post.

"Stations," Kai commanded quietly. As usual, he carried his twin crossbows and a pair of knives, but he was not planning on using them tonight. Tonight would be about air maneuvering and ballistics, which was why he was glad to see Deniev watchfully checking on the gunners and their equipment.

Rhynlyr was indeed flying very high, and the ships could not get enough altitude to fly over the Melkyr Mountains. Kai knew the range well, though, and led the way between the loosely spaced peaks. From there, he altered the *Defiance*'s course to approach the Inner City from the west.

Leaning over the side of the ship, Kai glowered at the damage the Enemy had done to Rhynlyr. Even in the dark, the destruction of the Dome and the Kingdom Bridge was painfully obvious. The urken had also thrown up ugly fortifications in the Inner City, cannibalizing building materials from what had once been trim shops and houses. Blackened craters scarred the streets, and even outside the city walls, green fields had been dug up to make way for garbage pits and trenches. As the *Defiance* flew low over the city, a stench of urken filth and rotting waste rose from the ruined city. Kai carefully guided the ship's helm, fury focusing him even more on the task at hand.

"Deniev," he instructed. "My map says there's a battery of cannons near the river. I'll steer for it, then give the firing order when it's in range."

"Aye, Commander," said Deniev. "We'll be ready."

The Vestigian fleet sailed silently into position. The sleeping city lay dark and quiet. That is, until the Vestigians' first round of explosives dropped.

From all four quarters of the city, bursts of fire went up, followed by rolls of thunder. The surprised urken screamed and wailed, and their reckless return shots went wide. Kai steered south, spotting the glint of cannons as he flew low over the river.

"Now, Deniev! Fire!"

The *Defiance*'s guns boomed. Plumes of earth and water shot up from the pummeled ground. Suddenly a huge spout of flame pierced the air, so high that Kai felt the heat on his face.

"Powder magazine!" he cried. "Well done, gunners!" The cannoneers let out a cheer.

Swiftly, Kai banked the ship to port, leaving the destroyed battery behind them. Time to locate the next target.

Across the city, he could see the other fleet divisions having equal success. Omondi's ships had struck a target near the old Council Row. From across the river, near Main Hall of the Academy, a billow of blue and green smoke went up. That had to be Calida, with a little help from Owen.

Suddenly a flash of light appeared beneath the *Defiance*. The enemy cannonball nearly missed the side of the ship, just clipping one of the wing sails. Kai sharply twisted the helm away from the surprise nest of cannons, shouting orders to his crew to trim the sails. When he looked down again, he saw a huge battery, at least twice as large as the one they'd just destroyed. Recovered from their shock, urken were forming squads and preparing the cannons for systematic firing.

"We'll see about that," Kai muttered. "Deniev! Ready the guns!"

Kai was wheeling for another round of fire when he realized his mistake. They were near the center of the city, southeast of the old Dome. Below them, surrounded by urken cannons, was a large warehouse. The firing order died on Kai's lips.

Not many people knew the exact location of the Atrium, the flying island's heart, but Kai had been an elite guard for the Council for many years. He had visited the underground bunker that housed Rhynlyr's lumenai, and he knew under which unmarked warehouse it stood. The site was remote enough that it had escaped the Lagorite attack on the Dome, and the bunker was sturdy enough to resist scattered overhead fire. But with enough targeted explosives, even the reinforced structure could not stand for long. If Kai had fired, he could have unwittingly brought down Rhynlyr. Which, he realized, was exactly why the urken had set up their biggest battery there. They were using the Atrium as a shield. They could fire on the low-flying Vestigian ships without fear of being shot at in return. Even as Kai had this thought, one of the ships in his division was struck by cannonball. The ship burst into flames as its lumena exploded, and it plunged down into the river with a jet of steam.

Clenching his teeth, Kai wheeled the *Defiance* around yet again. "Hold your fire!" he shouted. "They have the Atrium surrounded!"

Kai's mind raced. They could not take the Inner City by air, not while the urken held the Atrium hostage. They would need to approach that battery by land if they were to have any chance. Only then could they take out the cannons without risking the island's lumenai.

"Run up a flag signal," he called to Jariel. "Signal the others to regroup!"

Jariel scrambled to obey. Kai scanned the horizon for responding flag signals and found them. The other quarters of the fleet were pulling together over the city center. Perhaps they could still capture the city tonight.

Then Kai tensed. From the edges of the city, more ships were approaching. As they drew closer, he could see their crews. Urken, captained by taller leaders cloaked in black. The ships were coming at them in a pincer formation, perfectly positioned to broadside the boxed-in Vestigians.

"Prepare cannons!" Kai shouted. But the enemy guns were ready first. Splinters of wood filled the air like rain, and many Vestigian ships caught fire. Packed close together, some of the captains panicked. Trying to steer their ships clear, they ended up ramming one another, causing even more damage. Chaos reigned. Kai tried to keep a cool head.

"Fire!" he shouted. Deniev's gunners broadsided the nearest urken ship. A pair of cannonballs linked by a chain hit the mainmast with a sharp *crack*. A few moments later, the huge wooden pole teetered, then crashed down across the deck. The crippled ship listed steeply to starboard, threatening to tip its urken crew over the side. The crew of the *Defiance* cheered.

Kai did not cheer. Instead, he rapidly took in the situation. One good broadside was not enough to stop the losing tide of this battle. The fleet was herded into a corner. The enemies might have fewer ships, but they held all the advantages of positioning. Much as Kai hated to admit it, it was time to get out and rethink a strategy for another day.

"Retreat!" he shouted. Jariel dutifully ran up the red pennant. The Vestigians began to flee north, away from the Inner City. The urken gave chase, firing easily at the unprotected rudders of the retreating Vestigian ships. Several took bad hits, and a few crashed, flaming, to the island surface. Kai gritted his teeth. They needed a distraction to get them away safely. Perhaps if he could just pull away from the other ships, lead them off...

Suddenly, from the other side of the fleet, a streak of green lightning split the sky. Blazing in the night, Lady Lilia took to the air, her drawn katana funneling crackling electricity toward the enemy ships. The black-cloaked commanders on the enemy ships drew their own weapons. Lilia landed on an enemy ship and engaged one in combat, her body moving with superhuman speed and balance. Other enemy ships drew near, their commanders swinging across on ropes to join the fray.

"Retreat!" Kai repeated, seeing the opening. "Lilia is giving us a chance to escape. She can fly. She'll rejoin us later."

Seizing their opportunity, the Vestigian ships turned and fled. A few of the urken ships tried to follow, but now their leadership was distracted and their formation broken. The battered Vestigian fleet limped away, disappearing into the night.

*

"We were ambushed," Kai growled to the Council.

Ellie sat with the fleet commanders as they made their report to Admiral Trull. The Vestigian ships had returned to Dhar at dawn, and the commanders had called an emergency meeting while their sailors received rest and medical treatment. Meggie sleepily took notes and Alyce sat ready in case she was needed to sing. Ellie was anxious for a chance to ask about the rescue mission, but held her tongue as she noticed the signs of the commanders' struggle. All of them smelled of old sweat and gunpowder, and their nautical coats were stained with soot and in some places, blood.

"When we found out they had the Atrium hostage, we couldn't fire on the battery there without risking the entire island," Kai continued. "We tried to regroup and send in a land force, but the enemy fleet trapped us. We lost a lot of good ships and sailors."

"The enemy ships were crewed by urken but captained by Valsha," Lilia added, checking the long gash on her upper arm. Amazingly, it had already closed and was beginning to heal.

Ellie timidly raised her hand. "What's a Valsha?"

Lilia looked disgusted. "They are the Faithless Ones, the Enemy's captains and most powerful servants. They are not invincible, but their senior officers match Alirya in strength—for they were Alirya once, before they turned from Adona Roi to serve Draaken. You have seen one—the creature Nikira who led the attack on Rhynlyr."

Ellie felt a shudder pass over her.

37

"We'll need an entirely new strategy if we're to capture the Atrium," said Calida. "A way to get our footsoldiers in there without attracting the enemy fleet's notice."

"Yes," Trull agreed, his face grave. "We can begin designing a new strategy tomorrow. For today, though, see to your divisions. We need to take stock of our losses in sailors and equipment. And keep the troops' morale up. Though it's disheartening to lose a battle, remind them we haven't lost the war."

The commanders were starting to get up to leave when Ellie cleared her throat. "Um, Admiral Trull, sir? May I present my motion?"

"I'd almost forgotten. Go ahead, Ellie."

Nervously, Ellie described her dream of Freith and Connor. She emphasized the island's danger and the clarity of the dream vision. "So I recommend that we send an immediate rescue mission to Freith," she concluded.

The commanders looked at each other.

"It seems necessary," Calida said. "We are Vestigians, and it is our duty to send rescue."

"With caris powder as scarce as it is and communications with the Havens blocked, we must send the child Tal to heal the coral," said Kai. "It is a risk, of course, but we have little choice."

"With an Alirya bodyguard, he will be nearly as safe on Freith as here," observed Trull. "But what captain can be spared from the Rhynlyr attack to lead the mission?"

"The child's father," said Omondi calmly. "Jude has been a captain before. I will miss him on my ship, but he will be a bad doctor if he is only worried about his son from morning until night. Send him."

"It *would* save us having to spare a captain from our divisions," admitted Ahearn. "But what ship would he take?"

Kai smiled, but there was little humor in the expression. "The *Legend*, of course. It's too small for combat duty, and it's in good repair. Connor's not here to captain it, but Jude knows the ship well. And if you're all willing to spare a sailor or two, I know just the crew to send with him."

"Very well. Any objections?" Trull asked. In the silence that followed, Ellie mustered her courage.

"Um...Your Honors, I'd like to ask one more thing. Since...since this mission involves my brother, I'd like to ask...for permission to accompany the rescue mission."

Some of the councilmembers looked at each other. "You? Why? What could you do?" said Ahearn.

Ellie flushed. "Connor's my brother. I know where he is. I've also worked with this crew before. I'm sure my knowledge of the island would save the mission time. Please let me go."

Ahearn coughed into his hand. Omondi looked at her with confusion.

"No," Calida said sternly. "You are too valuable a resource to the Vestigia Roi for us to let you risk yourself in this way."

Ellie looked pleadingly at the Alirya advisor. "Lady Lilia? Wouldn't Ishua want me to help people on a falling island?"

Lilia's eyes held kindness and pity. "I think he would applaud your heart for rescue, Ellie," she said softly, "but not all tasks are for all people. I may not make decisions for the Council, but I encourage you to see all the good you may accomplish here."

Desperation rising, Ellie turned to Kai. Maybe he could turn the tables for her.

"Kai? You know I've always been part of the *Legend*'s crew. You know why rescuing Connor matters so much to me. If it were someone you loved in danger…"

Kai banged his fist on the table, his face red with suppressed anger. Ellie jumped.

"No!" he shouted, his voice rough with emotion and weariness. "Absolutely not. Others will execute this mission and do it well. It's foolish and selfish of you to even think of risking yourself in this unnecessary way. Your place is here."

"But…" Ellie felt tears prick her eyes.

"No. I forbid you to go. That is final."

Ellie pressed her lips together, trying to hold back the tears. She bowed and left the room quickly. She heard Alyce's voice calling after her, but she walked off down the cold hallway.

So they were all against her, then. Did it really matter? No. She had already made up her mind. She hadn't expected such a betrayal from Kai, though. Of all the councilmembers, she'd thought he really cared about her, that he'd understand her need to go after her brother. Well. If her former bodyguard thought he could *forbid* her to go, he was in for a surprise. One way or another, she was going to rescue Connor.

Chapter 4
Stowaway

Inside the dark hold of the *Legend*, Ellie hid behind a huge coil of rope. She set down her bundle beside her, feeling the lumpy shapes of her sketchbook and slingshot along with her spare clothes. Leaning against the rope, she closed her eyes, feeling pleased with herself. If the Council had really wanted to keep her from going on the Freith mission, they shouldn't have chosen a ship she knew so well. She'd simply waited until suppertime, when most of the Vestigians were in the dining hall, then snuck through the shadows to the *Legend's* gangplank, triggered the hidden latch on the weather deck, and found her way past the Oratory, the dining hall, and the library to the dark and silent hold of the ship. The crew would be setting sail later tonight. Ellie had thought about openly begging them to take her with them, but however much they sympathized with her, she knew they wouldn't disobey the Council's direct orders. She would just make herself comfortable and wait until the ship was too far out to turn back. Then, like it or not, they'd have to take her along. In the quiet darkness, Ellie drifted off to sleep.

The next thing she knew, the *Legend* was pitching and rocking, adrift on open air currents. The hold was still totally dark, but Ellie could hear the distant voices of her crewmates as they worked to keep the ship on course. Then bootsteps sounded on the stairs, and light appeared in the hold. Ellie held her breath. She wasn't sure how far out they were yet. The crew couldn't find her until it was too late to take her back.

"Ellie?" a familiar voice whispered.

Ellie blinked. *Jariel?* No one was supposed to know she was here. Were they looking for her on the Council's behalf?

"Ellie, it's me."

Ellie heard a few heavy items scoot across the floor. Then a face appeared directly over her, illuminated by a single candle. Ellie looked up at her best friend, speechless with something between shock and fear. Jariel grinned.

"Relax, you ninny. I haven't come to turn you in, if that's what you're afraid of." Jariel set down the candlestick and clambered over the heap of rope to sit beside Ellie.

"How far are we from Dhar?" Ellie whispered breathlessly.

"About twelve hours. Too late to turn back now."

Ellie exhaled. "How…how did you know I was here?"

Jariel gave her a look. "Where else would you be? Obviously you were going after Connor, and nothing in the sea or sky was going to stop you. When Alyce told me we were going to Freith and you weren't, I knew that just meant you'd be coming without permission. Plus the latch on deck wasn't quite shut. I came down here to check on you just after we set off, but you were asleep. Snoring, actually."

"And you didn't say anything?"

Jariel snorted. "What do you think I am? You're my best friend, and Connor's my shipmate. I want him found too."

Ellie leaned her head back. "So the others don't know yet?"

Jariel shook her head. "Not that I know of. Sunny's been sniffing around, so Owen might suspect, but no one's said anything. It's probably time you said hello, though."

Ellie took a deep breath and stood up, her stiff muscles complaining. "I suppose you're right. This should be interesting."

*

Vivian sat on one of the dormitory bunks, a curtain dimming the midday sun. She'd just finished feeding Tal, and now the baby was asleep in her arms, his body warm and limp as he nestled against her. She drank in the sight of him: his tiny eyelashes, the soft sheen of fuzz on his head, his mouth puckering as he dreamed. They were on their way to his first real rescue mission, and emotions washed over Vivian in quick succession. She knew and appreciated that her baby just might be Ishua's salvation for the islands. But she also felt suddenly, keenly, the tragedy of having a son with the gift of healing broken coral: someday she was going to have to let him use it. She just hadn't expected that day to come so soon. For this moment, though, he was just her precious baby boy, perfect in every way. She just wanted to hold him like this a while, imagine she could keep him safe forever.

Vivian startled as she noticed someone standing in the doorway. Jude was leaning against the doorpost, a particularly soft look in his eyes. Vivian loved the way Jude looked at his son, at her. She hoped Tal's eyes would turn out to be like Jude's.

"How long have you been there?" Vivian whispered, shifting Tal to her other arm as he squirmed in his sleep.

"Long enough," said Jude, coming to sit beside them. He kissed Vivian's hair and stroked Tal's curled fist with the back of one finger. "I want to memorize this sight. Tal is growing so fast. I don't want to miss a moment."

Vivian felt sudden tears start in her eyes, her heart swelling until it hurt. She would do anything to keep these two safe, to keep their family together even in these uncertain times. "I love you," she whispered.

"I love you too," Jude whispered back, smiling.

A knock on the door made them both look up. Tal woke at the sound and started whimpering. Vivian shifted him again as Alyce poked her head into the dormitory.

"Um...can you both come to the dining hall? I think you should see this."

Vivian followed Jude out to the *Legend*'s dining hall, where their crew sat around the table: Tal's winged bodyguard Hoyan, Alyce, Aimee, Owen, Finn, Jariel...and Ellie. Vivian's eyes widened. The children all looked solemn.

"Would someone like to explain what's going on?" Jude said after a moment of silence. His expression was controlled, but Vivian noticed the tight lines beside his eyes and mouth.

"I, um, found Ellie in the hold," Jariel blurted out.

"Can she stay, Captain?" said Finn. "It's nice to have her back on the crew."

"That is not the point," said Jude. He looked at Ellie, crossing his arms. The two had always been close, but Ellie had been expressly forbidden to come on this mission. And yet here she was.

Ellie cleared her throat, avoiding Jude's steady gaze. "I'm...um, I'm from Freith," she started unsteadily.

"Yes, we know that," Jude said. "The question is, why are you here when the Council gave you clear instructions to stay on Dhar?"

Ellie looked up, her usually mild blue eyes flashing. "Because Connor is on Freith," she said, now speaking clearly. "The Council must have told you about my dream. They agreed to send a rescue mission, but wouldn't promise to look for Connor. I can't let that happen. I *saw* where Connor is being held. Jariel knows the orphanage, but I know the city of Sketpoole. I can help you with the rescue mission, if you'll accept it. But one way or another, I'm coming with you."

Aimee squirmed at this declaration of defiance. Finn tried to suppress a spreading grin.

Jude ran a hand over his hair. "Ellie, this isn't a wise plan. Not only are you putting yourself in danger, but the rest of us could also face discipline from the Council when we get back. Not that we have any choice now. If Freith is falling, we don't have time to turn around and take you back. But know that when we return, we'll have no choice but to submit to the consequences—all of us."

Ellie bowed her head. "I know. And I'm very sorry to involve you all. When we get back, I promise I'll tell the Council that you didn't know I was here until it was too late. I don't mind whatever punishment they give me, as long as I can bring Connor back safe and sound."

Vivian couldn't agree with Ellie's methods, but she was impressed by Ellie's newfound courage and resolution. When they'd first met, the girl had been so shy and timid she could barely speak to a stranger without stammering. Now she was deliberately putting herself in the way of danger and punishment to save her brother. Love had made her a warrior.

"Well," said Vivian, "since everyone's mind is made up and we can't turn back, it seems the only thing left to do is make a plan for our mission. Ellie, perhaps you should start by describing your dream in detail."

Chapter 5
Ghosts

Kai sat down with the Council at dawn to begin work on a new battle strategy. A few days ago, their meetings had been buoyant and hopeful, full of anticipation that Rhynlyr would soon be reclaimed. Now, after yesterday's rout, they couldn't shake the gloom hanging over their heads. Besides, they had already been working for half an hour and Ellie hadn't shown up. Where was the girl? It wasn't like her to be late. Had she given up hope entirely?

As if thinking the same thing, Trull addressed the young messenger boy standing in the corner of the room.

"Messenger, please go see if Seer Reid is in her room. She's needed here immediately."

The boy darted out the door. Trull rolled his neck. "Of all the days to be late. We could use a seer's help right about now."

The Council room did seem different without Ellie's quiet presence. Kai fondly remembered watching her early lessons on Rhynlyr as she learned to harness the power of the great gift she'd been given. He'd started the bodyguard work for Ellie because the Council had ordered him to. But Ellie had worked her way into his heart until protecting her was a matter of care as much as of duty.

The messenger boy returned a few minutes later, looking confused. "She's not in her room, Your Honor."

Trull frowned. Meggie, fidgeting with her writing set, spoke up. "I know Ellie's habits pretty well, sir. May I have a look around for her?"

"Please," grumbled Trull as Meggie left.

"An absent seer. Just what we needed today," Ahearn agreed.

"We can start on the plans anyway," said Calida. "She can always check them later."

The commanders talked carefully through the various points of a land mission to capture the Inner City. The obstacles were obvious, which was why the plan hadn't been anyone's first choice. First off, the Vestigians would be sacrificing the advantage of their ships. Soldier to soldier, the urken forces greatly outnumbered them. There were also terrain difficulties to navigate, such as the large wall around the Inner City and any surviving nests of cannons between the wall and the heavily armed Atrium. However, Ahearn and Omondi were eager to try the land attack. With the least flying experience of all the commanders, the two of them couldn't wait to shift to their strengths.

The morning wore away, and it was nearly noon when Meggie returned to the chamber, a bewildered look on her face.

"Well? Where is she?" said Trull.

"That's just it," Meggie said slowly. "I...I can't find her."

"Where did you look?"

"Everywhere. I checked all the usual places—her room, the dining hall, the balcony where she tries for visions of Connor—plus every other place I could think of."

Kai had the feeling of standing aboard a ship that was rapidly losing altitude. Yesterday he'd reacted to Ellie's request in anger. He realized now that those feelings hadn't just come from her strategic foolishness—he'd been afraid for Ellie, afraid to let her go on a dangerous mission where he couldn't protect her. And because of his reaction, she'd done exactly what he feared. "I think I know where she is," he said slowly.

"Well, by all means keep it to yourself," said Calida sarcastically.

"She's aboard the *Legend*, headed for Freith."

"Impossible," said Trull. "We forbade her to go. She wouldn't disobey the highest level of Vestigian authority."

"Not unless her brother's life were at stake." Kai rubbed the bridge of his nose. "I know her. I should have seen this coming."

"What should we do?" said Omondi. "We need the seer's visions."

Kai sighed heavily. "Only one thing to do. I'll go after her. It's my fault. I drove her to this. I should be the one to bring her back." He started to get up from the table.

"No," said Trull sharply. "If Ellie is gone, it is a blow. We could have used her visions, and she will have to face discipline for her disobedience when she returns. But it is too late to go after her now. The *Legend* is nearly a day out, and we cannot spare you, or any other captain, to chase after it. We will have to do without Ellie's visions for the time being."

"But, sir—" Kai gripped the edge of the table hard. "She may be sailing into danger. The crew may not even know she's aboard. I have to go after her."

Trull shook his head. "Commander, I know you were once Ellie's bodyguard. But that is not your position anymore. Your duty is here, leading your troops to Rhynlyr. The Vestigia Roi is more important than any one of us."

Kai stood still, clenching his jaw so hard it hurt.

"Do you understand, Commander?"

Kai took a deep breath. He hated this, hated sitting here and discussing strategy while Ellie might be heading into danger. But little as he liked it, he knew Trull was right. Every leader was needed for the Rhynlyr battle. There was nothing he could do now but hope to Ishua that the other crewmembers would watch over Ellie and bring her back safely.

"I understand, Admiral." Kai sat stiffly back down.

By the end of the day, the commanders had assembled a new strategy. It was much more complex and dangerous than the initial air attack had been, but there was no other way to take the Inner City without risking the Atrium. They planned to strike in three days to let the Vestigian sailors recuperate from their injuries and put the enemies off guard.

Tired but restless, Kai headed for the practice yard. An open area had been set aside in the enormous ship hangar and stocked with a variety of practice weapons. A few sailors were already there, doing target practice at the archery range or sparring with staves or blunt swords. Kai shrugged out of his nautical coat and picked up a pair of practice knives, stretching his tense muscles.

Breathing deeply, Kai began to move through the forms of knife work that he'd first learned at the Academy. Before that, he'd started his military career as a street rebel on the Arjun island of Sikar. He'd been a young man looking for a cause, and the island's cruel and repressive governor had given one. Kai had joined a gang of other revolutionaries and begun his first fight for justice. They'd been young and idealistic, and they'd believed in their cause and their fellowship. But looking back, Kai regretted the methods he'd agreed to use. They'd terrorized government officials at home, wearing masks and throwing homemade explosives. It was that uncontrolled violence that had led to…everything else. All the loss that could have been prevented. When he worked with the knives, his mind in full control of his body, Kai felt that he was somehow atoning for that reckless past. Now, as a Vestigian, he knew exactly how to break an arm or strike a target if he had to, but he was no bonfire blazing out of control. He was a wind blowing through a narrow tunnel, a river regulated by a dam.

His practice knife struck something solid. Kai lost his balance and snapped out of his thoughts. Korrina stood there, blocking his weapon with a practice javelin. She wore that expression he knew so well, her eyes tough and hard, but a smile tugging at the corners of her lips.

"Spar?"

Kai wordlessly took a step back, adjusting his stance to work with an opponent. Korrina did the same. Kai evaluated her posture, looking for weaknesses. She'd come to the Vestigia Roi untrained, but she was a quick learner who wasn't afraid to take a beating. Kai had taken to working with her over the weeks and months, and her natural abilities had flourished so quickly that he could no longer afford to go easy on her. Their styles were very different—he preferred to moderate his energy, using an opponent's force against them, while Korrina tended to attack in a head-on rush that overwhelmed all opposition. But the very difference of their approaches had helped them both improve. As he faced Korrina now, Kai warned himself to be ready for anything.

Korrina made the first move. She darted forward, trying to use the longer reach of her weapon to get inside his defenses. Kai quickly blocked with one of his knives, twisting his body to make himself a smaller target. He made a lunge, keeping his knees bent to improve his balance and reach. Korrina quickly sidestepped around him, then grabbed her javelin pole in both hands and shoved Kai across his shoulders. Kai had been prepared for resistance from the side but not the front. He staggered backward a step, momentarily dropping his guard, and Korrina lunged in with the point of her javelin. Kai quickly rebalanced and spun out of the way on his back foot. Korrina's lunge overbalanced, and he smoothly grabbed her ankle and flipped her to the ground.

In another second she was up again. With a powerful leap, she jumped up and planted both feet on Kai's chest, kicking him backward. Now Kai was the one on the ground. He rolled to the side, narrowly avoiding the javelin point, and dove again for Korrina's feet. But this time she was ready, jumping out of the way. Pressing her advantage, she stabbed again and again with the javelin.

Have to get up, Kai thought. With a grunt, he rolled forward, jumping back to his feet. He spun, then slashed out with one of his knives. But Korrina's javelin was already there. The forceful parry sent the knife spinning out of Kai's hand. Grimacing, he adjusted to one weapon and lunged again. Korrina fell back step by step, and he advanced. Then, without warning, she blocked the knife and in the same movement struck Kai's arm hard with the pole of the javelin. With his arm momentarily numbed, Kai's next lunge was a fraction slower.

Korrina did not miss this fact. Sidestepping his arm, she pushed her javelin inside his defenses—and right up to Kai's throat.

Kai dropped his knife and raised his hands in surrender. "Good match."

Korrina lowered her javelin and smiled. "I am getting better, no?"

"Much better. I was fighting for my life. There's not much more I can teach you."

Korrina grinned with pleasure, sweat beading on her face and neck. There was a jug of water at the edge of the practice yard, and they both dropped down on a bench for a drink.

"You are worried about your friends," Korrina observed after a moment of silence.

"Is it that obvious?" Kai rubbed his face on his sleeve. "I found out this morning that Ellie stowed away aboard the *Legend*. I asked to go after her, but the admiral said I'm needed here." He sighed, pushing back his damp hair. "He's right, of course. It's just hard to know she might be in danger when there's nothing I can do about it. Ellie's safety was my responsibility for so long, and now I can't protect her at all."

Korrina nodded, tapping the end of her practice javelin against the floor. "That was how it was on Janaki, when the flying death came. Makundo, his wife and two children—they were like my family. I was alone before them. They gave me a home, I helped on their farm. And then the *mapepo*, the demon spawn..." Korrina's face grew hard, fierce. "Everything I loved, taken from me in one day. And nothing I could do."

"Except fight," said Kai.

Korrina nodded. "Except fight. That was why the Janakim began to sail—to make the demon spawn pay for what they did. Now Makundo is gone, but I still fight."

"Is it enough?" Kai asked, half to himself.

Korrina shrugged. "Sometimes. Sometimes when I fight, I can forget, at least for a while. But it does not help the dreams at night."

"And it can't bring back the dead," Kai murmured.

Korrina shook her head. "No. It can't." Her fingers twitched, and she loosened the band in her dark, curly hair, shaking it free. "Did you lose someone too?"

Kai looked across the practice yard at the handful of sparring sailors. "Yes. Many."

"Someone you loved?"

Kai felt a tweak inside, the pain of an old wound. "Yes." He looked up at Korrina, saw something gentler in her eyes—was it curiosity, compassion? She looked nothing like the girl he'd known long ago, when he was young and full of revolutionary ideals. But something about her expression reminded him of Tassa. She had the same warrior spirit, too. Kai pulled back sharply.

"No, fighting can't bring back the dead." He stood up, stiffly extending his hand to Korrina. "Good match."

Chapter 6
Rescue Mission

Four nights later, Ellie stood with Jariel at the railing of the *Legend* as the lights of Freith appeared in the distance.

"Freith," mused Jariel, twisting the end of her ponytail. "Can you believe we were right here a little more than a year ago? We've seen so much since then! Battles, falling islands, the Vestigia Roi rallying for war…"

"And we thought we were just transferring to a new school," Ellie sighed, leaning her chin on her hand. "I wasn't even sure then if the Rhynlyr Academy was a real place, or if it was just one of Miss Sylvia's stories." She looked over at Jariel. "I barely even knew you then. That's hard to believe."

"You didn't know you had a brother, either. Or your Sight."

"True," said Ellie. "You were my first friend at the orphanage—maybe the first real friend I ever had."

Jariel hugged Ellie. "And now look at us. Friends everywhere."

Ellie squeezed back. "I wonder what Miss Sylvia will say when she sees us. I hope she's all right. She used to take such good care of the island's coral."

"*I* wonder if those horrible Cooleys who returned you to the orphanage are still on Freith," said Jariel. "I want to give them a piece of my mind."

Ellie tensed. "I don't. Anyway, last I heard they were leaving Freith for the island of Bramborough. Who knows where they are now."

"Ellie, Jariel," Jude called softly from the helm. "We're approaching the island. Time to get ready."

Ellie felt a tingle run down to her fingertips. Not long now until she'd see Connor.

There was a cold wind blowing, and the crew buttoned their nautical coats to the chin. They carried only their weapons, a flask of water each, and several sets of candles and matches. Ellie also had her sketchbook containing the images from her dream. Vivian bundled Tal in blankets until nothing could be seen of him but his little nose, then strapped him to her back for the climb down the ladder. Hoyan stood nearby. The red-winged Alirya wore a plate of leather armor over his bare chest and carried a *guandao*, a long staff with a formidable curved blade on the end. The crew planned to visit the island core first, have Tal heal the coral, then approach the orphanage through the connecting tunnel in search of Connor. Alyce and Aimee would stay with the ship until the others returned. The falcon Zira was scouting the island to see if the way was clear.

Just then, Zira returned and landed on Aimee's shoulder. The bird and the girl shared a long look.

"Uh-oh. She says something is wrong down there," Aimee said, translating the bird's thoughts. "Where there should be a big hole, there's only flat land."

Owen frowned. "What's that supposed to mean?"

Jariel pulled out her spyglass and searched the surface of the island. "Well, for starters, I can't see the island core."

"What?" Jude borrowed the spyglass for a look. "It's hard to tell in the dark, but it might have been covered or paved over. That complicates things."

"How are we going to reach it, then?" said Finn.

"We could reverse our plan," said Ellie. "We could go to the orphanage first, rescue Connor, then use the orphanage tunnel to reach the island core. If Miss Sylvia is there, she might even be able to give us more information."

"I'd feel better if we took care of the coral first," said Jude, handing the spyglass back to Jariel. "But it doesn't look as if we have a choice. We'll go to the orphanage first."

The crew agreed. Ellie recommended that they let down the ladder near the harbor, on the outskirts of Freith. If the governor, Dorethel Hirx, had paved over the island core, he might also have soldiers watching it. He believed Vestigians, or Basileans, were a rebel group hostile to his government. But with Ellie's help, it would be easy enough for the *Legend's* crew to reach the orphanage via back streets, avoiding official attention. She felt reassured that she'd made the right decision to come.

Jude brought the lumena down to maintenance power and let down the rope ladder, then turned over the helm to Alyce.

"We should be back by tomorrow night, if not before," said Jude.

"Come back soon. Aimee and I will take good care of the old girl," Alyce said, patting the *Legend's* helm.

"Take care of Sunny, too, okay?" said Owen, scratching the shaggy dog's ears.

"I'll give him all the snacks and belly rubs he wants," Aimee promised.

One by one, the seven sailors began the descent down the ladder. Ellie remembered how terrified she had felt making that first, long climb up to the *Legend*. She still didn't love the unpredictable movements of ship ladders, but now it was all part of a familiar routine.

It was nearly midnight by the time they landed, and the city of Sketpoole lay quiet, the lights out in most of the drab buildings. As Ellie led the way down familiar cobblestone streets, she felt anxiety rise within her. It hadn't been so long ago that Ewart Cooley had torn up her sketchbook and thrown it into a mud puddle on these very streets. Would she somehow wake up to find that the events of the last year had been a dream—that she was right back to being an unwanted orphan?

As if sensing her unease, Finn flashed her a smile, his teeth white in the darkness. No, this last year hadn't been a dream. The friends beside her assured her of that.

As they turned a corner, the Sketpoole Home for Boys and Girls appeared at the end of the street. It was the strangest feeling to see it again. The tired old building looked exactly the same. Its walls were still in need of paint, and its chipped shutters still hung at crooked angles. Still, it had been home for a short but crucial time in Ellie's life.

A block from the orphanage, Jude pulled them all behind a building. "Remember: according to Ellie's dream, Connor is in the orphanage's back room. We don't know how heavily he's guarded, so we'll have to be ready. Jariel, Hoyan, you go ahead and scout. If all is quiet, Owen, you can pick the lock on the front door. We'll keep to stealth as long as possible, but the rest of you, cover us from a distance if there's trouble. Don't follow us in unless I give the signal."

They all nodded. Jude made a motion with his hand, and they headed forward. It felt strange to be sneaking up on the orphanage with all the lights off. Ellie wondered if anyone was here after all. Jariel and Hoyan hurried ahead, Jariel peering into the darkened front windows, and Hoyan flying over the building to investigate the back, but both returned with the same report: all appeared quiet and dark. Ellie picked a position behind a thick shrub in the front yard, settled a stone in her slingshot, and waited as Owen approached the front door. Producing a few slender tools from inside his nautical coat, he knelt down in front of the door handle. A bare minute later, the front door swung silently inward, revealing a dark front entryway.

Ellie leaned forward, watching as Jude, Hoyan, Jariel, and Owen entered the hall cautiously. A moment later, a light appeared in the hallway. Ellie tensed. Urken? The governor's soldiers? But no—a woman stepped into the light. Ellie knew that worn shawl, that frizzled head of hair. It was Chinelle, the very first person who'd welcomed Ellie to the orphanage. She'd done the cooking and washing, and Ellie had often helped her. Chinelle appeared to be the only person awake in the building. The middle-aged woman had a hand on Jariel's head, smoothing her red hair, and Ellie stood up from her hiding place. If Chinelle was still answering the door, the orphanage couldn't be under enemy control. Sure enough, a moment later Jude gave the all-clear signal. Ellie, Vivian, and Finn approached from their various hiding places.

"Ellie!" Chinelle exclaimed when she saw her. The woman's face looked a bit tense, but it was hard to imagine anyone being truly relaxed when a troop of armed visitors arrived in the middle of the night. "My, how you've grown. Won't you come in and introduce your friends? I'll fix you a cup of tea."

"You ought to have that lock on the front door replaced," Owen suggested, closing the door behind him. "It was practically standing open."

"You're probably right. That door's been here longer than I have," said Chinelle with a nervous laugh as they entered the dark kitchen. She lit a lamp.

As soon as the light flickered on, the cellar door banged open. A troop of soldiers surged forward, shouting.

"Run! Get back outside!" Hoyan yelled.

The *Legend*'s crew fled back toward the front door, the Alirya covering their retreat with the long reach of his guandao. Though her heart pounded with fear, Ellie also felt the sharp sting of treachery. Chinelle, of all people! Why would she betray them? The crew burst back out into the yard.

A Valsha was waiting for them there. He was a tall, pale young man with sharp cheekbones and a wicked smile. In his hands he held a flail, a long chain of biting metal links.

"Well, well," the black-cloaked man said. "What have we here?"

Behind them, Hoyan came through the front door, brandishing his guandao. At the sight of the Valsha, he spread out his red wings threateningly.

"Faithless One," he snarled.

The Valsha spat at Hoyan's feet. "Arcvon is my name, fool."

Hoyan's feathers ruffled. He pitched his voice to the crew. "Move out of the way."

Knowing they were outmatched in this fight, the crew obeyed. The two warriors circled each other, looking for weaknesses. Ellie remembered what Lady Lilia had said—that the Valsha had been Alirya once. Now that the two creatures were face to face, Ellie could see the resemblance—their finely sculpted features, their raw power—but also the total hatred between them. They were twins but also opposites—north and south, morning and night. And one was going to kill the other.

Arcvon slowly began to whirl his weapon in the air, the metal chain clicking as it gained speed. Suddenly he released it, striking for Hoyan's leg. Hoyan leaped into the air on his giant wings, dodging the blow. Arcvon whirled the flail again, this time flicking it in a different direction with liquid speed. It caught Hoyan's right arm, wrapping around him and locking. Arcvon jerked hard, and the Alirya fell to earth, landing on his back. The Valsha stepped closer, but suddenly Hoyan released a bolt of orange lightning that sparked along the flail's chain. The powerful shock threw Arcvon backwards, this time knocking him onto his back. As his enemy lay momentarily paralyzed, Hoyan freed himself and threw the flail across the yard. Lifting his guandao, he lunged toward the Valsha. Arcvon blocked the sweeping strike with a black swordbreaker just in time. He shoved backward, throwing Hoyan into the air and giving himself time to rise. Hoyan flipped in the air and kicked down hard on the Valsha, pushing him down again. Still airborne, Hoyan began to whirl the guandao at unbelievable speed, the blade-tipped staff becoming a silver tornado in his hands. Arcvon leaped to avoid a slicing cut, then jumped high in the air with a roundhouse kick, his boot smashing into the side of Hoyan's face. The Alirya dropped and rolled back to his feet. Another series of guandao strokes slashed at

Arcvon's arms, and the Valsha suffered a long cut before bringing up his swordbreaker to catch the weapon. He twisted and the guandao snapped in half, cutting the weapon to the length of a short sword. With Hoyan so close, the Valsha got in another strike, tearing at Hoyan's exposed side with the jagged edge of the blade. Blood as clear as water came from the gash. Wounded but undeterred, Hoyan flew into the air and brought his blade down with a sharp chop that missed Arcvon's neck by inches. Arcvon lunged out with his blade again, but this time Hoyan caught his wrist. The Alirya twisted sharply, producing a sharp *snap* from the Valsha's arm, then flipped him on his back. Arcvon lay on the ground for only a second, clutching his broken arm. In that second, Hoyan used his curved blade to chop off the disabled Valsha's head. Then the Alirya doubled over, pressing a hand to his gashed side as the Valsha's black blood soaked into the dirt of the orphanage yard.

During the fight, the soldiers from inside had moved into the yard. They wore gray uniforms with a stitched red arrow insignia, except for a man whose insignia was set in a gold pin. He stepped forward.

"What a diverting spectacle," he introduced himself, his expression cold and cutting. "I am Governor Dorethel Hirx. And one of you must be the Basilean seer Lord Draaken is so terribly interested in."

Ellie instinctively drew closer to her shipmates. Chinelle stood behind the soldiers, and the pain of betrayal stung Ellie again. But the maid was sobbing uncontrollably into her apron. "I'm sorry," she blubbered aloud. "They have Miss Sylvia and the children. They said they'd kill them all if I didn't bring you inside. I'm sorry."

Not betrayed, then, Ellie thought wearily. *Just fooled.*

"Silence," Hirx snapped at the maid. "You will all drop your weapons and identify the seer, one Ellie Altess, immediately."

"And if we don't?" said Finn.

The governor raised one eyebrow. "Guards, bring out our assistants."

A pair of soldiers left, then escorted three people outside. Ellie's stomach dropped.

The governor's assistants were Horaffe, Loretha, and Ewart Cooley.

Chapter 7
Betrayal

Ellie's former adoptive family looked almost the same. Loretha now wore an expensive satin coat with fur trimmings, Horaffe's hairline had receded a bit more, and Ewart was taller and slightly thinner, his greasy hair lying flat against his pimply face. But their expressions were still just as sour as they had been on the day they returned Ellie to this orphanage. They were still gambling with the world for all they could get.

"Which of these people is Ellie Altess?" said Hirx.

"Her," said Loretha, pointing to Ellie without hesitation. Her too-red lips pursed as if she'd tasted something spoiled. "I'd know her anywhere."

"And she's just as ugly as ever," Ewart snickered.

"Not as ugly as you'll be when I'm done with you," Jariel snapped, shouldering in front of Ellie. "And her name's Ellianea Reid, for your information."

Ewart took a step toward his mother.

"I...I thought you'd moved away from Freith," Ellie stammered.

"Well, we came back. Freith offered us better...opportunities." Loretha proudly smoothed the fur on her coat.

The governor silenced the conversation with a wave of his hand. He stepped closer to Ellie. "So you're the little minx who has caused Lord Draaken so much trouble. You don't look like much, but His Magnificence knows best." He turned to the Cooleys. "You will be paid for your services according to our agreement, but remain here until Lord Draaken's emissary comes to complete the transaction. You may be called upon to offer more information when she arrives."

"Nothing's complete yet," Jude warned. "You've left us out of your calculations. We won't let you take Ellie."

"Besides," Vivian urged. "Don't you know your island is falling? You're drifting away from the rest of Newdonia and toward the Edge right now. We can save your island if you'll help us."

Hirx smiled indulgently. "So thoughtful of you. But Lord Draaken has already thought of that. As soon as we deliver his prisoner, he has promised to stop our island's movement."

Owen snorted. "You really think he's going to keep that bargain?"

Hirx scowled. "Do not insult His Magnificence. Guards, escort the prisoners inside."

Hoyan, his face unhealthily pale, staggered to his feet, brandishing his broken guandao in one hand. "Not without a fight." Around Ellie, the other crewmembers adjusted their grips on their weapons.

"Well, if it isn't the crew of that pathetic little boat. What was it called again?"

Ellie's chest constricted at the sound of the smooth, silky voice. She didn't even need to turn around to know who it was.

"Ah, Your Eminence," said Hirx, his tone instantly turning simpering. "I was just explaining to the prisoners the wisdom of cooperating with the Lord of the Seas."

"We're not prisoners," Hoyan growled fiercely.

"Not yet," came the voice from behind them.

Slowly Ellie turned around. There was the familiar black-cloaked figure, her dark lips curved into a predatory smile. *Nikira.* The Valsha had tried to convince Ellie to join Draaken's side, nearly killed Vivian, and overseen the destruction of Rhynlyr. Ellie would have been happy never to see her again.

"Hello, Ellie," said Nikira. "It's been too long."

"Not long enough for me," said Ellie, taking a step back.

"Leave her alone!" said Finn, nocking an arrow to his bow.

"How sweet—you've brought all your little friends with you, Ellie. You *do* have a knack for getting others into trouble." Nikira's eyes scanned the little group, coming to rest on Vivian and Jude. "Ah. You again."

At that moment, Tal gurgled in the sling on Vivian's back. Nikira's face kindled with wicked delight. "And you have a baby now. I love babies. Give it to me."

"No," said Vivian and Jude in unison. Vivian angled her body to keep Tal away from Nikira. Jude stepped in front of her, staff balanced in his hands.

"Leave them alone, Nikira," said Hoyan. The Alirya's wings ruffled and rose. "If it's a fight you want, then fight with me." Ellie noticed he didn't mention Tal specifically. Maybe Nikira didn't know about the baby's abilities. If she didn't think he was important, perhaps she wouldn't single him out for capture—or worse.

"Very well," said Nikira. "If you insist." She let her cloak drop behind her with a flutter, revealing the hilts of two swordbreakers strapped to her back.

The *Legend's* crew stepped back, leaving Hoyan and Nikira alone on the field with the fallen Arcvon. Nikira took in the decapitated form with a sniff.

"Junior officers," she sniffed. "Never trust them with anything you want done." Her eyes slitted as she took up a crouching position. "Fool. I will make you suffer."

Hoyan lunged forward, slashing with his guandao, though his reach was now severely shortened. Ellie also took in the drastically slower pace of his movements. If Valsha were not invincible, could Alirya also be killed?

Nikira easily dodged Hoyan's swipe. She delivered a double jab with her swordbreakers, her movements swift and easy. Hoyan blocked the first, but barely dodged the second, receiving a nick on his forearm. He heavily lifted off the ground with his wings, dropping down behind Nikira. But she whirled, delivering a powerful roundhouse kick to his already injured ribs. The Alirya doubled over. Nikira prepared another double jab. Hoyan thrust out his guandao to block the blows. The first swordbreaker caught his weapon, snapping it in half and sending the blade spinning away into the darkness. The second caught him in his unprotected side, sliding in below his leather armor. As Hoyan stiffened, Nikira plunged her free swordbreaker into his other side. The Alirya dropped to the ground, his red wings crumpling over his limp body. He did not get back up.

Ellie stared, petrified, at the fallen Alirya. Nikira retrieved her weapons from Hoyan's body with two vicious yanks, the black blades dripping with clear blood. She sneered at the crew huddled together on the far side of the yard. "Who's next?"

Governor Hirx cleared his throat. "If I may, Your Eminence. Ellie, you have a choice to make, young lady. You can cooperate with the Lord Draaken, save the rest of your friends' lives, and avoid any more unpleasant…scenes," he said, gesturing at the two bodies lying in the yard. "Or you can put up a struggle, which will cost you dearly and ultimately prove useless."

"Maybe it's useless, but we'll make it as hard for you as we can," said Jariel, her voice a little shaky, but determined.

The governor shrugged. "Brave, perhaps, but foolish. There's also one more fact you should consider."

The governor clapped his hands. Two more guards marched out the orphanage door, holding two prisoners at knifepoint. One was the elderly Sylvia Galen, the orphanage keeper. The other was a little girl Ellie remembered from her time at the orphanage—Adabel, she thought her name was. Both stood very still, but Adabel was crying softly. A bruise darkened one side of Sylvia's face.

"There are two dozen more orphans in the back room," the governor explained calmly. "I'm fully prepared to execute them one by one until you surrender yourself."

Ellie stood in silent horror. Her friends' lives and the lives of all the orphans here depended on her choice. She glanced over and saw Jude's hand curl around Vivian's.

"I just have one question," Ellie said. "Where is Connor?"

"Connor?" The governor frowned.

"A…a prisoner who was kept here. Draaken oversaw him personally."

"Oh, the boy. He was only here a day or two. He's been moved now."

"You fell for the Lord Draaken's little ruse, then," said Nikira. "He said that the bait would bring you here. How like you *Ulfurssh*. So trusting. So stupid."

Ellie took a deep breath. So she'd put all her friends' lives in danger. And Connor wasn't even here. Well, she'd gotten them into this mess, and it was her responsibility to get them out. Terrified as she was of Nikira, Ellie knew what she had to do. Slowly, she bent down and set her slingshot on the ground.

"I will go with you," Ellie said. "Just leave the others alone."

Hirx nodded his approval. "They will be released once you are safely away."

Reluctantly, the rest of the crew also laid down their weapons. With an entire orphanage of hostages, there was little other choice. Hirx's soldiers hastily stepped forward to bind their hands and search them for anything else concealed. One found Ellie's sketchbook and handed it over to Nikira. She wrapped it in her discarded cloak as if afraid to touch it.

"I'm glad you chose sensibly," Nikira said to Ellie. "I don't have time to waste watching meaningless executions." She pushed a slender lead rope over Ellie's head, tightening it around her neck. "I have already spent far too long hunting you across all the archipelagos but one. Now it's time for you to see it. Don't worry. You'll like His Magnificence's domain beneath the sea." A slow smile curled her lips. "What fun we'll have."

"Is…is there any other way we may serve you, Your Eminence?" simpered Loretha Cooley, stepping forward. Nikira ignored her.

By the light of a lantern one of the guards held, Ellie could see the wrinkles on Loretha's face. Once Ellie had tried desperately to make this woman want her, but she hadn't and she never would. Now Ellie saw what a weary, anxious woman stood before her, always trying to angle herself onto the winning side. Suddenly Ellie felt only pity for Loretha. She might never become a better person, might continue trying to deceive and manipulate others as long as she lived. But this time she'd gambled on the wrong side. Draaken was not as generous a master as Loretha Cooley believed him to be.

"I forgive you," Ellie heard her own voice saying.

"You…what?" snapped Loretha, her expression indignant. "What right do you think you have…"

"Never mind," Ellie sighed wearily. "I forgive you for not being the family I wanted you to be. And I'm sorry for what's coming to you."

"What?" said Ewart.

"Shut up," Nikira growled with a tug on the rope. "The Lord of the Seas is waiting."

Ellie followed Nikira to a black carriage waiting in front of the yard. Governor Hirx motioned to his top guards, and together they hurried into a second one. As the carriage pulled away, Ellie glanced back at her friends standing in the orphanage yard. She hoped desperately that they'd be all right. It seemed unlikely at this point, but she hoped she'd be all right too.

At the docks, Nikira pulled Ellie out of the carriage and toward the strangest boat Ellie had ever seen. It was completely enclosed in black scales and had fins and two bulging glass eyes. Ellie might have thought it was a real fish if not for the gears and controls she glimpsed through the glass. A second fish-boat bobbed farther out in the harbor. Perhaps it had carried the unlucky Arcvon here. Nikira opened a well-sealed hatch in the boat's back.

"Get in," she told Ellie.

Governor Hirx, who had been standing by watching, cleared his throat. "A pleasure, a true pleasure, to assist the almighty Lord of the Seas. And...ah, about his plan to stop the island's drifting. When will that take effect?"

Sitting inside the fish-boat, Ellie waited to hear the answer.

"And just why would he want to stop it?" Nikira sneered. "Don't you know how he gets his soldiers?" She leaped into the boat and it jetted away, leaving Hirx and his men standing motionless on the pier. Ellie pitied them too. She could have told them that this was how the Enemy's bargains ended.

Ellie caught a glimpse of the open boat's interior. There were two seats and a cramped cargo bay behind them. In front was a box with a few levers and navigational instruments, reminding Ellie of the lumena controls aboard the *Legend*.

Nikira drew Ellie's sketchbook from her folded cloak. "What is this?"

Ellie reached for it. "It's mine. Just...sketches."

Nikira hurled the book away as if it burned her fingers. Ellie stifled a cry as the book hit the ocean surface, saturated with water, and slowly sank. "More of your detestable illuminations. Those polluted things have no place in Lord Draaken's magnificent domain."

Ellie sat still and numb as Nikira closed the overhead hatch, sealing them inside the fish-boat. The Valsha pushed forward on one of the control levers, and water covered the fish's glass eyes. Ellie's heart pounded. The boat was not just going forward—it was also going down.

They traveled in silence as the light from the ocean's surface gradually faded into darkness.

"You said you'd hunted me across all but one of the archipelagos," Ellie said at length, trying to distract herself from thinking about how much water was over her head. "But I've been to all of them: Newdonia, the Orkent Isles, the Numed Archipelago, and Arjun Mador. What did you mean?"

"Haven't you ever heard of the Lost Archipelago?"

"Well...I've heard of the Elbarra Cluster. But that whole archipelago was lost over the Edge."

"Is that what they told you? I suppose landwalkers would think that. For some Elbarra islands, yes, it was too late. But one was salvageable."

"Really?" Ellie felt a spark of interest. "Then...why is the archipelago called lost?"

"Because your stupid landwalker storytellers do not know everything."

"If it's not lost, then where is it now?"

Nikira pulled a cord, flicking on a ghostly white exterior lamp that illuminated the water in front of them. By its pale light, her face looked corpselike.

"You're about to find out."

Chapter 8
Coral

V ivian watched, frozen, as Nikira took Ellie away, followed by Governor Hirx and his top officers. Vivian was more than relieved that Nikira, ignorant of Tal's powers, had left the baby alone. But Ellie was gone, taken to some unknown base where they might never find her again. Everything had gone so wrong tonight. Vivian glanced at the still bodies of Hoyan and Arcvon still lying in the yard. Everything.

"You'll stay here until the gov'ner gets back," growled one of Hirx's remaining guards.

"But he said we were to be released," argued Jariel.

The guard looked confused and slightly uncomfortable. "He'll...decide what to do with you later. Keep quiet."

"But we may not *have* until later," said Vivian. "Your island is falling. We can save it."

"I said, keep quiet!"

The guard's words sounded angry, but Vivian heard the quaver in his tone. She guessed Hirx's departure had not been part of the plan. She also guessed that the governor would soon realize Draaken would not be able to save Freith—and then his only priority would be chartering his own escape. Perhaps in a few hours these half-dozen underling guards would realize they had been duped. She just hoped the island had that long.

The crew of the *Legend* was herded into the orphanage. The building had been ransacked—benches turned over, cushions cut open, stuffing tossed everywhere. A scattered supper still sat on the dining table, and the Cooleys sat down to it as the prisoners were marched to the back room. There, about two dozen young children and a gangly young man sat tied up, huddling close to one another for warmth and comfort. Vivian's heart twisted. They looked frightened and miserable.

The prisoners were left, bound, on the floor with two guards to watch them. Except for the sniffles of a few children, the room was dark and quiet.

The night hours slipped slowly by. The floorboards creaked as the guards shifted from foot to foot. The moon set, some of the children went to sleep, and Vivian could feel Tal squirming in his sling. He must be hungry by now. She worked at her bonds, wondering if she could somehow move him, but the ropes held fast.

Vivian cleared her throat and spoke softly to one of the guards. "Excuse me."

"Quiet," he growled.

"It's just...I need to feed my baby." As if to back her up, Tal began to whimper.

To Vivian's surprise, the guard did not bark at her again. Instead, his expression softened. "How old is he?" he asked.

"Nearly four months."

The military planes of the man's face eased into a small smile. "I have one almost the same age. A little girl."

"Do you?" Vivian smiled. "They're wonderful at this age."

"Aye. My girl learns somethin' new every day. Me and my wife don't get much sleep anymore, though." The guard gestured with his head. "Come on. There's a chair over here you can use." The second guard began to protest, but the first one cut him off. "It's only a baby, Orrick. They has to eat."

The guard helped Vivian to her feet, cut her bonds, and even gave her a blanket to wrap herself in. When she was finished, Vivian cradled the sleeping Tal, his chubby face slack and peaceful. The guard smiled at the baby.

"Fine lad. What's 'is name?"

"Tal," Vivian said softly. "What about your daughter?"

"Ania." The guard's face filled with pride. "I'm Royd."

Vivian was moved by a sudden compulsion. "Royd—aren't you worried about what might happen to Ania if we're telling the truth? If Freith really is drifting toward the Edge of the world? We have the solution. All we need to do is travel to the island core."

The second guard, Orrick, began to protest again. Vivian hurried on before he could stop her. "You could escort us. You wouldn't have to let us out of your sight. We can save Ania and all the other people on the island."

Orrick shook his head. "No chance. Gov'ner's orders."

"Now, hold on," said Royd. "Gov'ner didn't say we couldn't move 'em, just that we had to watch 'em."

"You wouldn't be disobeying your orders at all," Vivian pressed on in her most soothing voice. "We'd be with you the whole time."

Orrick frowned. "I don't like it. Sounds like funny business to me."

"But what if they's telling the truth?" said Royd, lowering his voice. Vivian could barely make out his words. "What if the island's falling, like they say?"

"Gov'ner wouldn't like it. I don't wanta lose my job."

"But the gov'ner ain't here, is he? Maybe he off and ran. Maybe he left us on a falling island to fend for ourselves."

Orrick shook his head again, but the gesture was less confident.

"There is a tunnel leading directly to the island core under this building," Vivian added. "We couldn't run away from you there, even if we wanted to."

"Maybe we better ask the others," said Royd.

Orrick said nothing, but he made a grunting noise that sounded vaguely like agreement. Royd left the room. Vivian strapped Tal to her chest and glanced anxiously out the window. Dawn was approaching. She hoped they would not be too late.

After several minutes, Royd trooped into the room, leading three more guards.

"Wirt, Orrick, and Royd'll escort you down the tunnel," said one of them importantly. "But no more'n three of you. And no trying to escape."

Vivian looked around. "Jude? And Jariel? You know the way, yes?"

Jariel nodded, and the three of them got stiffly to their feet. The guards cut their bonds, but surrounded them tightly.

"Do you have caris powder?" Sylvia whispered.

"We have something better," Jude whispered back.

"You'll need the key to the cellar door. Take it." With her hands bound, Sylvia awkwardly took a large pewter key from her apron pocket. Vivian tucked it into her pocket.

Passing through the dining room, where the Cooleys were asleep amidst the remains of their repast, Vivian, Jude, and Jariel headed down the stairs into the cellar, its shelves lined with sacks and jars. Against one wall was a thick door.

"That's what the key's for," Jariel said.

Vivian used the pewter key to unlock the door. It swung open into utter darkness.

"That's the tunnel?" said Orrick, a note of nervousness in his voice.

"Yes. It's safe, though," said Jariel. "And I've still got my candle and matches." She struck a light, and suddenly dirt walls appeared out of the dark. "Come on."

The tunnel was dark and seemed endlessly long. The three guards surrounded the prisoners as they marched through the darkness. At one point, Tal began to cry, and Vivian kissed his fuzzy head. She didn't particularly enjoy marches through tunnels, but she'd much rather be doing this than sitting in that dark room with her hands tied. With a pang, she wondered where Ellie was, and if she was safe. She wished there had been a way to prevent Nikira from taking her. They would have to form a rescue plan—just as soon as Tal could heal the coral and save the island.

At last the tunnel ended in a small hole. Jariel, Jude, and the guards wriggled through with little trouble, but Vivian had to pass Tal to Jude before she could fit. Before them stood an aging wooden door with a sliding bolt. One of the guards opened it to reveal a deep shaft with a spiraling iron staircase. Vivian looked down into the dark water of the island core. Sure enough, there was not the faintest glow of pink, healthy coral.

"What're you going to do?" asked Royd.

"This is where he comes in." Vivian gently unwrapped Tal from his blankets. The baby fussed as the cold air touched him.

"I know, baby. It's been a long night. Just a little while longer, and you can go back to sleep," Vivian crooned as she removed her own coat and boots. "Jude, if you could follow me down with the light?"

The guards and Jariel watched from the top as Jude and Vivian descended the winding staircase. Vivian took a few steps into the cold, dark water, shivering as her trousers soaked past the knee.

"Are you sure this is how it works?" Jude frowned. Vivian nodded, realizing that Jude had not yet seen his son's abilities for himself. She carefully lowered Tal into the water. The baby screamed when it touched his foot.

"Shhh," she soothed, his wails piercing her heart. "It'll be over very soon." She guided Tal's tiny, perfect toes toward the nearest branch of coral. Where the baby's foot touched, a flush of pink bloomed over the gray surface. As Tal continued to scream, life rushed back through the broken branch and the pieces fused back together. When the pink glow began to plummet downward, sending a new coral root toward the ocean floor, Vivian quickly pulled Tal out of the water and dried his foot on her shirt. She tucked him close and rocked him, soothing his cries. The regrowth of dead coral was truly awe-inspiring, but she wished that it didn't have to make her baby so cold and miserable. She turned to head back up the stairs and almost crashed into Jude. He was staring at

Tal almost as intently as on the day they'd first met. His fingers slowly reached for the baby's foot, still chilled from the water.

"So *that's* what the One Kingdom looks like," he breathed.

Vivian smiled and squeezed his hand. She remembered her own wonder when she'd first seen Tal's abilities. In spite of all the fear and danger, she couldn't imagine feeling any prouder of their extraordinary son.

As they climbed back up the stairs, Vivian saw Jariel and the guards looking down at them, their faces illuminated by the pink light rising from the core.

"Wow," breathed Jariel, tickling Tal's foot. "I knew you were special, but that was amazing!"

"Never seen anythin' like it," remarked Orrick.

"So now we're safe?" asked Royd.

Vivian nodded. "The coral is what anchors your island to the ocean floor and keeps it from going over the Edge of the world. Now that the coral is strong and healthy again, you'll be fine."

"Gov'ner never told us about that," grumbled the third guard, Wirt.

"You don't seem like dangerous traitors," said Orrick.

"That's because we're not," Jariel chimed in. "We never were. So will you let the others go when we get back?"

The guards looked at each other. "Gov'ner's not here to say no," said Wirt.

"Don't see no sense in holdin' prisoners who ain't done nothin' wrong," said Orrick.

"Me, I'd rather be catchin' some sleep in my own bed," said Royd. "'Leastways, if Ania lets me."

Morning had broken by the time the *Legend*'s crew returned to the orphanage, tired but satisfied. The guards soon agreed that the governor was not coming back, so there was no reason for them to stay or continue holding his prisoners. Forming a unit, they marched out the door and down the street. Royd tipped his hat to them as they left.

Vivian and Jariel quickly freed the others. Jude checked the children for injuries, though they were more tired than hurt. Chinelle, anxious to atone for her actions, put on a kettle of tea and took the orphans upstairs for some sleep. Sylvia, Finn, and Owen were greatly relieved to hear that Governor Hirx was not returning. The Cooleys, however, were visibly shaken.

"But he promised us payment!" Loretha whined shrilly.

"Well, Draaken also promised to save Freith, and look what happened with that," said Jariel dryly. "The Enemy isn't one for keeping his promises."

Loretha looked down her nose at Jariel. "And exactly who are you?"

Jariel crossed her arms. "Only Ellie's best friend. And you have a lot of explaining to do."

"Explaining about what? The governor asked us to identify the girl, and why shouldn't we? She was nothing but a violent menace in our house."

"Careful," Vivian warned. "Ellie has many loyal friends here."

"Ellie got what she deserved," sneered Ewart Cooley. "I'd turn her in again tomorrow."

Finn walked right up to Ewart. Without warning, he punched him squarely in the nose.

Ewart fell to the ground, howling and grabbing his face. "Owww! My nose! I think it's broken!"

"*I* wanted to do that," grumbled Jariel.

"Oh, my baby! My poor Ewart!" babbled his mother, pawing at the wailing boy as blood dribbled from his nose. Horaffe stood by, looking detached and slightly uncomfortable. Loretha pointed at Finn. "Somebody punish that boy! He's a monster!"

Finn stepped back, inspecting the knuckles of his harpist's hands. Jude cleared his throat.

"Finn."

"Captain." Finn didn't look at him.

"I trust you won't make a habit of punching civilians."

Finn's eyes flicked upward. "Not unless it's strictly necessary, sir."

Jude looked from Finn to Ewart. "Accepted."

Sylvia, her bruises sharply evident in the morning light, cleared her throat. "We have much to discuss. I suggest we move these people to the cellar while I consider their fate. They have caused significant property damage, and reparations will need to be made. Kyuler, will you escort them?"

"With pleasure," said the gangly errand boy. After being tied up all night, he looked positively overjoyed to lock the Cooleys in the cellar.

"Vivian, Finn, Owen, this is Sylvia Galen, Vestigian agent on Freith," said Jude, nodding respectfully to the older woman. "It seems a little late for introductions, but there it is."

"It's a pleasure to meet the person who sent us Ellie and Jariel," said Vivian.

"And a pleasure to meet their crew, though I wasn't expecting these circumstances," said Sylvia, patting Jariel's cheek.

"Sylvia, please tell us what happened here," said Jude. In the daylight, Vivian could see weary lines etched into his forehead. "We have two missing friends, a lot of holes to fill in, and not much time."

Sylvia nodded. "No time to waste, then. You'd better sit down." When the crew was seated around the dining room table, she launched into her story.

Chapter 9
Partings

Governor Hirx has been a pawn in the Enemy's hand as long as I've been on this island," Sylvia began. "He hunted Vestigians even before the Enemy kept a physical presence on the island. However, we used the tunnel to feed the island's coral and sent occasional recruits to the Vestigia Roi. Things escalated a few weeks ago when a party of urken marched openly through the center of Sketpoole. The governor added fresh *asthmenos* poison to the island core and sealed off the top, presumably on Draaken's orders."

"Nothing a few explosives can't handle," Owen interjected. "We'd have to rig it from outside, though. Blowing things up when you're inside them isn't usually a good idea."

"Last week, the Lagorites came here," Sylvia continued. "They forced us all to stay upstairs while they used the back room for a special prisoner."

"Was it Connor?" asked Jariel. "A boy with dark hair and blue eyes?"

"I couldn't get a close look, but that does sound like him," said Sylvia. "I'm afraid they treated the poor boy very harshly. Then they suddenly took him away. They boasted that he was bound for Lagora."

"Lagora? What's that?" said Finn.

"History has handed down the understanding that the lost Fifth Archipelago, the Elbarra Cluster, disappeared over the Edge back in the Second Age," said Sylvia. "But based on the snatches I overheard from our captors, that may not be the case. It sounds as if one of the islands may have avoided the Edge, sinking instead to the bottom of the ocean—which, as we know, is the Enemy's special domain."

"That must be where Nikira was taking Ellie, too," said Owen. "She said Ellie would like Draaken's 'domain beneath the sea'—though I don't think she will."

"Where is...Lagora?" said Jude.

"I do not know," said Sylvia. "I do, however, know the coordinates of the old Elbarra Cluster. That might be a place to start looking."

"An underwater prison," sighed Jude, rubbing his hands over his hair. "How are we going to reach it?"

"Let's tackle one thing at a time," said Vivian, patting his back. "Are we all agreed to go after Ellie and Connor?"

"Obviously," said Owen.

"First we have to tell the rest of the Vestigia Roi what happened here," said Jude. "They need to know that Freith is safe and that you haven't been harmed, Sylvia. We'll also have to report Ellie's capture and our suspicions about Lagora."

"I have an eyret bird," said Sylvia.

"Good. Before we write the Vestigia Roi, though, we should send the eyret to tell Alyce and Aimee to lower the *Legend* to sea level and join us here," said Vivian. "The ship is safe now, and they'll be worried about us."

"We also need to give Hoyan a proper burial," said Jude heavily. "The other creature too, I suppose."

"I'll help you," said Finn.

"The rest of us will help clean up the orphanage," said Vivian. "But Jude—there's something I need to talk to you about afterwards."

Kyuler went down to the harbor to collect Alyce and Aimee, who had landed the *Legend* and brought Sunny with them. By the time they arrived, Hoyan and Arcvon had been laid to rest in separate ends of the orphanage yard. Alyce and Aimee listened with horror to the story of Ellie's capture and also shared news from the docks. They had seen a ship, filled with soldiers in uniform, depart, along with some sort of a submersible boat that resembled a fish. A similar contraption still floated in the harbor.

"That adds credence to the sunken island theory," said Jude. "Perhaps the other boat belonged to the unfortunate Arcvon. It just might be our ticket underwater."

"It also confirms that our courageous governor sailed away from his sinking island, hoping to save his own neck," Sylvia said dryly. "I think he'll find the current much stronger now that we're closer to the Edge. Unless he's taken along some *very* skilled sailors, there is only one destination for that ship."

"It's a good thing the guards agreed to release us, then," said Jude. "Now that the island is safe, we can go in search of Ellie and Connor."

"Before we do, there's something else we should talk about," said Alyce, looking at Aimee.

"Not again," Aimee grumbled. Zira sat on her shoulder, looking equally unhappy. "I already told you. I'm not staying."

"But with so many littler kids here, don't you think you ought to stay and help look after them? Isn't that a good idea?" said Alyce, a forced brightness in her voice.

"No. It's a bad idea," Aimee glared.

Vivian studied Alyce with compassion. So she planned to go after Ellie and Connor, but didn't want to lead her little sister into danger. It was noble, but Vivian guessed at the pain it was costing Alyce.

"Actually, I was going to ask you something else, Aimee," Owen said. "I can't take Sunny, Moby, and Pinta with me on this mission. It wouldn't be safe for them. Since I have to leave them here, I need someone to take good care of them. Would you do it, Aimee? Sunny already likes you a lot." As if in agreement, Sunny laid his chin on Aimee's knee, thumping his shaggy tail on the floor.

"Me? Take care of Sunny?" Aimee's grumpy expression melted into one of delight.

"Well, and Moby and Pinta, too."

"Yes! I'll take the best care of them. I promise," said Aimee, dropping to the floor to hug Sunny. Zira flapped to a safer perch on the back of a chair as Sunny licked Aimee's face. "Is that okay, Alyce? Can I stay?"

Alyce tried to smile through the mist brimming in her eyes. "Yes, of course, Aimee. It's okay."

Chinelle went to gather supplies for the *Legend*'s voyage and Sylvia sat down to notify the Vestigia Roi of the new developments. Meanwhile, Vivian pulled Jude out behind the orphanage building, where there was a mostly fallow winter garden and a pen with two goats, along with the two fresh graves.

"We have a choice to make before we set out, Jude." Vivian took a deep breath, wishing she didn't have to say this. She had Tal out of his sling now and cradled him against her shoulder. "Especially after what Alyce and Owen have done—protecting their loved ones by leaving them behind—we cannot ignore it any longer. I'd hoped to keep our family together a little while longer, but this next voyage is likely to be dangerous, and I can't put Tal at risk. I think we should leave him here with Sylvia."

Jude was silent for a long moment, running his hand over a garden fencepost. "Why with Sylvia?" he asked eventually. "What if you were to stay here with him? It would certainly make me feel better."

Vivian sank down on a bench. Her trouser legs were stiff with dried seawater, and she felt drained of energy after the sleepless night full of terrors. She pulled Tal close, and Jude sat down beside her.

"I want to stay with Tal. I want to so much." Vivian dashed tears from her face. "The thought of leaving him behind, of wondering if...if we'll ever see him again..." her voice broke. "But I can't stay behind, either. How could I send you into the Enemy's stronghold alone? Especially because I'm the only one who speaks the urken's language. Besides, what would I tell Tal when he's older? How could I raise him to be a brave and kind Vestigian if he knew I had run away when Draaken's power threatened our world?" Vivian felt like she was babbling now, but she didn't care. She felt as if her heart were being pulled inside out. "No. You and I both have gifts that may help the mission succeed, and we'll need each other's help. While leaving Tal behind is the last thing I want...it is the only choice I can live with." Her voice choked up, and her arms tightened around the baby.

Jude said nothing. Instead he pulled her close, wrapping both her and Tal in his arms. Vivian could feel his tears in her hair.

"Sylvia will take care of him," Vivian continued when she could speak again. "She's a faithful Vestigian and has a lot of experience with children. When it's safer to travel, we could ask her to take him back to Laralyn and Deniev. If…if anything happens to us, I know they'd care for Tal as their own." Just voicing the possibility sent a fresh stab of pain through Vivian.

"I do not want this either," said Jude after a long moment of silence. "But Vivian—you are the bravest and wisest person I know. Your gifts would greatly help this mission. Much as I want to keep you out of harm's way, who am I to stand in the way of the One Kingdom? And if that is decided, then we must certainly leave Tal here with Sylvia. She will take care of him."

Vivian leaned her head against Jude's shoulder, tears seeping from under her eyelashes. This choice seemed right, seemed obvious. Why, then, did it hurt so much?

About an hour later, the Legend's crew assembled in the front hall of the orphanage. The eyret message was on its way to the Vestigia Roi, a cart stood ready to take the crew back to the harbor, and Sylvia had agreed to let Tal stay, along with Aimee and Owen's animals. Vivian held the fed and sleepy baby in the crook of her arm, trying to memorize every contour of his tiny face.

"We should get under way," Jude said reluctantly. "Ellie and Nikira already have a sizable head start."

"Bye, Liss." Aimee sniffled and hugged Alyce.

Alyce was doing her best to keep from crying. "Bye, Aim. Take good care of Owen's pets while we're gone."

Owen set Pinta in Aimee's palm and ruffled Sunny's ears. "Yeah. I'll miss them."

Aimee nodded. "I will. I promise."

Vivian knew she could put it off no longer. "I love you so much," she whispered to Tal, covering his face with kisses. "Whatever happens, hold that in your heart. It will always, always be true."

Jude touched the baby's soft cheek, letting Tal grip his finger. "Not for long, son," he crooned. "We'll be back before you know it."

"And don't grow too much while we're gone," Vivian choked out. "I don't want to miss a thing." Tal just blinked and waved his little fists in the air. Before she could change her mind, Vivian handed him to Sylvia, who easily settled the baby into her arms.

"So you are the one who can heal the islands," Sylvia said, smiling into Tal's face. "You remind us that the One Kingdom is coming soon."

"Take care of him," Vivian managed, her voice broken. "You have all the instructions about Laralyn and Deniev, I know, but we'll be back for him soon."

"Of course you will," said Sylvia, patting her cheek. "And don't you worry. I've cared for a great many babies here. He'll have lots of new friends and all the goat's milk he wants. This precious little one will be safe with me. Now, go find Ellie. We'll be waiting when you get back. May Ishua protect you."

As the crew stepped outside the orphanage, Vivian saw the Cooleys in the front yard, glowering as Kyuler handed them hammers and nails.

"What do you mean us to do with *these?*" came Loretha's shrill voice.

"Something useful, for a change," Sylvia answered. "Your old employers did quite a bit of damage to this place with your help. Now it's your turn to make it right. Kyuler will oversee your work when he gets back from the harbor." She looked at Ewart's scowl, a bit bent out of shape around his swollen nose. Sylvia chuckled. "Cheer up, young man. A bit of wholesome work fixes many problems. And goodness knows you have a few that need fixing."

As the cart pulled away from the orphanage, Vivian waved until Tal, Sylvia, and Aimee were out of sight. After they turned a corner, she leaned her head on Jude's shoulder. "I hope they stay safe—Tal and Aimee and Sylvia and the rest," she murmured. "Especially Tal."

"Me too," said Jude. He looked at her. "Do you realize this island is where it all began for us?"

"What do you mean?"

"Our story. This is where Sylvia met Ellie. If Ellie hadn't come aboard the *Legend*, then she wouldn't have found you on Mundarva. And you wouldn't have found me. And none of our adventures together would have happened."

"Well, I'm glad they did," said Vivian, kissing his cheek. "If we have to face dangerous times, there's no one I'd rather share the journey with."

The cart drove through the narrow, cobbled streets of Sketpoole until it reached the dingy harbor. Trash bobbed on the water, along with the *Legend* and the abandoned submersible boat. Kyuler helped the crew load up their supplies, then headed back to the orphanage. Finn and Owen lashed the fish-boat behind the *Legend* for towing. They'd decided to take the voyage by sea, so as not to miss any signs that might come from underwater, and the submersible boat might come in handy later.

Once the ship was rigged up and ready, Jude charted a course for the coordinates Sylvia had given them.

"Let's hope this works," he said. "Set sail!"

The crew scrambled to trim the sails, and the *Legend* started out of the harbor toward the lost island of Lagora. Toward Ellie and Connor. They hoped.

Chapter 10
Trapped

Kai stood in the hold of the *Defiance* along with a hand-picked sabotage force of a dozen sailors. Five days had passed since the first failed attack. Now, traveling almost silently and without lanterns, the Vestigian ships again flew low over Rhynlyr. In addition to his usual pairs of crossbows and knives, Kai and his team had been outfitted with a variety of small explosives, courtesy of Calida and her ballistics team. They wore grease paint to help them camouflage in the darkness.

The Outer City lay quiet. Kai and Omondi's ships let down their ladders about a quarter mile outside the Inner City wall. Scouts had reported that a number of cannon nests remained inside the wall, and the four gates were heavily guarded. But the Vestigians weren't going in by the gates. Not all of them, anyway.

Leaving Deniev in charge of the *Defiance,* Kai descended the ladder with his sabotage team. On the ground, they fell into formation with Omondi and a dozen of his best troops, including Korrina. They carried nothing but their weapons, planning to travel light and swift. Korrina had a bundle of javelins strapped to her back and a pair of long knives at her belt. Her hair was bound up in a tight black wrap that heightened her impression of fierceness.

Kai glanced to the north, where Ahearn's entire division was disembarking from their ships. They would wait a quarter of an hour, then launch a ground attack on the nearby Water Gate. Calida's flying ships, accompanied by Kiaran, would cover them with cannonfire from above. The Vestigians didn't actually need to take the gate, though they hoped to. Their real mission was to draw out the urken and keep them busy while Kai and Omondi's sabotage force neutralized the cannons around the Atrium. Once the Atrium was secured, the fleet could safely bomb the urken's other batteries and retake the island.

Omondi hurried forward with three other Nakurans, running from cover to cover until they reached the shadow of the western wall. It was time for the Nakuran prince to do what he did best. Lassoing the wall's sturdy stone crenellations, the climbing team maneuvered up, finding footholds among the rough stones. Cautiously they topped the wall, their bows drawn. Kai watched as they silently brought down a pair of unlucky urken guards. Other than that, their section of wall was deserted.

The ruckus of battle sounded in the distance. Ahearn's troops must have reached the Water Gate. Omondi motioned to Kai, and he led the rest of the sabotage team forward. Swiftly they began to climb the wall. The rough surface and the Nakurans' assistance sped up the process, and soon all two dozen sailors were up. From this high point, Kai quickly scanned the city. Battalions of urken were rushing toward the embattled Water Gate, where blasts of cannonfire now announced Calida's presence. Kiaran's blue lightning strikes split the air. If the

Enemy's flying ships were anywhere nearby, hopefully the Vestigian fleet would draw them out, too.

The sabotage force hurried down a stone staircase, and Kai took the lead. Having spent a good seven years as a Dome guard, he knew every route through the Inner City, or used to before the city was bombed. He dispatched two scouts to run ahead, then led the main force toward the Atrium. As they hurried past charred buildings, reeking of urken filth and defaced by urken scrawls, Kai cursed under his breath. This was the Enemy's way. He could neither create nor build; he could only steal and twist what Adona Roi had made. Well, Rhynlyr would not remain in his power much longer.

They were over halfway to the Atrium when Kai's scouts returned. Out of breath, they reported that they had run into a pair of urken sentries. They'd taken one out before it could make a sound. But the other had gone down with a cry that attracted attention. Kai cursed again as he heard footsteps beginning to pound in nearby streets. Now they'd have to hurry.

"This way!" he hissed.

Switching routes, Kai avoided Council Row and wound his way through back streets, hoping to avoid pursuit. But two blocks from the Atrium, the sabotage force ran right into an oncoming troop of about two dozen urken.

"Archers!" Kai shouted.

Immediately Kai and the other well-drilled Vestigian archers dropped to one knee, letting a volley fly. A number of the Enemy's hideous creatures dropped, their wails piercing the night.

"Charge!" commanded Kai. Knowing they would not have a second chance to fire, the archers switched to hand-to-hand weapons and attacked. The urken had been surprised by the archers, but now they were ready. The beasts were not swift, but they had long arms that wielded their jagged swords with terrifying power. A sailor fell with a shriek, his skull crushed by a blow. Kai punched an urken with one of his knives, then tripped another beast and cut its throat. A third creature slashed at Kai with a hooked sword, but he sidestepped and cut off the hand that held the sword. Out of the corner of his eye, Kai saw Korrina punching and stabbing with a pair of javelins, driving the urken in terror before her. All that sparring practice was paying off—for both of them.

At last the few surviving urken realized they were beaten. Dispersing, they bolted in terror. Kai led the twenty remaining Vestigians forward. They turned a sudden corner, and there was the Atrium: an unmarked warehouse just east of Council Row, its once-white walls now smudged with smoke and scrawled over with urken obscenities. And surrounding it were a dozen long-barreled cannons, manned by at least three dozen urken.

Ducking behind the corner of a building, Kai nodded at the crew. They acknowledged, readying their weapons for a charge. Kai lobbed a smoke bomb into the midst of the urken. Surprised, some of the cannoneers began to fire into the smoke. Kai and his crew flung themselves to the ground as the guns fired wildly. A shell hit the corner of the building over them, and shards of wood rained down. Kai readied another smoke bomb, preparing to charge the cannons, when he suddenly stopped.

Ships crewed by urken flew overhead. At the helm of one stood a black-cloaked Valsha, a woman with high cheekbones and sharp features. Apparently Ahearn and Calida's diversion hadn't worked—or had been defeated.

One of the enemy ships fired across the square, exploding a building in front of several Vestigians. Korrina tackled Kai to the ground as huge stones flew through the air.

"Surrender!" the Valsha called, her voice carrying effortlessly. "We have guns trained on your precious lumenai. You cannot approach."

Kai scrubbed dust from his face, clenching his teeth. "Korrina," he said under his breath. "On my move, follow me. Bring the others." She nodded sharply.

"And if we don't surrender?" Kai shouted back to the Valsha, fiddling with something at his belt.

"Then you will all die."

"Not if I have anything to say about it," Kai muttered under his breath. With one swift move, he yanked a pair of smoke bombs from his belt and threw them in opposite directions. Two clouds of smoke burst, swirling together and hiding the Vestigians.

"Go!" Kai shouted. Urken cannons fired at random, and the Valsha's voice shouted angrily over the chaos. Kai hurried in the direction of the Water Gate, hoping against hope that Ahearn and Calida's attack had opened it as an escape route. But as they neared the gate, Kai skidded to a stop. Two more urken airships hovered there, cannons still booming as they fired on the retreating Vestigian forces. Urken swarmed over the wall in both directions, hunting for any stragglers. Their escape route was cut off.

Kai heard footsteps in the streets behind him. They were also being pursued.

Beside him, Korrina's eyes glinted in the light of the explosions. "We will fight," she growled.

"No," Kai shook his head. "We will die, and our deaths will cost the Enemy nothing. I have another idea." He drew a special crossbow bolt from his quiver, then fired it straight up. A trail of purple smoke shot high into the air. Moments later, a matching signal went up from outside the city walls. Kai nodded.

"Follow me."

Once again the Vestigians ran through the darkened streets of the Inner City. They stopped in the square where the Dome had once stood. The once-beautiful building had been struck by a firestar, crushing its glass roof into a crater. But Kai led the sailors to the north side of the ruined building, scanning the foundation for something. There. He rammed his shoulder into a slab of stone, and it budged. The handle was gone, but the side door was still standing. Kai pushed at the door again, and this time Korrina and Omondi helped him. The heavy door gave, revealing a dark set of stairs.

"Inside. Hurry," Kai hissed, urging the sailors forward. He waited for them all to enter before he followed, shoving the door shut and bracing it from the inside.

The underground room was completely dark. The heavy breathing of the weary sailors sounded unnaturally loud. Omondi struck a match.

"Where are we?" he asked.

The tiny orange flame revealed a low-roofed stone room. A few crates were stacked against a wall, but otherwise the room was empty. The air was cold and musty.

"We're just below the service entrance to the Dome," said Kai. "The old Council's cooks used to store supplies down here, but it was also meant as a refuge for the Council in case of emergency."

Omondi's match guttered out.

"So what do we do now?" said Korrina's voice.

"We wait," said Kai, running his hands over his head. "We cannot attack the Atrium while the enemy ships are guarding it, and we cannot remove the enemy ships without our own fleet. But Calida and Ahearn have apparently been routed, which also leaves the city gates blocked and the walls guarded."

"So we are trapped here until the fleet sends us help," said Korrina.

"I signaled the fleet, so they know we're alive," Kai agreed. "But yes. We have to stay hidden until reinforcements arrive."

"Are there any supplies?" asked Omondi.

"Light another match," said Kai. Using one of his knives, he pried open the crates against the wall. One held dried meats and fruit, and another contained sealed jugs of water. Kai guessed the provisions would last the sailors a few days if they were sparing. He hoped that would be enough.

"We should post a guard," said Korrina. "To warn us of danger or if help comes."

Kai agreed, dispatching a single sailor as Omondi distributed small rations of food and water. Exhausted, the sailors settled down to eat and rest, sitting in the dark to conserve matches. Kai felt too tense to sleep. He volunteered to take the next watch in two hours, then leaned against a wall, cleaning his knife blades vigorously.

He felt the air stir as someone sat beside him, and though it was dark, he knew it was Korrina.

"Well done," she whispered close to his ear. "This is a good hiding place."

Kai blew out a breath of air, cleaning his knife blade with the edge of his shirt. "I feel like a fool," he whispered back, keeping his voice too low for the others to hear. "I led us into a dead end with no escape. Now we're trapped here."

"And what would have been better? That we all die in the street?" Korrina snorted softly. "*That* would have made you a fool."

The corners of Kai's mouth turned upward in spite of himself. "I'm glad most of us made it here safely. I just wish we'd been successful in retaking the Atrium. We were so close."

Korrina's hand slipped into Kai's. "We *will* take it," she whispered. "The fleet will come back for us. Then we will recapture the Atrium and the island."

Kai squeezed Korrina's hand, taking comfort from its warmth and strength. "Thank you. I'm just sorry to drag you into all this. Though I'm not sorry you're here…with me."

"You cannot drag me into anything. I am here because I choose to be," came Korrina's whisper. "And I am not sorry either."

Kai felt the weight of her head as she leaned against his shoulder. Warmth bloomed inside his chest, a flicker like the orange light from the match. Perhaps being trapped underground wasn't the worst fate in the world.

Chapter 11
Ships

Recording minutes for a one-person Council is the most mind-numbing work ever invented, Meggie thought. She had been sitting in this chair, her writing set idle on her lap, for the past hour while Admiral Trull went over paperwork. Silently. Alone.

Meggie was just going to ask if she could be dismissed when Trull planted his big fist on the pile of paper in front of him.

"What am I doing here, Meggie?" he growled.

"Do you—want me to write that down in the minutes, sir?"

"No." Trull rubbed the bridge of his nose. "I'm asking you."

"Well…" Meggie set down her pen, considering her words carefully. "You're looking after the civilians on Dhar and keeping Council business running while the other commanders are…"

"Out fighting," Trull finished. "Doing their duty. Doing *something*. While I'm here with this…" he gestured at the mound of documents in front of him. "Paperwork."

"I know a thing or two about paperwork, sir," said Meggie, tapping the writing desk in front of her.

Trull jerked his chin at the writing desk. "Do you…like your work?"

"I won't say it's the same as working on Council business directly, sir. But I am grateful to be here and help out, even indirectly."

"So you actually like all...this?" He gestured at the pile of papers.

Meggie shrugged. "I'd never done anything useful in my life before serving on the Council. I liked hearing about real Vestigians' problems and thinking up good ways to fix them. I liked debating and figuring out good answers. The paperwork is really just a tool to make that happen. Maybe I'll be able to stand for a proper Council seat, someday when the Vestigia Roi is safe and has actual elections again."

Trull raised his eyebrows. "Politics for you, eh? Who'd have thought Consul Radburne'd have a daughter who wanted to fill his shoes?"

Meggie felt a wave of heat flush her face. "I'd prefer to think that I fill my own shoes, sir. I do not support my father's decision to turn traitor."

"Of course not. Well, glad somebody likes all this governing business. Me, I can't wait for the day when I have my feet on a deck again. Since you like the paperwork so much, why don't you help me with this? You can read some of the documents, pass over anything that needs a decision." Trull pushed a stack of papers toward Meggie.

"Really, sir?" Meggie felt her heart leap.

Trull shrugged. "It's not as if you're recording many minutes today."

It was some time later when Meggie heard a knock at the door and looked up. She'd been so absorbed in a report on flour supplies that she wasn't sure if hours or minutes had passed. It felt so good to be doing something useful rather than just recording other people's conversations.

"Come in," said Trull.

Commanders Ahearn and Calida appeared, along with Deniev and the Alirya Kiaran. Calida's face was dark with smoke, and Ahearn had a bandage wrapped around his head.

"What happened? Where are the others?" Trull stood up.

Meggie reluctantly slipped back into her recorder chair. This was bound to be important.

"The sabotage force was captured," Calida practically spat. "Our diversion worked for a while, but then some of the enemy fleet broke away. We saw them hover over the Atrium, which must have halted Kai and Omondi's progress."

"But the Lagorites rallied and pushed us back from the gate. We were forced to retreat," said Ahearn, glowering fiercely.

"Someone fired a distress flare, so at least part of the sabotage force is alive, but they're trapped in the Inner City," Deniev added.

"We must free them. We still need a ground force to liberate the Atrium," said Trull.

Calida and Ahearn exchanged a glance. "Our ships took heavy damage last night," Calida explained. "The Enemy's firepower was concentrated on them as part of the diversion. We cannot sail back into the city until repairs are made—not for several days at least."

"Those trapped soldiers don't have days!" Trull banged his fist on the table. "Even if they're still alive, they'll starve or be picked off by urken in a day or two. We have to get back over there."

"Show me more ships, and we'll go tonight!" Calida barked back. "But we cannot attack with broken masts and sails full of holes."

Trull began to pace. "We've already drained our resources from the islands. There are no more ships or sailors."

"Then we're grounded here while the others suffer and die," growled Ahearn.

There was another knock at the door. A young messenger stepped inside and cleared his throat awkwardly.

"Er...sorry, Your Honors. But...we've sighted flying ships on the horizon, coming from the east. They're headed this way."

"From the east, you say?" Trull frowned. "How many?"

"Ten, Your Honor."

Meggie thought quickly. They'd already agreed that no more recruits were coming. All the existing Vestigian ships were accounted for. Did that mean these new ships belonged to the Enemy? Were they seizing the Vestigia Roi's moment of weakness to attack Dhar?

Deniev crossed his arms. "If they're enemies, we can't just wait for them here. Vellir is full of civilians."

"This isn't going to be pretty if they're looking for a fight," said Calida. "I wish we had time to make some repairs."

"We'll have to make do with what we have," said Trull grimly. "Let me sail out with you."

"You're needed here, sir," said Ahearn. "Someone must get the civilians to shelter in the underground bunker."

"All right," Trull agreed grudgingly. "I'll give the order. Meggie, you're with me."

Calida, Ahearn, and Deniev headed back to the hangar with Lilia and Kiaran. Meggie followed Trull to ring the alarm bell. The loud clanging sound brought scores of civilians flooding into the dining hall. In his booming voice, Trull instructed everyone to retreat to the bunker.

Meggie watched a wave of panic rush over the crowd as they began to surge down the passageways. Halfway down, she found Katha.

"What's going on?" Katha demanded.

"There are some ships headed this way," Meggie explained. "It's probably nothing—just a misunderstanding."

"Or it could be enemy soldiers coming to murder us!" Katha wailed.

"Shhh! Keep your voice down," Meggie hissed. "It's no use panicking. We've just got to stay calm and wait."

Though all of Vellir was built into Saklos Mountain, the bunker was buried at the very base. The long room's walls were made of solid stone, and its single door, equipped with three steel bolts, was as thick as a man's arm was long. It had been designed as a last retreat in case of attack. But as Meggie ushered little children, elderly people, and mothers with babies into that dark underground room, it felt more like a tomb than a refuge. As the door's triple bolts slammed shut one by one, Meggie sat down beside Katha on the cold floor, trying to keep her own panic at bay. Laralyn and Gresha joined them. A few dim lanterns flickered in the oppressive darkness. In her mind's eye, Meggie vividly imagined the fleet being blown to smithereens. The sentries might have seen only ten enemy ships, but what if those were simply bait to lure the Vestigian fleet into a larger ambush? How long would it be until they heard the howls of urken in the passage just outside? Hardly realizing it, she reached for Katha's hand and squeezed.

"Ow, don't pinch," muttered Katha, but she squeezed back.

Then someone began to sing. At first it was a dull, flat sound muted by the low-ceilinged stone room. But then more voices joined in, and together they found the places where echoes could collect and rise and push the walls away.

Listen, O heavens, and hear the Song.
The good king's making-words,
Listen! They fall like the rain.

All things call him Maker
All life looks to him for food and breath.
The good king makes all things,
All things beautiful in their right time.

He makes all skies and clouds,
The moon and stars call him Father.
The rain is his gift, and the ocean it fills,
The sun is his too, when the storm has passed.

Still clinging to Katha's hand, Meggie joined in. It was the same passage of music that had been sung the night of the Rhynlyr attack. How strange it felt to sing it now, in a stone bunker deep underground. Yet wasn't it the very same Song that kept the heart of the Vestigian resistance beating?

They sang until one of the lanterns burned out and Meggie's throat felt rough and dry. Silence fell. Gresha began to whimper and reached for Katha, who pulled her onto her lap. Meggie wondered at her sister. She could be a sniveling pest one moment, then a perfectly calm and comforting presence the next.

The silence was broken by a banging on the door. Everyone froze.

Boom. Boomboomboom. Boom.

Meggie listened more carefully. The signal for safety was one tap, followed by three, then one, then two, then three again. It was a complex enough pattern that no enemy could guess it by accident. When she heard the last three raps on the door, she looked at Admiral Trull, who got up and crossed the chamber. With all eyes on him, he slid back the bolts, one by one.

Ahearn, Calida, and Deniev stood in the doorway, along with a detachment of other sailors. None appeared wounded. Ahearn's face was calm enough, but Deniev was glowering fiercely.

"Is the way clear?" said Trull.

"We're no longer in danger of attack, Your Honor," Calida reported. "But the sailors think there's something you should see before you clear the people to leave the bunker."

Deniev looked at Katha and Meggie. "You should come too."

Meggie frowned at Katha. Why them? Neither was officially on the Council anymore. Heart pounding, she got up and followed the councilmembers back up the passageway.

When they reached the hangar, Meggie saw ten additional flying ships crowded alongside the battered fleet. They looked trim and well repaired, and their crews sat against the wall, hands on their heads. Even from a distance Meggie could see they were human, not urken.

As Trull approached, a Vestigian sailor prodded a prisoner to his feet. The man stood up slowly. His back was to Meggie, but there was something familiar about his white hair, his stance.

He turned around.

Katha fainted dead away. Deniev caught her before she hit the ground. Meggie's stomach balled into a cold fist.

"Father?"

Chapter 12
Visions

llie must have fallen asleep, because she awoke with a jolt as the fish-boat stopped.

"We're here," said Nikira.

A crack of light opened in the undersea darkness. Nikira steered the fish-boat into it, and a hatch shut behind them. There was a low rushing sound, and through the glass eyes of the fish, Ellie saw the water drain from around them. When the sound had stopped, Nikira opened the door.

They were in a dimly lit bay that felt damp and smelled like old shoes. Nikira tugged on the rope around Ellie's neck, leading her through two sets of doors, and Ellie hurried to keep up. On stepping through the second set, Ellie stopped and stared.

"Welcome," said Nikira, "to the island of Lagora."

They stood at the edge of a city that was completely sealed off from the outside ocean. Under the high, domed ceiling was a glowing globe like a sickly, greenish sun. Translucent cords trailed down from the light source, reminding Ellie of enormous jellyfish tentacles. Under the globe, the city had a thick central pillar of twisting chambers and passageways, its exterior ribbed like the skeleton of an enormous eel. On the ground level of the city, open spaces were filled with dark, slimy-looking plants that gave off a putrid smell. One large patch was full of nothing but pale, glowing flowers that reminded Ellie of the souls she'd seen rising from the fall of Mundarva long ago. Goosebumps rose on her arms. She was a prisoner in Draaken's city at the bottom of the ocean. She wondered if the master was currently in residence.

Nikira led Ellie toward the eel-like passageways, moving past groups of urken tending the reeking gardens. Valsha officers oversaw the work. Some of them rode giant spiders; others tapped black whips in the palms of their hands. All nodded respectfully to Nikira as she passed. Ellie wondered how powerful Nikira was among them, and what kind of prize or promotion she had been promised in exchange for capturing Ellie.

"Observe the genius of Lord Draaken," Nikira said as they passed through the city. "Lagora is the jewel of his domain."

"How...did it come to be?" Ellie asked, trying to sound innocent and curious. Maybe she could learn something useful.

"I have already told you of the sunken island of the Elbarra Cluster, a pathetic speck of land," Nikira said, a swagger in her step. "But Lord Draaken did the impossible, transforming it into a city not merely habitable but brilliant. The island can be raised or lowered at will and boasts devices landwalkers could never dream of."

"Like that?" Ellie nodded toward the jellyfish-like globe with the tubes running down.

"That is one. Lagora's lamp provides light and energy for other devices, such as the Genesis Engine, the pride of Lagora." Nikira gestured toward a gleaming metal tower, equipped with dozens of attached tubes and chambers. "The process of transforming fallen souls into urken once claimed great amounts of Lord Draaken's time and energy. However, he has finally completed a machine that can produce soldiers swiftly and efficiently, making his military resources endless. All he needs are fallen islands to harvest."

Ellie glanced back at the garden of pale flowers, a second wave of shivers seizing her. So *this* was the place where Draaken brought souls lost over the Edge, transforming them into mindless creatures for his army. And now he could do it faster and better than ever.

Nikira was in raptures now. "This is the foremost kingdom on earth. When Khum Lagor comes at last, this city will be the model for all that come after."

Ellie stared out at the dead city. Its artificial lamp could never hope to compare with the brilliant sunsets she'd seen on Rhynlyr; its rotting gardens would never grow the sweet, ripe oranges she'd tasted on Vahye. In fact, Lagora was nothing more than a poor, twisted imitation of the world Adona Roi had sung into being. What must it be like to live down here, in this dismal hole, cut off from sparkling rivers and growing trees? Ellie almost felt sorry for Nikira and the others who lived here. "You really don't know what you're missing."

Nikira gave a sudden yank on Ellie's leash, forcing Ellie close and making her gasp for breath.

"What do you know? What good is beauty without the power to rule it?" Nikira started walking again, yanking Ellie behind her. "This way. Lord Draaken won't be kept waiting."

They entered one of the eel-like passageways. The wall pillars had a wet, slick texture and allowed very little light to pass between them. The putrid stench of the city followed Ellie and Nikira as they climbed the steeply sloped passageway. As they neared the top, they turned off into a room that was completely dark. The air was damp and cold. They stood in silence for a moment.

"Well," came a voice from the darkness. The tone was deep and silky, and it sounded as if it were coming from everywhere at once. It turned Ellie's hands clammy and filled her heart with a dread she couldn't pinpoint. "If it isn't young Ellie. The ssseer."

Nikira abruptly knelt and yanked on the leash, pulling Ellie down with her. Caught off balance, Ellie fell to the floor and lay flat, oppressed by the fear in the room as if a heavy thing were sitting on top of her.

"Well done, my Valsha," the voice said to Nikira. "You will be rewarded. Leave us now."

Nikira's footsteps retreated as red and yellow lights flickered awake. Ellie felt the cord being removed from her neck. A cold hand lifted her chin.

"Child," said the voice. Her heart pounding, Ellie forced herself to look up. The man bending over her had a round, balding head, thick black eyebrows, and golden eyes. His long black robe was trimmed with wide yellow bands down the front.

"Rise," he said. Not taking her eyes off the man, Ellie slowly got to her feet, realizing with surprise that he stood only a few hands taller than her. Looking into his eyes, she found it suddenly difficult to think or form words.

"Wh-who are you?" she stammered at last.

"I am...someone with an eye for talent," the man said with a smile. "My business is matching people with opportunities that suit their gifts. And your gift is quite unique." He clasped his hands behind his back and began to pace slowly, his silken robe whispering on the floor.

"You are a person who has always looked for a family, a place to belong. Again and again you have been abandoned. Yet you have this gift, this Sight, that would make you an indispensable part of any crew. I treat my crew like family. And I'd like to invite you to join my family." He smiled, showing teeth that were ever so slightly pointed. He began to pace again, elaborating more on his plan. But Ellie stopped listening. Instead she began to hum from the Song.

Instantly, the short man began to melt and stretch in her vision, transforming into a huge black serpent with yellow stripes. It turned to look at her with its yellow eyes and let out a low hiss. The Song caught in Ellie's throat, and the snake changed back to a man.

"You're…Draaken," she managed.

The man's smile had a nasty edge now. "Yesss." He melted back into serpent shape, though Ellie was no longer singing. "And I am Draaken." Now he changed shape into a man with a checkered shirt and dark curls. *Ishua?* "And I am Draaken." Again he melted, and Ellie saw Jariel standing before her, red ponytail swishing. "And I am Draaken."

Her mouth dry, Ellie suddenly realized why Draaken was called the Deceiver. She quickly began to sing again. Though Draaken continued changing forms, now all she saw was the constant serpent.

"You can't deceive me," Ellie said. "My Sight shows you for what you are."

Returning to the shape of the bald man, Draaken cocked an eyebrow. "That may be true. But I will give you only two choices, little seer. You can willingly use your talents to help me and gain a secure place in my family. Or I can gain your assistance by force. But that would be the less comfortable option. For you, at least."

Ellie shook her head. She dreaded what Draaken might do, but the choice was obvious. "I'll never help you, no matter what you do to me. I'd rather die."

Draaken's lips curled into a sharp smile. "What a small imagination you have. I never said I'd harm you personally."

Behind him, four urken guards under the command of a Valsha appeared, pushing back a retractable wall. In the next room, Nikira was calmly sorting sharp metal tools by the light of a small, glowing fire. In front of her was a raised stone slab with someone strapped to it. The prisoner looked at Ellie, and her knees almost buckled.

"Connor!" she screamed.

"As I said, you will assist me one way or another," Draaken said calmly. "If you cooperate willingly, you will enjoy status and privileges like my other favored servants. If you waste my time with struggles or delays, Nikira has been authorized to torture your dear brother to the limits of her extensive creativity, all without granting him the relief of death until I give the command. It is up to you to determine how much he suffers."

Ellie could hardly breathe. Facing her own suffering or death was nothing compared to this. For herself, she would bear anything rather than help Draaken. But to see her brother in danger was an entirely new level of fear. "Connor," she whispered again.

Draaken grinned, baring his sharp teeth. "Do I take that as your agreement?"

Stunned, Ellie mutely followed Draaken over to the adjoining room, which held a stone pillar, a lectern, and a jumbled heap of books. As she passed Connor, Ellie grabbed his hand where it was strapped down. It was as cold as the stone table.

"Are you okay, Connor? Are you hurt?" she blurted.

Connor's gaze was strange, blank. His eyes, the mirror image of her own, were so familiar, and yet there was no glint of recognition in them.

"Leave me alone," said Connor's voice. It sounded dull and empty.

"Connor, what's wrong with you?" She gripped his hand. "It's me, Ellie!"

"Get away from me!" Connor snapped.

"What have you done to him?" Ellie looked at Nikira, panic rising. "Bring him back!"

Nikira simply rearranged an assortment of pokers in the small fire as the urken guards dragged Ellie to the stone pillar and handcuffed her to it. On the wall before her was a huge map of Aletheia with all its islands. The locations of Rhynlyr and the Havens were closely kept secrets, and the flying islands almost never appeared on non-Vestigian maps. But apparently Draaken had found them all and added them to this map.

Draaken slipped a pair of spectacles with thick gold rims and tinted lenses onto Ellie's face. "Remember: cooperate, and Connor remains healthy and whole," he warned. "Don't make him suffer."

Ellie's throat closed as she looked at Connor. His empty eyes stared at the ceiling. He didn't struggle as Nikira arranged her instruments of torture.

Ellie looked to her other side and saw a man being led into the room, his hands tied. He looked Nakuran and had obviously suffered starvation and torture. An urken guard bound his foot to the heavy lectern, then picked up a book from the huge pile in the corner. Ellie glimpsed one of the pages. *A Song Book*. Nikira had once tried to kill Vivian for one. Now Draaken had an entire hoard of them, probably plundered from Rhynlyr.

"Are you ready to show us your talents?" Draaken grinned wickedly.

The urken guard set the Song Book open in front of the human prisoner, then flicked a whip across his back. The man did not cry out—he looked like he had suffered so much that he barely noticed more pain. He opened his mouth, and in a hoarse rasp like the grinding of rusty gears, he began to sing. However unlovely his voice, the Song still had an effect. The urken in the room cowered down to the floor, and Nikira swatted the air, as if troubled by a pesky insect. Ellie's vision shifted, and as she looked at the wall map, she saw gold lines begin to form around Rhynlyr. It was a fairly commonplace vision, much like the ones she'd seen during Council meetings over the past few months. But the second Valsha in the room stepped up to the wall map and began to trace over the gold lines in charcoal pencil.

Wait, Ellie wondered. *How can he see my vision?* Could the tinted glasses—could Draaken have figured out a way to *project* her visions for others to see? But if the Enemy could see what she saw, he'd be able to predict, perhaps even sabotage, the movements of the One Kingdom! Ellie squeezed her eyes shut, turning her face away from the map. She couldn't let him do that.

No one raised a hand to strike her. Draaken didn't even yell at her to continue. In fact, the Nakuran man kept on scraping out the Song as if nothing had happened. But from behind her, she heard a whimper that swiftly built into a cry. Connor!

Ellie twisted around just in time to see Nikira press a red-hot brand from the fire into the exposed sole of Connor's foot. Her brother let out a scream that pierced Ellie's heart, and the room filled with the sickening smell of burnt flesh. Looking away, Ellie closed her eyes, tears leaking through her eyelashes.

Forgive me, Ishua. I can't watch them torture my brother.

Then she opened her eyes and let the visions come.

Chapter 13
Second Chances

Meggie stared at the white-haired prisoner, his hands still on his head. He had grown a beard, and his cheekbones stood out from a thinner, harder face. His stooped shoulders and suntanned skin made him look older. But those blue eyes, that straight nose…he was, without a doubt, her father, Errol Radburne. The man who'd betrayed the Vestigia Roi into enemy hands.

Katha, recovering from her faint, ran into his arms. "Oh, Father! You're alive! We've been so worried about you."

He pulled her close, kissing her golden hair. "I'm so glad to see you safe." He extended his free arm. "Meggie?"

Meggie stood rooted to the floor. Emotions churned inside her. She wished she could be as glad as Katha was to see their father alive and safely returned. But all she could see was his face at the last ceremony on Rhynlyr, the way he'd cowered with fear as he confessed his complicity with Draaken. In the more than nine months since then, Meggie had learned to live without him. She had risen to leadership in the Vestigia Roi, helped rally the army to take back their home, and seen many people die from war and sickness in the process. And here, standing before her, was the man responsible for their suffering.

Trembling with rage, Meggie turned away from her father. She couldn't look at him.

"Well," said Admiral Trull, crossing his arms. "If it isn't Errol Radburne." Without taking his eyes off the prisoner, he addressed the commanders. "Report."

"When we confronted the group of ships, they surrendered unconditionally, sir," Calida reported. "They offered no resistance."

"We didn't resist because we came to help," said Radburne, releasing Katha. "These sailors are Vestigians who were kept as prisoners in the Ilorin Reformatory. They fought to free Ilorin from the Enemy and came here to help take back Rhynlyr for the Vestigia Roi."

"How did you find us here?" glared Trull.

"Vellir's location is no secret to any councilmember," said Radburne. "With most of the other Havens captured, it was a logical guess."

"Which means the Enemy probably knows all Vellir's secrets by now," grumbled Deniev. Meggie had never seen the man in such a dark mood, but he had nearly given his life as a rearguard on Mharra, helping the Vestigia Roi escape from urken. She supposed Deniev had good reason to be angry at her father.

Radburne shook his head. "I have sold no more secrets to Draaken, I swear it. I know my actions on Rhynlyr were wrong, and I have paid the price over these many months. But I am here now to make it right, and so are these sailors. We were prisoners under the Enemy, and we have no love for him. We will do whatever it takes to prove our loyalty and rejoin our fleet."

Trull snorted. "We'll see about that."

"I've never seen this man before, but I know what we do with traitors on Innish," said Ahearn. "Once they've betrayed, you can't trust 'em again."

"How can you say that?" Katha exclaimed. "You don't know him! Whatever he did in the past, he only did to protect Meggie and me. You can't blame someone for trying to protect his family. Isn't that what all of us are doing here?"

"No," said Admiral Trull, "we are trying to reclaim the island that he traded away, and we are *not* all engaging in treachery to do it. Whatever your father's motives may have been, it was his duty to protect the Vestigia Roi—a duty he held in contempt."

"If we trust him, he'll just bide his time until he can sell us to the Enemy again," warned Deniev.

"On the other hand, he brings ten fully crewed ships in good repair," said Calida. "They could be the salvation of our troops on Rhynlyr."

"We will discuss it more and come to a decision by morning," said Trull. "Meanwhile, keep these prisoners under guard aboard their ships. Meggie, Katha, notify the civilians to remain in the bunker overnight. Then report to the Council chamber. Your opinions will be wanted."

Katha hugged her father and kept looking back at him over her shoulder as she left, but Meggie wouldn't meet his eyes. She walked away quickly, forcing Katha to trot to keep up. When they'd turned a corner, Katha grabbed Meggie's arm.

"Meggie—do you really hate him so much? He's our *father*. It's like he's come back from the dead. Don't you care? I thought we'd never see him again."

Meggie looked away. "Maybe that would have been better."

Katha looked as if she'd been slapped. "How can you say that? Don't you remember the way things used to be?"

"I remember him dragging us around to official dinners and parties, always trying to get us to meet the right people. I remember him being gone all the time. I remember him surrendering to our greatest enemy."

"No, no, before all that, before Mother died. I know I'm older, but it wasn't so many years ago. Don't you remember when he'd take us down to the Kingdom Bridge to feed the ducks, or give us coins to make wishes in the fountain outside the Dome? Do you remember the tea parties we used to have when we were little, how he'd make our dolls talk and tell jokes? You used to laugh so hard your tea would come out your nose," Katha giggled.

Meggie did not smile. "It still doesn't excuse what he did."

"Maybe not. But is that a reason not to care about him? Everyone makes mistakes, but it doesn't mean there's no good left in them. Father did something wrong, but the Vestigia Roi needs him now. I need him. And you do too. Give him another chance."

Meggie shrugged off Katha's grip and continued down the passageway.

With the civilians settled in the bunker for the night, Meggie and Katha offered their perspectives to the Council. Katha gave her father a glowing character reference and urged his immediate pardon and release. The councilmembers then peppered Meggie with questions, but she avoided direct answers. She didn't know what to think. How could she recommend forgiveness for a man who had sacrificed his fleet to the

Enemy? On the other hand, Katha's words nagged at her. The rest of the Council was also divided. Ahearn urged punishment for the traitors, while Calida kept pressing the issue: if they were to rescue the missing troops on Rhynlyr in time, they needed fresh ships and sailors right away. The two Alirya remained neutral, reflecting that while people could change, it was also possible for them to slide back into old habits. Trull could not seem to decide. The discussions stretched into the night, but they reached no decision.

"Let's reconvene at dawn," said Trull at last. "We're getting nowhere without any rest. Think it over and be back here in the morning."

Meggie didn't return to the bunker, but went instead to the small room she shared with Katha. At least she wasn't afraid that the Ilorin sailors would murder her in her sleep. Katha fell asleep quickly after smearing her face with beauty cream and rolling her hair in curlers. But Meggie couldn't settle down. She kept thinking about Katha's words, about her father holding out his arm for her. But then she saw him surrendering to Draaken all over again. Who was this man? Did he deserve a second chance?

Finally, Meggie gave up on sleeping. She got dressed and went down to the ship hangar, addressing the sentry guarding her father's ship.

"I'd like to speak to the prisoner Radburne."

The sentry frowned. "Can't do that, miss. I have these prisoners under guard until dawn."

Meggie wet her lips. "I'm here on behalf of Admiral Trull."

The sentry raised his eyebrows. "Well, if that's the case, you can see him in the captain's cabin right away. I'll bring him up."

Meggie felt a twinge of guilt for the lie she'd told. She hoped it would be justified—that she could learn something tonight that would help the Council. But was she really so different from her father, using dishonest means to achieve a goal? The thought nagged at her as she sat down in the captain's cabin, twisting her fingers together.

After a few moments the door opened, admitting the sentry and her father, who was still bleary from sleep.

"Want me to stay, miss?" asked the guard.

"No, thank you. Please wait outside."

Radburne sat down, but Meggie couldn't stay in her chair. As soon as the guard was gone, she stood and began to pace.

"Meggie—" her father began.

She held up her hand. "Don't try to sweet-talk me. I want answers." Her father fell silent, and Meggie continued to pace. Finally she stopped and turned to him.

"*Why?*" The word escaped from her throat, half question, half moan. "Why did you do it—betray Rhynlyr, betray us all, to the Enemy? How could you?"

Her father bowed his head. "I...I had a dream. Draaken threatened to kill everyone on the island, starting with...with you and your sister, unless I—"

"Yes, yes, I know," Meggie snapped. "Lilia told us what you said that night. But...the whole island? The Vestigia Roi? You handed it all over, because of what? A dream?"

Her father lifted his eyes. They looked older now, humbler. "I know that to you, what I did seemed foolish, even selfish. And I will be the first to admit—I betrayed my sacred trust as a member of the Council. But…" he sighed, studying her face. "There was no way I could let any harm come to you or Katha. Perhaps…perhaps before your mother died, I might have been braver, might have looked for other ways to protect both you and the island. But…" the lines around his mouth and chin began to melt. Was he going to cry? "With your mother gone, you and Katha are all I have left. You are my everything. I did the only thing I thought I could to save you."

Meggie turned away, afraid the tremble in her own chin would betray her. "And did you think about how hard it would be for us? Trying to rebuild our lives, knowing that our father was a traitor and a servant of Draaken?"

"I am no servant of Draaken," her father's voice ground out. "I was weak for giving in to his demands, but I never pledged myself to his service. Meggie, I am sorry, so sorry, for the grief I caused you and your sister. I did what I thought was best for you at the time, but I see now that it was not the right path. I have suffered much for it, and I have changed. Won't you give me a chance to show you how much I've changed, Meggie?"

Meggie crossed her arms, squeezing her sides as if to hold herself together. Her eyes felt hot and dry.

"All right," she said at last. "I don't forgive you and I don't understand you. But I'll suggest that the Council give you another chance." She opened the door, and the sentry came in to return the prisoner to the hold. As he passed Meggie in the doorway, her father brushed her hand.

"I'm so proud of you, my daughter," he said. "The Vestigia Roi are lucky to have you as a leader."

Meggie did not reply. She left the ship and headed back to bed. But it was a long time before she fell asleep.

Dawn came quickly. Meggie joined Katha, Calida, Ahearn, Trull, and the Alirya in the Council chamber. The commanders discussed their positions, which were essentially unchanged from last night. Calida wanted to send the prisoners on the Rhynlyr rescue mission; Ahearn didn't want to trust them, at least not until Rhynlyr was safely reclaimed.

"If I may," Meggie ventured. "My opinion may not count for much, but I've done some more thinking since last night. I wish Ellie were here, so she could see the prisoners' true intentions and the One Kingdom's path. But since she's not, I think we have to focus on what's really important—retaking our home—and decide the best we can. We need these reinforcements if we're going to free our troops on the island and liberate the Atrium. So whether or not they deserve it, I do think we should give the Ilorin sailors another chance. Just like falling islands, maybe people can be rescued or change their course. We've all made wrong choices, but that doesn't mean we can never make right ones again." Out of the corner of her eye, Meggie saw Katha smiling.

Trull nodded. "Well said. I would normally question your objectivity on this matter, since the prisoners are led by your father. But I know that you have not always supported his actions and do not accept his word uncritically, which inclines me to agree with Calida. Our need for fresh ships and sailors is immediate. These sailors surrendered to us without resistance and have every reason to want to prove their loyalty. Now that we have a majority vote, I will order that they be freed and dispatched to Rhynlyr right away. As a precaution, I will send them under the command of existing captains, including Ahearn and Calida."

"Let's hope we don't regret it," grumbled Ahearn.

At noon, Meggie stood in the hangar with the Council, watching as the new ships sailed off to Rhynlyr. From aboard a ship called *Fortitude*, Radburne turned and gave the Vestigian salute, looking straight at Meggie and Katha. Katha sniffled and waved her handkerchief. Meggie did not feel Katha's effusive emotions, but she did return the salute. She hoped that this time her father would honor its meaning.

*

Ellie forced her eyes to stay open. She had no idea what time it was or how long she'd been strapped to this stone pillar, her visions projected for Draaken to see. The assisting Valsha was busily tracing over the golden lines on the wall map, most of them converging on Rhynlyr. Ellie wondered if the Vestigia Roi were renewing their assault on the island. She might have felt hopeful about that if she'd had room for any feeling other than weariness. Her body felt as if she'd run around an entire island and climbed a dozen ships' ladders, and her mind felt weary too. She had been using her Sight nonstop for what must have been many hours, obeying whenever Draaken ordered her to magnify or slow down a vision. She'd resisted his first request, but the screams that instantly came from Connor were more than Ellie could bear. Though her brother's mind was so disturbed that he could not recognize her, Ellie still could not cause him suffering.

She was beginning to wonder how long her strength would hold, though. Her head felt muddled and foggy, her fingers and toes far away. She remembered Zarifah saying that too prolonged a vision could weaken or even kill her. Ellie knew how to stop the visions, but she couldn't do it now, not while the Enemy had Connor in his power. Yet she felt weak enough to collapse. She wondered what it would be like to die while Seeing. Would she feel pain? Or would it be more like falling asleep when she reached the end of her strength? She felt too tired to care.

But Draaken looked displeased. As the Valsha scribbled over the vision lines, the bald man paced, his brows puckered. The lines leading to Rhynlyr were growing ever stronger and more numerous—a fairly clear sign that the One Kingdom was moving in that direction. Either the Vestigian army was currently conquering the island, or it soon would be.

Finally Draaken stopped pacing. "Enough!" he barked.

The Nakuran singer, who looked nearly as haggard as Ellie felt, went silent. Ellie sagged in her bonds as the vision vanished. She was suddenly aware of a throbbing headache and an abyss of exhaustion. Draaken threw a glance her way.

"Release her bonds," he snapped to a nearby urken, which was coming out of its cowering position now that the music had ended. "Let her rest. I need her fresh for later."

An urken removed the spectacles from Ellie's face and released her handcuffs. Ellie dropped to the floor, too drained even to stretch out into a more comfortable position. Draaken, Nikira, and the other Valsha gathered around the wall map, and Ellie tried to listen to their plans. But exhaustion took over. She was asleep before two sentences had been exchanged.

Ellie's dreams were a sequence of choppy, seemingly random images: the wintry mountains of Dhar, a fiery explosion, a lumena flickering out, an enormous wave rolling out to swallow all the islands. There was a garden with a high hedge, a tree whose enormous flowers bloomed in every color, and a black dragon fighting a man with a sword that blazed with white fire. And then Ellie was underwater, swimming desperately, but unable to breathe or find the surface—until a hand closed around her wrist and pulled her up into the air. Gasping, she saw Ishua's deep brown eyes. "All will be well," she heard him say.

And then she was awake, a pair of hands dragging her up from the floor. She wondered for an instant what all those scenes had meant. But she soon forgot about the dream as an urken forced a spoonful of dark green paste into her mouth. Ellie nearly gagged on the taste of old fish, but somehow managed to swallow. The food and rest, while not nearly sufficient, lifted her weariness a little. At least her knees didn't buckle as the urken handcuffed her to the stone slab once more.

Draaken approached, fixing Ellie with his yellow eyes. "Well, little ssseer," he said, acting strangely jubilant. "You've been quite helpful so far. Thanks to you, I realized we've been thinking small— much too small. That's about to change."

"Is Connor all right?" Ellie demanded.

"Of course. And as long as you continue to cooperate, he will continue to be all right." Draaken's eyes glittered as he slipped the projection spectacles back on Ellie's face.

Fighting tiredness and a rising sense of guilt, Ellie looked back at the map. Now the island of Rhynlyr was almost all golden. Maybe the Vestigia Roi had reclaimed it at last! But if the Vestigia Roi had won, then why did Draaken want her to keep Sighting the island? And why did he look so happy?

Chapter 14
The Atrium

Kai snapped awake as the door to the underground hideout banged open. Korrina, who had been asleep sitting up with her head on his shoulder, also woke, rubbing her eyes at the sudden burst of light.

The sailor who had been on sentry duty ran in. "Ships!" she cried. "Help has come!"

Everyone scrambled to their feet. Having spent a day and a half underground with short rations and constant darkness, the sailors were eager to get outside. Korrina hastily strapped her javelins to her back.

"See? I told you they would come for us." She tossed a smile over her shoulder at Kai as she headed out. Kai was right behind her. He would be glad to get back on mission again, but there *were* some things he would miss about his time in this bunker.

Sure enough, two overhead groups of ships were converging near the edge of the city. About ten Vestigian vessels, in surprisingly good repair after the beating they'd taken two days ago, were drawing the enemy fleet away from the Atrium. Now was their chance.

"Get back to the Atrium as quickly as possible," Kai murmured to Omondi. "We'll attack the cannons, then get inside and take control of the island as quickly as possible."

"Good," said Omondi. "Let's go."

The sailors hurried through the quiet streets. The air attack was an excellent distraction, but it sounded like it was turning into a fierce battle. Cannonfire rumbled and streaks of colored Alirya lightning split the sky. As the sabotage force neared the Atrium, Kai hurried ahead and checked around the corner of a building. The same nest of about a dozen cannons was there, but only about two dozen urken remained with them.

Kai retreated to join the others. "I think we should change our strategy," he whispered to Omondi. "You too, Korrina. There are fewer urken here now. All we need is one group to get behind the cannons and pick off the soldiers. If we split our forces into three groups and attack from different sides, we can divide their fire. I'll take the center and create a distraction."

Omondi and Korrina nodded, dividing up the remaining sailors and slipping off to approach the Atrium from other directions.

"We're *trying* to be noticed this time," Kai told the six sailors in his group. "Make plenty of noise. Any explosives you still have—fire them two at a time. We want to distract the urken while the others break through their defenses. But when the cannons start firing, take cover."

Kai waited until he saw the barest flicker of movement from another side street—Korrina's detachment. Then he signaled his soldiers.

The Vestigians jumped out with a yell. They fired bows at the unsuspecting urken, felling several before they could react. The sailors hurled explosives, causing bursts of light and smoke and even blowing up one loaded cannon. Then they jumped back behind the shelter of a building, flattening themselves to the ground. One sailor was not fast enough and fell victim to a cannon shot.

The diversion worked. As the cannon smoke cleared, Kai spotted Omondi and Korrina's detachments simultaneously charging the cannon nest. Korrina jumped over a cannon barrel and took out an urken gunner with her javelin. One cannon fired, mowing down three more Vestigians, but the rest made it past the artillery pieces. Attacked from two sides, the urken fought back hand to hand, their cannons now useless. Kai signaled his sailors, and they rushed in to join the others.

The two fighting forces were nearly equal in size, and the determined Vestigians soon finished off the urken. Briefly wondering why such a small detachment of urken had been left to guard the Atrium, Kai glanced back at the sky. The enemy ships were still occupied, one vessel going up in an orange ball of flame. That meant there was still time to get to the lumenai.

The warehouse around the Atrium had no doors. Its only entrance was a trapdoor on the roof—one of several precautions to protect the lumenai. But Kai wasn't about to be deterred, not now. One of his sailors gave him a leg up, and Kai jumped, catching the edge of the roof and pulling himself up. On the roof, he ran into a pair of urken just coming out of the trap door. One swung at Kai's head with its sword. Kai ducked and gave the urken a sweeping kick to the ankles, knocking it off its feet. As the second beast lunged for him, Kai dodged, letting it overbalance and fall. With both enemies prone, Kai dispatched them with his two knives.

More Vestigians were coming up behind him, and Kai checked the trapdoor. The inner ladder had been kicked aside, but the drop was only eight or ten feet, and he couldn't see any more urken inside. Kai jumped down and set up the ladder for the others. It was old and a bit rickety, but it should hold.

A metal door led down a set of stairs to the control room. Kai knew that the door had a bar on the inside, which could make entry difficult. But to his surprise, the door stood ajar. He frowned. First the small urken force outside, now an open door. After fighting so hard to defend the island, why were the enemies making it easy for them to reach the lumenai now?

"Come on," Korrina nudged him from behind. "We have work to do."

Cautiously, Kai led the way down the stairs, a half dozen sailors following him. Just three urken guarded the control room. Kai stabbed one in the neck just in time to see Korrina give the second a javelin strike and the third a headbutt.

The Atrium, the beating heart of Rhynlyr, was a round room with panels of brass levers and dials along the walls. In the center was a large glass tank with at least ten lumenai inside, any one of which gave enough power to keep a Vestigian ship aloft. The glowing, fernlike plants waved gently in the water, but their fronds looked slightly wilted and droopy. Kai touched the glass of the tank, and sure enough, it was uncomfortably warm. The lumenai were drained from sustained exertion and needed relief soon, but they were not as far gone as Kai had feared. Rhynlyr wasn't going to fall today. There was still time to return the island to its proper altitude and refresh the lumenai.

Posting a few guards at the top of the stairs, Kai examined the brass controls. He'd sailed on a number of different ships and had a fair bit of navigation experience, but this panel was more complicated than anything he'd ever seen. Soon he realized that each lumena had a separate power throttle in addition to other dials for more specific functions. Sticking to the main purpose, Kai spoke to Korrina over his shoulder.

"Help me lower these power throttles down."

Grabbing a brass lever, Kai gradually eased it back from full power, releasing the pressure on one overtaxed lumena. Korrina started on another one. A row of gauges on the wall showed pressure needles returning to moderate positions. Kai felt an almost physical sense of relief. "It's done. The lumenai still have enough power. The island will be all right."

Korrina laughed and bear-hugged him, knocking him off balance. "You did it!"

Kai caught her shoulders and grinned. "*We* did it. It might take a few hours, but Rhynlyr is on its way back to a normal altitude. It's only a matter of time before we drive out the rest of the urken and recapture the island."

Then the floor lurched. Kai and Korrina were thrown against the control panel.

"What was that?" said Korrina.

Kai checked the controls. "Everything looks normal."

There was a second shudder, and Korrina rubbed her ears. "The pressure just changed."

Kai's stomach flipped over as the control needles suddenly began to flutter like jittery insects. "We're...losing altitude, fast. We're *falling*."

"But you said the lumenai still had enough power!" said Korrina.

Kai spun back toward the center of the room. "They do! The plants are healthy; the power should still be there!"

Korrina turned back to the control panel, shoving the brass levers forward. "We have to get the island back up!"

The levers moved, but the gauges did not respond. Kai shook his head in disbelief. "Something's gone terribly wrong. We have to get everyone off the island. *Now.*" He pulled Korrina away from the control panel and ran up the stairs, barking orders to the other sailors and hoping desperately that the Vestigian ships were still close enough to see a distress signal. But what if they'd retreated—or been destroyed? Kai and his sailors would be trapped on a falling island. *Please, Ishua. Send us a ship.*

Omondi was already on the roof of the warehouse, pulling sailors to safety.

"Omondi! Signal the fleet with a flare!" Kai shouted up to him.

The Nakuran man fired a purple-smoking arrow into the air. "A ship is coming!" he shouted. "Come up!"

Kai glanced around. All the other sailors were up, but he didn't see Korrina. Blast, where was she?

"Get aboard!" Kai shouted to Omondi, then dashed back down to the control room. He found Korrina shoving at the control levers, trying one last time to force more power out of the lumenai.

"It's over!" Kai shouted, pulling her away. "Something's failed! We have to get out!" He half-dragged her up the stairs, pushing her onto the ladder ahead of him. But the rickety ladder had endured too many climbers. It gave a loud *crack*, then buckled and collapsed under Korrina. She broke her fall with a smooth roll. Dust and fragments of plaster fell from the ceiling as the warehouse shook.

Heart pounding, Kai sized up the distance to the trap door. It was too far to jump, and their comrades outside had already evacuated the roof. Without the ladder, Kai knew he and Korrina couldn't both make it out of the warehouse.

But one of them could.

"Here," he knelt down, cupping his hands. "I'll give you a boost."

Korrina glared at him. "And how are you going to get out?"

"Don't worry. I need you to get out of here."

"I'm not leaving you here."

"Have a ship throw me a rope, if you can. But *get on a ship.* There's no time."

"No. I'm staying with you."

Kai ground his teeth desperately. How could he convince her to do this? "Please, Korrina. I need to see you do this. Do it for me, if you won't do it for yourself."

Korrina hesitated for one moment, emotions speeding across her face. Then she knelt down in front of Kai, took his face in her hands, and kissed him hard. Letting him go, she stepped into his interlocked palms. Kai stood up quickly, launching her into the air. Korrina caught the edge of the trapdoor and pulled herself through. He saw her disappear.

Good.

Kai let out a deep breath. He was alone, trapped in a doorless warehouse on a falling island. His ears popped with the rapidly changing air pressure. He knew that the ocean could not be far below, and that there was no way to survive such an impact. He was going to die.

But, strangely, he was not afraid. He felt satisfied. Korrina was boarding a ship. She was safe, and nothing else mattered.

I love her, Kai thought wryly. *Fine time to realize it.*

Then a rope ladder came snaking through the trapdoor.

Kai asked no questions. He grabbed the ladder and began the fastest climb of his life. When he cleared the trapdoor, he saw that the ladder came from a flying ship far overhead. Korrina clung to the ladder just a few feet above him.

"Will this work?" she shouted over the wind. She must have tossed the ladder's end into the warehouse for him.

Clinging desperately to the ladder, Kai looked up at her and thought he'd never seen anything more beautiful in his life.

"Yes. This will work," he managed.

Kai and Korrina were halfway up the ladder when there was an ear-splitting *crack*. Kai looked down at the battered landscape of Rhynlyr, the city streets and green meadows pockmarked with craters and crooked urken shelters. But as Kai watched, it all began to fold in the middle, like a closing book. The landscape crinkled and buildings began to slide toward the center.

There was a tug on the ladder. The ropes must have snagged on a falling building. The ship above them listed, dragged down by the extra weight. Kai quickly drew one of his knives and slashed at the ropes below his feet. The tail of the ladder dropped away, and the ship righted itself.

"Hurry!" he shouted up to Korrina. "Climb!"

Korrina was just a few feet away from the ship's hull when, with a rumble, a gaping fissure began in the center of the folding island. It widened, running from end to end of the island and pulling apart mountains from meadows, Academy from Dome, following the line of the Alluvia River. With a terrible grinding and crashing sound, Rhynlyr gave one last shudder and cracked completely in half. The two halves dropped out of the sky like a bird pierced by an arrow and hurtled toward the sea. Kai heard his own voice, a strangled cry of horror and grief.

He saw the pieces of Rhynlyr strike the water before he heard them. Geysers of spray shot up hundreds of feet in the air. The sea gave a roar like a wounded monster. Massive waves rose and rolled out like a host of siege towers bent on destruction. Debris from the island floated a short while, then sank slowly into the foaming sea. Rhynlyr was gone.

Kai stared at the ocean, hoping that he would blink and the terrible scene would vanish. Surely this could only be a hallucination brought on by hunger and fatigue. But the churning water, the floating wreckage, the great waves all stayed. This was real.

Hands from inside the ship—Kai saw the name *Fortitude* on its side—pulled both of the climbers to safety. Numbly, Kai looked around and once again thought he was hallucinating. Why else would he see Radburne, the traitor, pulling Kai to his feet inside a Vestigian ship?

"Kai," said Radburne, his blue eyes earnest in a soot-streaked face. "I'm glad to see you alive."

Kai couldn't produce a single word. He just stared.

"He needs rest," said Korrina. "He has hardly eaten or slept in three days."

Radburne nodded. "You can take a crewmember's bunk. You'll need your energy to report to the Council later."

Kai allowed himself to be guided to a bunk, where he lay down for a while, but sleep was impossible. He kept replaying the panic of the lumenai not working, the shock of Korrina kissing him goodbye, the island's fall. Then there was Radburne's face, a ghost from the past. Eventually Kai got up. Tired as he was, he could not rest. Nabbing a piece of hardtack from the galley, he went up on deck. Fresh air and a view of the sky always helped calm him.

But Radburne was standing beside the helm of the ship, with a glowering Deniev steering. When Kai saw the former councilman, a muscle tightened in his jaw. Radburne looked as if he had aged ten years in the last ten months, but his profile was unmistakable. As a Dome guard, Kai had once taken orders from this man, only to watch him betray the fleet Kai loved. Because of Radburne, countless Vestigians were dead—whether in the first attack on Rhynlyr, from the underground fever, or in recent battles. Many children were orphans because of his betrayal. The man had much to answer for. Kai turned his back and walked to the ship's bow, where Korrina was looking out at the approaching shape of Dhar. He stood beside her for a while, saying nothing.

"Are you all right?" she asked.

Kai nodded. "Thank you…for throwing me the ladder back there. You saved my life."

Korrina looked out at Dhar. "What was I supposed to do, leave you behind? I owe you my life, too." She looked at Kai, her dark eyes piercing. "Why did you do it? Send me up when you thought you would be stuck there?"

Kai tried to speak, but the words gummed up in his throat. The truth of what he wanted to say was so enormous that it stunned him.

137

He'd promised himself he'd never love anyone again—not after he'd watched Tassa die, captured and executed by the ruthless governor of Sikar, along with some of the other rebels. Kai remembered the moment with crystalline sharpness. He remembered standing helpless in the crowd as the prisoners dropped from the scaffold, high on the city wall where everyone could see and no one could reach. Fighting for justice, avenging himself on a system that had taken the lives he'd loved, was the only cause that had given Kai enough hope to go on. But from that day, he'd barred those feelings, that risk, from his heart. He would never be such a fool again, he'd thought. But then Ellie had started it, cracking open the door with her thoughtful eyes and her innocent trust. The crew of the *Legend* had wedged open the cracks a bit more, giving him a family to belong to for the first time in years, welcoming him in, giving him people to care about and protect. And now there was this woman beside him— fierce, teasing, passionate. Korrina had risked her life to stop Rhynlyr's fall, had endured days underground without a word of complaint. She was the one who laid her head on his shoulder in the dark, whose quick javelin moves and sharp wit always caught him by surprise. Why had he given her a boost out of the warehouse when he thought he'd be left behind to die? Because he couldn't bear the idea of a future without her in it. He knew he could face death as long as she was safe and well.

But the words wouldn't budge. Kai cleared his throat, trying to dislodge them.

"I couldn't leave a comrade behind," he said finally. "It was what any captain would have done for their crew."

"Oh."

Kai hated the note of disappointment in Korrina's voice. *Fool, just say the words.* He opened his mouth to try again, but the ship's lookout interrupted. "Land ho!"

"We should get ready to land," Korrina said. "The admiral will want a full report."

Chapter 15
For King and Kingdom

When the returning commanders gave their report, Meggie was so shocked she dropped her pen. Ink splattered on the tidy Council minutes.

"*Gone?*" she blurted out. "How can Rhynlyr be *gone?*"

Admiral Trull gripped the edge of the table, his knuckles white. "So you're telling me that the island we have worked for months to recapture—our home—has fallen into the sea."

Kai, Ahearn, Calida, and Omondi sat around the table, avoiding eye contact. Kiaran and Lilia stood by the wall, arms crossed and wings folded.

"Yes, sir," Calida finally acknowledged.

Trull banged his fist on the table. "How can this be? We have sacrificed everything to retake Rhynlyr! What happened?"

"I was in the Atrium, sir," said Kai. "The lumenai were taxed, but not nearly at the end of their strength. We operated the controls to return the island to its normal height. But then…we lost power. It was as if something else were overriding us. We tried everything, but there was no way to stop the island's fall. At last we were forced to either evacuate or be killed. Korrina was there if you need a second witness."

"And you *saw* the island fall," Trull said, sounding dazed.

"With our own eyes," Omondi confirmed.

"Then…was it all for nothing? Everything we've fought for?" Meggie squeaked. She knew she shouldn't be talking in a regular Council meeting, but she couldn't help it. She felt numb and sick at the loss of her home.

"I don't know," said Kai gravely. "We don't have enough information yet. I want to find out *why* the island fell. Rhynlyr should have stayed aloft, but it didn't. If there's something sinister behind this, other flying islands could also be at risk."

Trull nodded slowly. "I want to question Radburne." Stepping outside, he asked a young messenger in the hall to summon the former councilman.

A few minutes later, Radburne stepped into the chamber. He glanced at Meggie, and she met his eyes for a moment.

"Radburne," said Trull, a gruff edge in his voice. "You helped execute a successful rescue of our ground troops, and that has done something to restore our trust in you."

Radburne nodded humbly. "We lost three ships and several dozen sailors, but it was our privilege to serve the fleet, Your Honor."

"You already know that Rhynlyr has fallen. Kai has informed us that the lumenai were healthy and should have kept the island aloft, yet they failed anyway. We need answers. If you know anything that might help us, this is your chance to prove your renewed loyalty to the Vestigia Roi."

"That is disturbing news indeed," Radburne frowned. "I do not know if it will help you, but I can tell you the story of my captivity. Some points may prove relevant."

"By all means," said Ahearn.

"When I was on the Council before the Rhynlyr attack, I sent ten ships to quell a rebellion at the Ilorin Reformatory," Radburne began. "On the way, they were hijacked by urken, then used to attack Rhynlyr from the air."

"I remember that part," Trull muttered.

"During the Rhynlyr attack, I was taken prisoner. The Enemy claimed to have my daughters hostage, but I had seen them slip off into the crowd, with several Dome guards to help them escape. So I let the Valsha Nikira take me without a fight, hoping it would distract her and give the girls a chance to get away safely."

Meggie wrote that down in the Council minutes. She hadn't known that part of the story.

"I was a prisoner for nearly eight months," Radburne continued. "First I was taken to Draaken's underwater base. It is called Lagora, and it was built from an island rescued from the Lost Archipelago. Now it is the movable headquarters of the Enemy. There I met Draaken face to face, which I sincerely hope I will never have to do again. He tried to win my trust by dazzling me with the wonders of his island. He told me he was nearing completion on a new device called the Genesis Engine, which would eliminate the slowness and inefficiency of making urken. Given enough souls harvested from falling islands, the Genesis Engine could provide him with a constant and virtually unlimited supply of soldiers. On Lagora, I also saw an enormous collection of Song Books, doubtless plundered from Rhynlyr, though I do not know what Draaken wanted with them.

"When the Enemy thought he had won me to his side, he questioned me closely about the mechanics of flying islands and lumenai. But once I knew my daughters were safe, I refused to give him any more information. I was never disloyal to the Vestigia Roi in my heart, and I vowed to make up for the ways in which I had harmed the fleet. When Draaken realized that I would not help him, he put me to work as a slave on Lagora for months. During that time, the small urken fleet captured several more flying ships. With this larger fleet, the Enemy wanted to capture more Vestigian prisoners and territory. I made a gamble and told him that Ilorin was an island ripe for the harvest—a prison full of Vestigian traitors ready to defect. However, I knew that no matter my grievances against the Vestigia Roi, I would never actively side with the Enemy to fight against my own people. I wagered that the Ilorin prisoners would feel the same. In the end I was right. Draaken sent me to guide ten flying ships to Ilorin. On the island, I managed to incite the prisoners to fight, telling them there was still hope for their redemption if they fought now for the Vestigia Roi. Most, if not quite all, joined me. Together we overpowered the urken and captured both the island and the ten ships. Then we set out in search of reconciliation with the Vestigia Roi."

"That, too, was a gamble," said Trull.

"I know," said Radburne, lowering his eyes. "I had no reason to expect that we would be welcomed back. But I hoped. I hoped that Ishua's fleet, which goes after drifting and doomed islands, would not give these wanderers up for lost."

Meggie looked at her father with new respect. She'd never heard him talk like this before. Yes, he had committed crimes and betrayed the Vestigia Roi. She could never forget that. But it seemed that he had truly changed. He had been willing to defy the Enemy and sail into danger to make up for the damage he'd done. He wanted to renew his commitment to Ishua.

"Your service is appreciated," said Trull, a gentler tone in his voice.

"But that still does not tell us why Rhynlyr fell," said Ahearn.

"It might," said Kai. "We know the Enemy was interested in flying islands and lumenai, and that his power has increased through the Genesis Engine. Though we may not know all the details yet, I would stake my life that the Enemy caused Rhynlyr's fall one way or another."

"There is also the matter of the captured Song Books," said Kiaran, speaking up for the first time. "We know that the Enemy cannot create, but only twist what Adona Roi has made through the power of the Song. Perhaps the Enemy has captured the Song Books in an effort to twist the Song's power to his own ends. I do not know if such a thing is possible. But I do know that the Enemy would love nothing better than to turn Adona Roi's great masterpiece into a weapon to use against him."

There was a knock at the door, and a messenger entered.

"Message, Your Honors." The young boy handed a tiny slip of paper to Admiral Trull. "Eyret bird came just a few minutes ago."

Trull unrolled the paper and read it. Meggie watched as the admiral's face contracted into a sharp frown. He dropped the message on the table and began to pace, blowing out a long breath.

"What is it?" said Omondi.

"It's from Freith. Our rescue mission," Trull said, his jaw working. "Apparently Freith is secure, but Hoyan is dead and Ellie was captured by the Enemy—taken, they believe, to Lagora. The *Legend*'s crew is going after her. The child Tal has been left on Freith for safety."

There was a moment of silence as the Council took in this barrage of news. Lilia bowed her head and murmured a few words, perhaps in tribute to her fallen comrade.

Kai's jaw tightened as his fists clenched on the table. "I was afraid of this," he said, his voice low and husky.

"But why?" said Calida. "What use would Ellie's visions be to Draaken?"

"There's the Lagorite prophecy, for one," said Meggie:

For the triumph of Khum Lagor
Look to the Ulfurssh for eyes of water.
For the victory of Draaken
The child of visions is the key.

"And Ellie's visions show the direction in which the One Kingdom is moving," said Lilia. "If he could force her to cooperate…"

"…say, by threatening her brother…" said Kai.

"…he could learn what we're about to do before we do it, then sabotage our plans. He probably knew about the Rhynlyr attack ahead of time," said Calida.

Meggie paled. "The Song was used to create the flying islands. If Draaken knew we were going to attack Rhynlyr and has the Song Book, could he have somehow…reversed it? Used the Song to undo Adona Roi's work?"

There was a long pause.

"If this is true—if Draaken somehow reversed the power of the Song to drop Rhynlyr out of the sky—then it's just the beginning," said Trull, his face suddenly haggard.

"The more islands he can destroy, the more souls he can twist into urken, strengthening his force even more," Kai added.

"The other Havens could be next," said Ahearn.

"Dhar must evacuate immediately," said Calida.

"But where do we go?" said Omondi. "All the Havens are in danger."

"A sea-level island," said Ahearn. "What about the one the *Legend*'s crew rescued—Freith? They said it is secure."

"We may be able to send our weak and sick there for safety," Trull said gravely, "but we cannot hide forever. If Draaken has Ellie, the Song, and the Genesis Engine in his grasp, it is only a matter of time before he unmakes the entire world as we know it."

"Then how can we win?" Meggie asked bleakly. "The Enemy holds all the cards."

"Not all," said a voice from behind her. Radburne laid a hand on his daughter's shoulder. "We still have our own prophecy:

When all the islands rejoin
And Aletheia again is One Kingdom,
The Captain of Winged Armies
Will return to rule his own.

"But our islands are falling from the sky," said Trull, his head bowed as he leaned on the table. "How can the One Kingdom come if the islands are lost?"

"We do still have Tal. According to the message, he is safe," said Kai.

"And there is more than one way for islands to rejoin," said Radburne. "It is beginning even now. Look around this room."

Meggie followed her father's sweeping gesture. The Vestigian commanders sitting side by side hailed from every archipelago of Aletheia. The whole world was represented in this room.

"If we are willing to stand together under Ishua's banner, then reunion has already begun," said Radburne. "All that is left is to decide how we will stand for our King and Kingdom."

"For our King and Kingdom," Trull murmured in affirmation.

"But how can we fight an enemy who knows our moves before we make them?" said Ahearn. "His next strike could be anywhere. We cannot defend every island, especially if we cannot trust our lumenai."

"We could take the offensive," Kai said slowly. "If we cut off the snake's head, it cannot strike."

Calida raised her eyebrows. "You think we should make an outright attack on Draaken?"

"What choice do we have?" said Kai. "We could stake out a defense on a floating island, buy a little time while we wait for Draaken to take over the world. Or we can go to him. Sabotage his next move. Strike at the heart of his power. If we can rescue Ellie, capture the Song Books, or destroy that Genesis Engine, we might even have a chance of defeating him. But even if we can't defeat him, I'd rather die fighting than hiding like a rabbit in the ground."

"Where is Lagora?" Omondi asked. "Can you lead us there, Radburne?"

"The island moves, but I can take you to its last known location," said Radburne. "It is all too likely, however, that the Enemy will see us coming and intercept us."

"Then let him," said Kai. "Only one of the prophecies can come true. Either Khum Lagor or the One Kingdom is coming. Even if we cannot win, I say we fight to make it the One Kingdom."

Kiaran nodded. "To the One Kingdom."

The rest of the Council got to their feet. "May it be found!"

Trull nodded. "Let's rally the Vestigia Roi."

Chapter 16
Lagora

Ellie knew something was wrong when she saw Rhynlyr flicker on the map. She was exhausted again, her mind as numb as her arms and legs.

"What are you doing?" she demanded wearily, the glasses continuing to project her visions on the wall.

Draaken ignored her. His eyes watched the wall map hungrily as he paced behind the singing Nakuran man. As the Song reached a crescendo, Draaken finally pushed the man aside, taking his place at the lectern. He inhaled, as if gathering himself for a great leap. Then came one of the strangest sounds Ellie had ever heard.

Draaken began to sing.

His voice was neither very beautiful nor very ugly—in fact, it was perfectly ordinary. And it was the very same Song of Ishua Ellie knew so well, the Song that had sparked her gift in the first place. And yet the sound was completely horrible. Draaken changed the tone somehow, turning the strong and confident music into something that sounded like jeers and taunts, as if every line were being mocked. It jarred Ellie's bones, and she squirmed away from the sound, wishing she could cover her ears.

To make matters worse, a cloud of darkness began to swirl around Rhynlyr on the map, as if a terrible storm were brewing. The cloud blotted out the golden arrows of Ellie's vision until at last it swallowed Rhynlyr entirely. Where the island had been, there was now only a dark pit, an empty blackness. Only one spot of gold was left, and it was toward the east, close to Lagora's location.

"What's happening?" cried Ellie. "What have you done?"

Draaken stepped back from the lectern, smoothing down his robe with satisfaction. Dark shadows ringed his eyes, and a faint pattern of black scales had appeared on either side of his face. Whatever he had just done had exhausted him, yet he looked very pleased with himself.

"Khum Lagor is coming," he said cheerily, as if discussing what was for breakfast. "The island of Rhynlyr has fallen from the sky. I have reversed the song of the Ulfurssh to destroy their own homeland. The other flying islands will follow, once I have taken some rest and you have shown me where the One Kingdom's next goal is. A very tidy solution, really. All made possible because of you, child of visions."

Ellie felt a wave of despair wash over her. Rhynlyr—*fallen*? Her home, the island the Vestigia Roi had fought so hard to recover was...gone? Guilt stabbed through her. Up to now, she had only been able to think of protecting Connor and herself, of getting the two of them out of this alive. But now she realized how much more was at stake. The One Kingdom itself was at risk, poised to either stand or fall. Her friends were out there, fighting for that Kingdom. And Ellie had been directly fighting against it. She glanced desperately over her shoulder at Connor. She loved him terribly; she wanted to save him from pain. But was she really willing to betray the Kingdom in a desperate barter for their lives? Even if she was, what made her think

150

Draaken would ever let them go? After what she'd seen on Freith, she already knew how well the Deceiver kept his promises.

Much as she wished for another way out, there was no good or easy option. Her only choice was between bad and worst; between excruciating pain for herself and her brother, and hopelessness and defeat for the whole world. She took a deep breath to steady herself.

"I won't help you anymore."

Draaken cocked an eyebrow. "Really? Don't you remember how much…inconvenience that choice will cause?"

Ellie clenched her teeth tightly for a moment. Then she shook her head, tipping her face forward. The gold-rimmed projection spectacles clattered to the floor. Looking Draaken in the eye, Ellie stomped on the lenses. Glass crunched under her boot heel.

"I belong to the One Kingdom. I have failed it before, but I will fight for it now."

For a terrifying moment, Draaken was silent. The scales darkened on his cheeks. His lips twitched, then relaxed again.

"Well," he said, his purring voice now concealing a bladed edge. "We will see about that. I will have my smiths make a new pair of spectacles to replace the ones you have so carelessly broken. In the meanwhile, you have already shown me valuable information. A ship is headed this way, and aboard it are some that you love."

The nearby glimmer of gold. Could it be the *Legend*, come to rescue her and Connor? Ellie visualized her crewmates' faces with a prickle of hope—and fear.

"We will see if you still hold to your ideals when these friends, too, suffer for your stubbornness."

"No!" Ellie gasped. "There's no one coming. The gold spot didn't mean—"

"So honest," Draaken clucked sympathetically. "Your fear tells the whole truth. I look forward to welcoming these friends of yours—and seeing how much pain you will put them through."

*

The crew of the *Legend* had been sailing southeast for two days, urging the ship to maximum speed and constantly looking for signs of Lagora. Having just finished trimming the mainsail, Vivian fingered the metal rattle Owen had given Tal. She had discovered it in her pocket after they'd set sail, and now she was glad she had it. These days, she felt as if she were spending all her time worrying about someone—Tal, Ellie, Connor—and it was nice to have something to hold that reminded her of her baby. Not an hour went by when she didn't think of him. Was he warm enough at night? Did Sylvia know just how he liked to be rocked before he went to sleep? Vivian was glad to know he was safe, yet every day she wished that working for the Kingdom hadn't meant separation from her son.

As the afternoon sun sank low, Jariel and Finn were up in the rigging, tightening a sail binding, and Alyce was in the galley getting supper ready. Owen was fishing over the side of the *Legend* to supplement their food supplies. Jude stood at the helm, checking a compass reading. Vivian noticed his frown, and she climbed the steps to the quarterdeck.

"What's the matter?"

Jude didn't look up from the compass. "Besides the fact that our friends are prisoners of the Enemy, our son is on a faraway island, and we're fighting a war we may not win?"

Vivian stood behind him, slipping her arms around his waist. "Besides those things."

Jude relaxed slightly, lowering the pitch of his voice. "We're nearing the coordinates for Lagora."

"And you're wondering what exactly we do once we get there."

Jude nodded. "The submersible boat can get us underwater, but...what if we can't find the island? What if it's not *there?*" His voice was hollow with desperation. "What if we can't rescue Ellie and Connor?"

Vivian was silent for a moment, pressing her cheek against his back. "We will search for them as hard as we can, with all the resources we have. And...that is all we can do." She sighed. "So much is beyond our control."

"Aye," Jude sighed, turning to wrap his arm around Vivian's shoulders. His face looked lined, tired. "So many things."

Suddenly Owen let out a shout. "I caught something!" he yelled. Finn and Jariel climbed down to the deck, their sail work finished. Owen's fishing line was taut, and he struggled to pull it out of the water.

"Wow, it looks big," said Finn. "Maybe it's a shark."

"Or a whale," said Jariel. "Need some help?"

Owen was getting red in the face as he wrestled with the line. "Sure. This has to be something huge."

Jariel held on to Finn, who held on to Owen. Alyce came over to help too. Together they leaned back, straining to bring the fish out of the water, but it stubbornly stayed down.

"What kind of fish *is* this?" grunted Jariel.

"If it doesn't come up soon, we should cut the line," said Jude. "Either the hook's stuck on a rock, or it's a fish too big for us to handle."

"Let me try just a little more," begged Owen. "I've never caught anything this size before."

The children pulled and struggled, but to no avail. Jude went to get his knife to cut the hook free. Suddenly the line slackened.

"Is it coming up?" said Owen.

"I think we lost it," said Finn.

Then something began to emerge from the water, still attached to Owen's line. At first, it looked like a floating clump of seaweed. But as it rose out of the water, it became a shrub, then a hedge, then a tree. By the time Jude returned with the knife, Owen's catch was the size of a house. The crew stared as the thing continued to grow. It was domed in the middle but flatter at the edges, like a monstrous hat. Its surface was spongy and green, like moss or an amphibious hide. Finally it stopped, looming over their heads like a mountain.

"Well, Owen," Finn breathed. "I do believe you've caught us an island."

"Do you think it's Lagora?" said Alyce.

"I don't know of too many other underwater islands," said Jude.

"Then how do we get inside?" said Jariel.

"I'll go ashore, look for some sort of opening," said Jude, reaching for a rope to tie around his waist.

"Let me," said Finn. "I'm lighter, and besides, you're the captain."

Jude didn't have a chance to answer. The island suddenly groaned, and several huge, yawning hatches creaked open.

"Well, there's our way in," said Alyce.

"I don't like it," Owen frowned. "It's too easy. Something's not right."

"But if this is Lagora, then Ellie and Connor are inside," said Jariel. "We have to go after them. That's what we came for."

Jude nodded. "I don't like it either, but I think Jariel's right. This might be our only chance to get inside. The *Legend* should just fit inside one of those hatches."

Vivian nodded. "Then let's go gather our weapons."

Jariel and Finn scrambled to haul in the sails as Jude spun the helm to change their course. Since they wouldn't be needing the submersible boat now, Owen cut it loose while Vivian led Alyce belowdecks to collect the crew's weapons. The assortment of knives, staves, and arrows seemed like toys against whatever might be waiting for them inside Lagora. Yet there was no other choice.

They returned to the deck just in time to see the *Legend* sail into one of the island hatches. The ship just fit inside, the mainmast missing the roof by inches. No sooner had the *Legend* docked in the shallow water inside than the back hatch began to slide shut behind them. Vivian's heart sank as she watched the patch of daylight shrink to nothing. She'd known that they had to enter the island if they were to save Ellie and Connor, but she would have felt better if the escape route had stayed open.

Once the hatch was completely shut, pale greenish lights flickered to life. Vivian could see the water beneath the *Legend* draining away, leaving the ship beached in the sealed chamber.

"What do we do now?" said Alyce.

"There are some doors," said Jariel, pointing through the gloom. "We should probably try those first."

"Be wary," said Jude, gripping his staff. "We don't know what kind of traps or deceptions the Enemy has prepared for us. Don't let your guard down."

"We won't," said Owen, stuffing his pockets with explosives.

There were two sets of watertight doors, but neither one was locked. The crew stepped into a small, shadowy alcove, and all of them took in their breath at what they saw.

"Lagora," breathed Jariel.

In many ways, the city looked like a normal island. But everything on it was either artificial or twisted in some way. A large, jellyfish-like globe gave off a sickly light that offered neither warmth nor cheer. Spreading gardens grew dark and slimy plants that gave off a putrid smell. Draaken might have established a habitable environment under the sea, but it would be a miserable place to live.

"Phew," said Jariel, wrinkling up her nose at the smell. "Why bother growing such awful-smelling plants?"

"Fresh air, probably," Jude whispered. "Without them, everyone down here would suffocate. They may provide food as well, though I can't imagine it's very appealing."

"Where do we go next?" said Finn.

"I think we should try those," said Owen, pointing to a tangle of upward-rising passageways that looked like long, thin skeletons. "If I had Ellie and Connor prisoner, I'd keep them in a dark room somewhere high up."

"Good thinking," said Jude. "Keep to the shadows. Follow me."

Vivian brought up the rear, making sure none of the children fell behind. The crew ran, crouching, behind a wall of glass tanks containing all manner of sea creatures: tiny black octopi whose trailing arms left black slime on the glass, slithering eels with electric sparks flickering from their fins, starfish with bladelike claws extending from each point. Vivian shuddered.

"I wonder what those are fo—" Owen was cut off as Jariel yanked him back into the shadows. A tall man in a black cloak walked by, leading a giant hairy spider, huge as a draft horse, on a chain.

"Just grand," Jariel muttered. "More Valsha."

"Let's get to the tunnels," said Jude quietly. "It's darker in there. We'll be less exposed."

When the Valsha had passed, the crew crept up to the skeleton-like passages. The floor and wall pillars of the passage were slick, as if the entire structure were made from the innards of some sea creature. They ran into no trouble, but soon realized that tunnels branched off in many directions. With no map or guide, Vivian wondered, how were they to find Ellie and Connor? The enclosed hallway soon forked, and the group stopped.

"Which way do we go?" said Alyce.

"I have no idea," said Jude. "Both have about the same upward slope."

"I hear voices up the left passage!" whispered Finn suddenly. "Sounds like a lot of urken coming this way."

"Go right," Jude hissed, and the group hurried that way. The rib-like pillars grew closer and closer together, and it became darker and darker. The tunnel forked again, and again they halted.

"Which way this time?" said Finn.

"Look, a light," said Alyce, pointing down the left passage.

"Is that good, because we can see? Or bad, because it might mean enemies?" said Owen.

"It could just be a wall lamp," said Jariel. "And I'd rather not go down a tunnel where I can't see anything."

"She has a point," said Vivian, looking down the right-hand passage. Just a few paces down, all light disappeared. It looked like an entry into nothingness.

"Well, we can try the left-hand way," said Jude. "But be quiet and careful. If we hear any noises, we'll turn back and try the other passage."

Silently the group moved forward. The light did not move, and Vivian felt calmer. Likely it was just a torch in a wall sconce after all. Suddenly she stopped.

"I heard a cry," she whispered.

"Me too," said Finn. "It sounded like Ellie."

"Keep your weapons ready," said Jude.

The crew advanced. Vivian's nerves were on edge. Were they about to find their friends? Were they about to be ambushed?

The light did, in fact, come from a wall lamp. They turned a corner and saw the pale greenish glow, which gave all the crewmembers' faces a sickly cast. For a terrible moment, Vivian imagined them as corpses to be turned into urken. If they failed on their mission, was that what awaited them? Would Tal be left alone to grow up as an orphan? Vivian pushed the thought out of her mind. She needed to concentrate so they could rescue Ellie and Connor and get out of here alive.

Another side tunnel branched off. From the dark opening came another scream, this one in a male voice.

"That's Connor," said Jariel. "Hurry!"

They followed a few turns of the tunnel until it suddenly opened up into a larger space. Jude held up his hand, and the crew cautiously passed through the entryway, brandishing their weapons. The room was dark except for the light of a lantern held by a standing figure.

The figure turned to face them.

"Connor!" Jariel shouted.

In the greenish light of the lantern, Connor looked pale and gaunt, but his blue eyes burned with pale intensity.

Lowering her short sword, Jariel ran toward him. "You're alive!"

Connor stiffly allowed her to embrace him, his eyes staring straight ahead. But before she could pull away, Connor's arm locked around her throat. Jariel struggled.

"Connor! It's me! What are you doing?"

Vivian and the other crewmembers surged forward to help. But before they could reach Jariel, Connor drew a short, slender knife, holding the terribly sharp point to Jariel's throat. Jariel went still, tears trickling from the corners of her eyes.

"Drop your weapons," Connor demanded flatly.

Jude dropped his staff to the floor. The others followed his example. Vivian felt numb with shock. Connor was one of their own. How could he threaten Jariel?

Jude spoke in his most soothing voice, though Vivian could sense his tension just beneath the surface. "Something's going on here that I don't understand, Connor. Why don't you let Jariel go and tell us what it is?"

A crisp, chilling laugh came from somewhere in the darkness. Out of the shadows appeared urken mounted on huge crabs, their pincers like swords. Vivian glanced over her shoulder. More urken blocked the doorway. Last of all, a tall, black-cloaked figure stepped into the lantern light. Vivian's stomach flipped over.

"Nikira," Jude hissed between clenched teeth.

"The island of Lagora bids you welcome, honored guests of my master," the Valsha crooned. "He thanks you for jumping so readily into his trap."

"I knew something was wrong," Owen mumbled.

"If this is how you treat guests, I'd hate to be your prisoner," said Finn.

"Our hospitality is not to your taste? That's a shame, since you'll be staying a while," Nikira purred, her tone thick with sarcasm. Then she barked a command to the urken in a different language. Some of the creatures approached to search the crew and bind their hands. They confiscated Owen's supply of explosives. Finn started to struggle, but Connor pulled his knife closer to Jariel's throat, and Finn went still. When the last crewmember's hands were tied, Nikira nodded.

"You may release the girl now, Connor. Tie her hands."

Mechanically, Connor obeyed.

"Not so tight, you nincompoop," Jariel growled. Connor did not respond.

Nikira said something else in the harsh urken language, and the *Legend*'s crew was marched single-file back down the passageways to the ground level of Lagora. They were shoved together into a small, dank cell with a damp floor and a low roof. There was one small, heavily barred window, but the air coming through it was putrid with the smell of the plants outside. The breathing of the six crewmembers was loud as they settled into the cramped space.

"Well, this is nice," Alyce muttered.

"What did Nikira say to the urken, Vivian?" Jude asked. "Could you understand the language?"

"More or less. Nikira ordered them to lock us up until someone was ready for us. She used a title I didn't understand."

"Could it be Draaken himself?" Jude wondered aloud.

"Goody," said Finn. "Just what we needed."

"At least they're not going to kill us outright," offered Vivian. "And maybe Draaken will bring Ellie with him."

"He'd better not have messed with her brain the way he messed with Connor's," Jariel grumbled.

"Maybe there's a way to break the Enemy's hold over Connor," Owen said quietly. "I know what it's like to lose control of your own mind. And I know it can be reversed. At least, with me it could."

"We just have to figure out how," said Finn.

Silence stretched out. Vivian felt Alyce lean against her shoulder. The other crewmembers also drew close to one another, oppressed by the dark and the cramped space.

"I wish we'd never come here," Alyce said miserably. "I know someone had to, but I wish it had been someone else—someone stronger and braver. We weren't prepared for this."

"I think all of us—everyone in the Vestigia Roi—feels unprepared for this war sometimes," Vivian soothed. "We all wish someone else could take our place."

"But if everyone waited for someone else to stand up to Draaken, he'd win without even a fight," said Owen.

"Exactly," said Jude. "We may not be able to defeat him. But we *can* resist, show him he can't take whatever he wants so easily."

"But how are we supposed to rescue Ellie and Connor?" said Alyce. "We're just six people. And now we're trapped here too."

"We'll watch for openings, take any chance we get," said Jariel. "If there's a way to rescue Ellie and Connor, we'll find it. But even if we can't, that doesn't mean we shouldn't have come. We're doing this because it's who we *are*. We're rescuers and sailors of Ishua. Even if we're not the bravest or the strongest, we don't give up on our friends or on those who need us, no matter what it costs."

Alyce turned her face into Vivian's shoulder. "I just wish it didn't cost so much. I want to survive and get out of here. I want to see Aimee again."

"We all do," said Vivian softly, her heart aching. She, too, longed to know she'd make it back to Freith, feel Tal's weight in her arms again. "Believe me, we all do."

*

Meggie looked around the ship hangar, watching as the crowd of civilians and sailors boarded ships. By nightfall, the fortress of Vellir would be empty. If the Council's theory was correct and the Enemy could now reverse the Song's power, then no flying island—or flying ship—was safe. Dhar's civilians were headed for the safe island of Freith, and the other Vestigian-held Havens of Amalpura and Ilorin had been ordered to evacuate as well. The rest of the fleet, sailing by water instead of air, was headed southwest to the last known coordinates of Lagora.

Across the hangar, Meggie could see a group of captains conferring. The commanders—Kai, Calida, Ahearn, and Omondi—were leading their usual divisions, and Admiral Trull was finally joining them for active duty. The Council reasoned that every sailor was needed for this last desperate gamble, and if they lost, there would be no Vestigia Roi left to govern—not for long, anyway. In spite of this grim line of logic, the admiral looked positively joyful with anticipation.

Meggie was headed to Freith with the other civilians. Not only was she untrained in combat, but as Council recorder, she'd been placed in charge of eyret communications. If they won the battle, the fleet would join the civilians on Freith. If they didn't…Meggie preferred not to think about being the last Vestigian leader in a world controlled by Draaken.

Katha appeared at Meggie's side, her hair perfectly curled and arranged atop her head. Meggie rolled her eyes. Her sister couldn't even take a serious sea voyage without primping. Still, Meggie was glad her sister was coming to Freith. Katha, it turned out, had a knack for managing little kids. And with the sheer number of children coming on this voyage, some of them without parents, that wasn't a job Meggie wanted to be stuck with.

"Look," Katha pointed. "There's Father."

From across the hangar, Radburne approached. He was dressed in nautical uniform once more. He and all the Ilorin sailors had been officially reinstated as Vestigians and assigned to Trull's division for this battle. In recognition of his bravery during the Rhynlyr mission, Radburne had been named captain of the ship *Fortitude*. It was a much lower position than he'd ever held on Rhynlyr before the attack, but Meggie saw a new lightness in her father's bearing. He looked happy to be serving the fleet he loved after being away for so long.

Radburne smiled as he approached Meggie and Katha.

"Well, my girls," their father said. "It's time to go. My crew is all ready to get the *Fortitude* under way." He set a hand on each of their shoulders. Meggie would have pulled away from the gesture a few days ago, but now it felt comforting. He looked at each of them in turn. "Stay safe. And know that I love you above all. I'm proud of you, always. Remember that."

Katha dabbed at her eyes with a handkerchief. "You be safe too, Father," she sniffled.

Meggie had planned what she was going to say, but when she looked at her father, she lost the words. Instead, she hugged him. She felt his arms go around her, cautiously at first, then holding on tight.

"You did it," she whispered.

"Not yet," said her father. "We've still got one more battle ahead of us."

"No," said Meggie. I mean—*you* did it. You kept your vows."

She let go at last, and her father chucked her under the chin, as he used to do when she was small. "I told you I would if you gave me a chance, didn't I?"

Meggie nodded slowly. "I'm...I'm proud of you."

Her father's mouth twitched into a smile even as his eyes filled up with tears. "Thank you, Meggie. I will do my best to keep it that way from now on." He kissed her forehead, then Katha's. "Until we meet again."

A few hours later, Meggie stood beside Katha on the deck of one of the Freith-bound convoy ships. Katha was humming softly to calm someone's fussy baby. The ships rolled gently on the nighttime ocean, and their lanterns flickered like fireflies over the water.

How small they look against the great dark, Meggie thought. *Will our fleet be able to defeat the Enemy? Or will Khum Lagor swallow up the One Kingdom at last?*

Chapter 17
Sea Battle

Two days later, Kai stood at the bow of the *Defiance,* scanning an empty plain of ocean. The Vestigian fleet had followed Radburne's directions and sailed for the island of Lagora. Now they had arrived, and the ships' masts clumped together as densely as a floating forest. But there was no sign of an island.

Admiral Trull, who seemed delighted to be back on active duty, was proceeding as if Lagora would magically appear. His ship, the *Intrepid,* ran up flag signals for the fleet to divide. The agreed-upon plan was for the fleet to separate into four quarters, each one led by a commander. Under each commander was a captain with orders to break away from the main group in case of an attack. By spreading out, the fleet hoped to gain more mobility and better odds of survival if part of it was destroyed.

Trull himself commanded the first quarter with Ahearn as his captain. Ahearn had less seafaring experience, but he was battle-tested, and his presence encouraged the sailors from the Orkent Isles. The Alirya Kiaran also sailed with them.

Calida commanded the second quarter with Radburne as her captain. Sailors from Newdonia answered to them. Kai thought he would never forget the former councilman's expression of shock and gratitude when the admiral had named him to the post. Restoring Radburne to a position of leadership had certainly been an act of faith on Trull's part. But the former councilman had shown great bravery and loyalty since his return to the fleet. Kai only hoped that would continue to hold true.

Kai himself commanded a third quarter of the fleet with Deniev as his captain. Under them were sailors from Arjun Mador, and Lady Lilia accompanied them. In his quarter, Kai was testing out a new tactic. He'd placed several singers aboard every ship, each singer equipped with an amplifying trumpet. Whether Kai's idea would work remained to be seen.

The final quarter of the fleet was under Omondi's command with Korrina as his captain. Kai spotted her halfway up the rigging of her ship, the *Venture*. She barked orders to her lookout, then scrambled back to the helm. Kai felt a spasm of regret, one of many he'd had over the last few days. He'd known since Rhynlyr that he needed to talk to her—needed to ask her if she felt as he did. The question chafed him like a ship's rope. And yet he'd avoided it with all his might, throwing himself into voyage preparations, strategy meetings, anything to get away from the conversation. Fear consumed him, greater than anything he'd ever felt before a battle. How could he risk his heart again in this way? What if he'd misunderstood Korrina's signals? What if she laughed at him for daring to reach for a woman so queenly and magnificent, so far above him? What if she scorned him? Or—worst of all—what if she said yes, and then he lost her like he'd lost Tassa? Kai felt as if he were walking into a battle without weapons, without armor, opening himself to the fullness of pain he'd spent years shutting out.

And yet, as he watched Korrina prepare her ship, Kai felt a deep ache somewhere near the center of his chest. He had not spoken. And now he and Korrina were both sailing into a battle that might cost either or both of them their lives. Could it possibly hurt more to stay silent than to speak? To fall in battle without ever telling her that she had become the wind in his sails, the magnetic north of his compass—that he'd loved her since the day she blackened his eye on Nakuru?

Kai's mouth tightened. He wished he could speak now, make right what he'd neglected. But he could not. He promised himself that if he survived this battle, he would not waste another moment.

As the quarters of the fleet separated, the sun rose higher, reflecting brightly off the sea, and the wind picked up. Kai watched conditions warily. Greater wind speed could be an advantage if the fleet needed to make a quick leeward move. Then again, it could make tacking difficult if enemies got upwind of them. But there was still no sign of Lagora. Kai wondered if Ellie and Connor were still on the island, and if the crew of the *Legend* had managed to reach them.

As planned, the deep *boom* of a cannon sounded from the admiral's flagship, and a plume of spray exploded from the empty ocean. If Draaken's headquarters were nearby, he would know he had company.

Nothing happened. Kai's thumb anxiously rubbed at the *Defiance*'s helm. There was no time to waste in looking for Ellie, Connor, and the crew of the *Legend*. If Lagora had moved on, it was time the fleet moved on as well.

Then the water began to churn.

Kai felt the *Defiance* roll gently with the wave. Something was rising to the surface—something big.

"Steady," Kai urged his sailors. They shifted nervously, hands on their weapons. Lilia stood calmly by the railing.

The object rising out of the water looked like nothing more than a clump of seaweed at first. But it kept rising until it was the height of a man, a ship, a small mountain. It was an island emerging out of the sea. It had to be Lagora.

Kai gave instructions to his navigator, who ran up a flag signal. Trull's response came quickly. *Yes.*

"Ready starboard cannons," Kai instructed his crew. As the *Defiance's* guns rolled out, Kai gave instructions to the singers. "At my signal, begin the Song. Use the trumpets to amplify your voices. Don't stop until I give the command." He turned back to the gunners. "Fire the cannons one at a time."

The *Defiance's* first cannon went off with a sharp report. A plume of spray went up a dozen yards short of the island. The landmass shifted direction, moving away from the blast. The second cannon fired, sending up another jet of water. The island moved steadily forward.

Perfect. The island had positioned itself between Kai's ships and Trull's.

"Fire!" shouted Kai.

Kai's and Trull's quarters of the fleet caught the island in a crossfire. Great patches of its mossy covering flew into the air. The island shuddered, then sank back below the surface. The Vestigian sailors cheered.

Then, from where the island had submerged, scores of boats began to rise to the surface. Some were shaped like black-scaled fish, and their hatches opened to reveal Valsha commanders. Other huge, pod-like wooden boats contained at least fifty urken apiece. And in the water, a different kind of host was amassing: an army of deadly sea creatures. There were crabs with giant pincers and eels with enormous fangs. There were swimming spiders, large and hairy as ponies, and jellyfish whose diaphanous tentacles sparked with lightning. There were tiny squid spurting puffs of phosphorescent ink, starfish with bladed claws, a group of sharks that swam with powerful strokes, and a skeleton whale with burning red eyes. And in the air above them were the buzzing scorpionflies that could temporarily paralyze a hand or arm with a single sting. Draaken had sent out his full force. He could intend nothing but the total destruction of the Vestigia Roi.

The Enemy's forces split, one group heading toward each quarter of the Vestigian fleet.

"Ready your weapons!" shouted Kai. All around him, sailors gripped their swords, bows, and spears. Lilia had her drawn katana in hand and her jade-green wings open.

"They have helkath," she said quietly. "I will deal with them, and with the Valsha."

"Be my guest," Kai answered grimly. "We'll have our hands full."

The first wave of creatures swam into range.

"Fire!" Kai shouted. His quarter of the fleet released a volley. The explosives burst among the sea creatures, shredding their front lines. But the enemies scarcely seemed to notice. The Valsha, commanding from the rear, continued to issue orders, driving the army of sea creatures forward. Behind them, the great boats filled with urken approached. Kai could see the leering beasts brandishing grappling hooks and ropes, ready to board the Vestigian ships and attack hand to hand.

"Singers! Now!" Kai commanded. The small choirs in Kai's fleet quarter began to sing. The trumpets they held to their mouths amplified their voices, sending the notes skimming over the waves. Though the music seemed odd in a battle, Kai found himself energized by the strains of the Song. At the same time, the attacking urken began to cower and wail. The Valsha were forced to drive them on with whips and shouted threats. The distraction left the sea creatures in momentary chaos and gave the Vestigian ships time to fire another volley. Kai watched with satisfaction as one of his ships scored a direct hit that swiftly sank one of the urken pods. Urken desperately flung themselves into the water and fell prey to the vicious sea creatures. Draaken's creatures seemed to have as little love for their allies as they did for their enemies. In his own quarter, Kai saw Deniev harpoon a giant shark that swam too close to his ship. A swimming spider set its sticky feet on the hull of the *Defiance,* and Kai shot one of its huge eyes with a crossbow bolt. The creature fell back into the water with a shriek.

But the distraction did not last long. The Valsha forced the urken forward in spite of their fear of the Song. And vigilant as the Vestigian archers and cannoneers were, more and more urken pods emerged from underwater. The Genesis Engine must be hard at work. One urken pod reached the side of the *Defiance* and threw a ladder tipped with hooks over the railing. Urken began to swarm onto the deck.

Sailors fought back with staves, clubs, swords, and bows. The singers, unarmed except for their voices, backed toward the ship's stern in terror, their music faltering. Lashing the *Defiance*'s helm in place, Kai blocked the urken's access to the singers. He fired off several crossbow shots before drawing his long knives. Ducking an urken's blow, he twisted its sword arm away, then caught it in the throat with a knife blade. But the urken held the advantage of numbers. At the *Defiance's* bow, a Vestigian sailor was knocked backwards into the water. He screamed pitifully as dozens of jellyfish wrapped him in their deadly embrace, leaving him paralyzed as sharp-toothed eels swarmed in to tear him to pieces. Kai looked away as the man's screams went silent.

At that moment, Lilia spread her feathery wings and leaped into the air. The Alirya in flight was majestic, her wings larger and more powerful than any eagle's. She lifted her katana, and a bolt of green lightning crackled down its length. Two helkath fell to the deck of the *Defiance,* visible only in death as their butterfly-like wings shriveled into the swollen bodies of black spiders. Kai kicked them off the ship before the bodies could scorch holes in the deck.

But Draaken's resources seemed endless. The ink of the tiny squid was corrosive, wearing down the hulls of the Vestigian ships as if they had spent decades in the water, weakening them against enemy fire. Kai instructed three gunners to stand guard over the *Defiance's* rudder. If that were destroyed, they would be dead in the water, unable to steer at all. The rest of the crew continued to fend off the urken, sea spiders, and giant crabs attempting to swarm the deck. Directed by the Valsha, Draaken's creatures attacked with single-minded ferocity. Scorpionflies stung sailors at random, diverting their attention and crippling their limbs. A few ships away, Kai saw Deniev's right arm go limp, forcing him to use his left for fighting.

"Lilia! Distract the Valsha!" Kai cried.

High in the air, Lilia switched direction. Kai briefly noticed that Kiaran was also airborne, his blue lightning also employed against the invisible weapons of the enemy. Lilia dove straight for one of the fish-boats where a trident-wielding Valsha had just stood up to shout an order. The Valsha hurled one of the bladed starfish at the Alirya, but Lilia blocked the flying missile with her green-glowing sword. Sparks flew into the air as the two supernatural beings clashed. The fish-boat bobbed and rolled in the water, but neither fighter lost their footing. Kai wanted to watch the rest, but the pincer of a giant crab nipped his ankle. He pulled back, then tried to stab it with one of his knives. But the creature's shell was too thick. Kai sidestepped another pincer swipe, then feinted and pierced the crab's eye. As the creature shrieked, Kai flipped it over the railing and back into the water, where a shark made quick work of it.

And still the swarm of sea creatures came on. Everywhere ships were being boarded, and the Vestigians were growing tired while the enemies had a neverending supply of fresh reinforcements. Kai's own limbs felt heavy, but there was no time to rest. He scanned the battle, realizing the Vestigians needed a new strategy if they were to survive this. But what other resources did they have? They were already using all their soldiers and weapons, and those were not enough. If this had been an air battle, their lumenai would have given them more options, but…

The lumenai.

Kai sprinted to the bow of the *Defiance,* dodging blows and cutting down two urken as he went. He unlatched and yanked open the trap door in the ship's deck, and brilliant white light poured out. Kai dropped to his knees beside the trap door, grabbing a nearby pair of wooden paddles. Kai lifted out the lumena with the help of one of his sailors. As the glowing fern emerged, the battling urken recoiled from its light. Careful not to touch the lumena, Kai slipped a loop of twine over one of its branches and swung the plant overboard. Several of his sailors cried out.

"What are you doing?"

"That's our only way to get airborne again!"

"Trust me!" Kai called. "Stay focused!"

Sailors aboard nearby ships watched the *Defiance*, confused. Kai signaled Lilia, pointing at the lumena in the water.

"Tell the other ships to do the same!" he called.

Soon Deniev's ship tossed its lumena into the water as well. An unlucky eel, swimming between the two charged ferns, died instantly from a powerful shock. The other Vestigian ships began to catch on and throw their lumenai overboard as well. Each lumena created a new point of contact, weaving a deadly electric web underwater. Anything that swam between them was electrocuted. A paralyzed crab sank beneath the waves, then several spiders. One of the fish-boats was caught, and a crackle of white lightning danced over its metal surface, sending up sparks as it charred the sensitive instruments inside.

As the lumenai did their work, Kai seized a moment to take in the damage. The lumena current had immobilized almost all of the fish-boats, and many of the Valsha had been forced into the clumsy wooden urken pods, limiting their abilities to move with and direct their battalions. Many of the enemy sea creatures had backed away to a safe distance from the electric current. Vestigian sailors were now turning the tide of their hand-to-hand battles, pushing urken stragglers into the water and cheering victoriously.

Lilia landed on the deck beside Kai. He ran his hands through his hair, exhaling slowly. "I thought we were lost."

Lilia frowned and pointed to the place where the submersible island had last been seen. "We still might be."

The seawater was dark, but something even darker was rising to the surface. At first it looked like a long, thick stream of oil. But Kai frowned. It didn't move like oil. In fact, its slippery motions looked almost...alive.

Then it surged out of the water.

A cataract of water rushed off a gleaming, scaly back, ridged with wicked-looking spikes. Trailing streamers hung from its jaws, its teeth as large as whaling harpoons. Its belly was striped brilliant yellow to match its slitted eyes.

A water dragon. An *enormous* water dragon. Kai's mouth went dry as he sized it up.

"Ishua, save us!" cried one of Kai's sailors.

Chapter 18
Aletheia Illuminated

Ellie had been given more of the wretched-tasting green food and another rest from her visions. But as a pair of hairy-armed urken forced her to her feet and handcuffed her to the stone pillar once more, she still felt exhausted. Draaken appeared and held out a new pair of spectacles.

"If you are quite finished delaying our progress, we can begin where we left off."

Ellie turned her face away. "I told you, I won't help you anymore."

Draaken shook his head sadly. "So selfish. I thought the Ulfurssh were supposed to be generous creatures, but you seem to care only for yourself." He snapped his fingers, and Nikira stepped out from a side passageway. "Bring in our guests."

A few minutes later, Nikira returned, leading a giant spider on a chain as if it were a pony. When Ellie saw who was with her, she gave a strangled cry. Connor marched beside Nikira. He was unbound now, but his blue eyes were still vacant, empty. Behind him, roped together in a line, were Vivian, Jude, Jariel, Finn, Owen, and Alyce. Their hands were bound in front of them, and they looked dirty and tired. Jude had a black eye forming. A troop of urken surrounded them, along with several crabs with pincers as long as Ellie's legs.

"Ellie!" Jariel cried out. An urken backhanded her fiercely across the face, and she stumbled. Ellie struggled against her handcuffs, but couldn't move.

"Bow before His Magnificence, Draaken, Lord of the Seas!" Nikira barked to the prisoners. Draaken advanced, a smile of calm malice on his face.

No one moved.

Draaken's smile remained, but it grew tense. At a flick of his hand, urken grabbed the prisoners, shoving them to their knees.

"Some Lord of the Seas, if you have to force people to bow to you!" Finn shouted.

Ignoring him, Draaken returned to Ellie and leaned down in front of her. She shuddered as the pupils of his yellow eyes became vertical slits.

"I hope you'll think very carefully about disobeying me again," he said, his voice silky and menacing. "If you do, you will be the murderer responsible for your friends' deaths."

Draaken tried to push the spectacles onto Ellie's face. Caught between two terrible choices, Ellie squirmed weakly. "No," she protested, her voice barely audible. Draaken nodded to Nikira, who made a quick gesture to one of the urken. Grinning fiercely, the beast brought down a thick whip with a barbed end across Vivian's shoulders. She stifled a cry, and Jude flinched visibly.

It had been hard enough when only Connor's life had been at stake. Now seven lives besides Ellie's own hung in the balance, not to mention those who were not here. How could she condemn little Tal to grow up as an orphan? Ellie knew what that life was like, and she could never inflict it on him. There was no way out, no choice to make. Ellie bowed her head. *Ishua, help us, for we are lost.*

Weakly, Ellie tipped her chin up, allowing Draaken to slip the spectacles back on her face. He nodded approvingly. "That's better."

Looking wearily back at the wall map, Ellie saw bright lines and sparks swirling around their current location. She frowned. Those couldn't be islands. Were they ships? Had the Vestigia Roi come to rescue them? Hope and horror struggled within her. How could the battered Vestigian fleet stand against Draaken's might, especially with the endless soldiers produced by the Genesis Engine?

Draaken smiled at the map. "Ahead of schedule." He nodded to Nikira. "Urgent business calls me away. While I regret that I will not be able to finish supervising Ellie's visions, I entrust the task to your capable hands, my chief Valsha. The seer is to be kept alive and her visions recorded. If she resists, the other prisoners are yours to do with as you see fit. When my business at the surface is complete, I will be ready to execute the final stages of Khum Lagor. If you serve me well in this last effort, I will make your promotion permanent, and Ellie will be your personal prisoner." Nikira bowed gratefully. Draaken swept a glance around the prisoners, lingering on Ellie. "Remember. Mercy is your choice." With a last flash of his pointed teeth, he swept out of the room.

When Draaken was gone, Nikira looked at Ellie with malicious delight. She walked slowly around the empty stone table where she had tortured Connor, fingering one of her long, jagged swordbreakers. "Well, you heard His Magnificence. Are you going to cooperate, or shall we begin the fun for today?"

"What...what business called him away?" Ellie said, hoping to stall for a little time.

"Nothing *you* need to know about," Nikira snapped, stalking up to the wall map. Then she turned. "On second thought, your little talent might help turn the battle to his advantage. There is no way you can interfere from down here anyway." Nikira signaled a pair of urken, who turned a large crank mounted on the wall. A pair of stone-colored panels slid away from a glass ceiling, revealing a view of the outside ocean. Lagora must be near the surface now, because it was light enough to see, and wavery blue reflections rippled over the room. Through the glass, Ellie could see the shadows of Vestigian ships. But she could also see Draaken's army mustering to meet them, and the sight filled her with fear. There were many fish-boats like the one that had transported her here, each one carrying a Valsha commander. Larger, pod-like boats carried squadrons of urken, freshly produced by the Genesis Engine. And numberless sea creatures, horribly mutated, swarmed in the water. The Vestigia Roi could never survive such an onslaught. Draaken did not intend them to.

The floor suddenly shuddered. Ellie stumbled, and only the handcuffs kept her from falling. Was the fleet firing on Lagora? In any case, Nikira did not seem pleased. She snapped her fingers, and the weary Nakuran singer began his work again. As the Song began, Ellie looked through the ceiling panel, her mind racing as her vision transformed the sea creatures into even more hideous monsters. Should she obey Nikira and help Draaken destroy the Vestigia Roi and the One Kingdom? Or should she resist and watch her friends be executed in front of her? What other choice could there be?

Nikira's eyes slitted. "Don't be difficult, Ellie. Someone you love will regret it."

She strode over to the line of prisoners. Alyce was bound at the end of the line, and Nikira cut her free with one stroke of her swordbreaker. Alyce whimpered as Nikira hauled her forward and pushed her to her knees.

Ellie looked into Alyce's terrified eyes, and her breath caught. *Ishua, where are you?* She desperately wished the Captain of Winged Armies would come bursting in, his starry armor and bright sword flashing. But she could see no glimpse of him. There was only Ellie, the timid orphan, left. Her and her gift.

Her gift.

With the lives of her friends, her fleet, and the One Kingdom hanging in the balance, rescue came down to Ellie. But maybe Ishua had already planted in her the strength to do what must be done.

Suddenly she wasn't afraid.

Nikira raised her swordbreaker over Alyce's neck.

Alyce squeezed her eyes shut.

Ellie began to sing. Her voice rose over the Nakuran man's, her gaze fixed on the wall map. The spectacles projected her visions, and Nikira's blade paused in midair.

Come awake, O sleepers,
from the silence of night.
Dawn rises,
new life from fire!
Rise up, O golden ones,
keep time with the music.

Come follow the Kingdom
to its glorious day.

Ellie's voice was parched, but she sang with all her might. The vibrant new Song words that had come to the Vestigia Roi on Mharra held just as much power here. The golden swirls of Ellie's vision flared to life. The urken in the room cringed away from the sound, but Nikira watched the map curiously, turning her attention away from Alyce.

Ellie sang faster and louder. The golden lines formed a border around the edges of the map, weaving themselves into an intricate pattern. Inside the frame, bold strokes of color in every shade began to flood the map. There was Academy green and the silvery green of caris leaves and the forest green of Innish tapestries. Orange poured in, the color of Jariel's hair and of the lava on Mharra and of the fruit in Vahyan orchards. Purple like the last flush of a Rhynlyr sunset. White like the marble buildings on Mundarva, or Korrina's flashing smile. Yellow like the lemon tree in Jude's old greenhouse or Sunny's shaggy coat. Pink like a glowing branch of healthy coral. And blue wove through it all, the color of the sea and the sky and of Ellie and Connor's eyes. The colors of everyone and everything Ellie had met since joining the Vestigia Roi swirled together, creating an illumination unlike anything she'd ever seen before. It was Aletheia illuminated—the One Kingdom as Ishua saw it, as glorious as it had once been and would someday be again. Ellie's eyes teared up, but she could not look away from the blazing illumination.

Then she heard screams. Around the room, the urken covered their faces as they howled in pain, blinded by the illumination. Nikira, too, had her fingers over her eyes. Her swordbreaker fell to the floor as her face contorted with pain and rage.

In the moment of chaos, the *Legend's* crew struggled to escape. It was impossible, though—they could do nothing while bound together in a line. But Alyce, her hands still tied in front of her, made a grab for Nikira's fallen swordbreaker. Running to the others, she slashed Jariel's bonds, who in turn cut Alyce's. Her hands free, Alyce hurried to set loose the rest of the crew and the Nakuran singer while Jariel gathered up the knives, whips, and hooked swords the urken had let fall.

Connor still stood near the crew. He did not move, but the empty look was gradually draining out of his eyes. He looked around slowly, his face taking on an expression of confusion and horror.

"Where am I?" he said hoarsely.

Jariel, dumping an armload of weapons in front of the crew, slapped Connor's face. "We're in the Enemy's lair, you dimwit! And that's what you get for threatening me!" Then she threw her arms around him in a bone-crushing hug. "And that's what you get for staying alive."

Connor stared at her, not quite sure what had happened.

"Get up, you fools!" Nikira screamed at the urken. Shielding her bloodshot eyes from the illumination, she staggered over to Ellie and forced a gag into her mouth. Ellie choked, and the Song ended. The urken staggered to their feet. The Vestigians, now armed, gathered into a circle with their backs to one another. Connor, wielding an urken sword, joined them.

The Nakuran singer stood frozen by the lectern, watching the scene in terror.

"Fight with us!" shouted Jude.

"You're nothing!" Nikira snapped back. "Stay where you are!"

Slowly, the weak, starved Nakuran man pushed away from the Song Book he'd been singing from for days. In spite of his frailty, he stepped in front of the lectern, raised his fists, and took a fighting stance. With a snarl, Nikira sprang toward him, grabbing a second swordbreaker from a sheath on her back. The Nakuran man tried to duck, but he was too weak to move quickly. With one smooth stroke, Nikira struck the man's head from his shoulders. Ellie tried to scream, but her gag muffled the sound. Nikira whirled, blood dripping from her weapon.

"Who's next?" she hissed.

"You are!" shouted Jariel.

"For the One Kingdom!" Jude yelled.

The urken rushed at the *Legend*'s crew. With a shout, the crew fought back. The urken were bigger than most of the children, but desperation gave the Vestigians strength. Their borrowed weapons flashed through the air.

As her friends battled with the urken, Ellie struggled to escape her bonds. The handcuffs chaining her to the stone pillar were metal, and she couldn't squeeze out of them. Nikira, hanging back from the main battle, approached her menacingly.

"You'll pay dearly for this little interruption, brat," she snarled. "When the Lord Draaken gets his hands on you…"

Suddenly Nikira yelped as a whip curled around her from behind.

"Leave her alone!" Vivian gave the weapon another crack. "You're a coward and a monster. And if you don't like pain, you shouldn't threaten my family."

While Nikira was distracted, Ellie felt her metal wristbands wiggle. Looking down, she saw Owen, hidden in the shadow of the pillar, picking the lock with the tools from Connor's former torture chamber.

"Shhh," he whispered. "Almost there."

A few seconds later, the cuffs popped open, and Ellie yanked the gag out of her mouth and the spectacles off her face. She stuffed both in her shirt pocket. Owen handed her an urken knife, and together they charged into the battle.

The *Legend's* crew was fighting with all the fury of cornered animals. Jude's sword swung in deadly arcs. Jariel tumbled nimbly between enemy stabs and swipes. Connor slashed and punched, pushing an urken directly into Jariel's waiting sword.

Finn was facing down an urken mounted on one of the giant crabs. The creature snapped its pincers, sharp enough to cut him in half. Finn danced out of reach. Suddenly the sound of a second crab's pincers came from behind the first beast. The crab turned to look, and Finn seized the moment to leap on its back. He shoved off the urken rider and clung to the crab's shell.

"Got you, didn't I?" Finn mimicked the pincer noise again, this time coming from his own mouth. Enraged, the crab spun in circles, snapping helplessly at the air. Finn tried to stab straight down, but the crab's smooth, flat shell was too hard to pierce. The creature bucked, trying to shake Finn off.

"Go for its eyes!" Connor shouted over the noise of battle.

Finn leaned forward until he could see the crab's eyes. Then he drove his knife home. The crab gave a squealing noise and bucked even more violently. Finn lost his grip and flew into the air, but managed to somersault and land on his feet. After a few more lurches, the crab dropped to the ground and lay still.

"Thanks!" Finn shouted to Connor.

The urken were losing ground, beaten back by the Vestigians' ferocity. But Nikira was not finished. Leaping onto her giant spider's back, she urged it forward. Its many-jointed legs were tipped with metal spikes. Jariel had to leap out of the way to avoid being trampled. Owen scrambled under the table where Connor had been held. From her mounted position, Nikira slashed fiercely with her swordbreaker. Jude barely escaped its point connecting with his throat, instead ducking to receive a gash on his upper arm. Connor tried to reach Nikira with his sword, but the spider kicked him away, tearing Connor's leg with its spiked foot.

After fending off an urken with her knife, Ellie studied the spider's movements. The crew couldn't get close to Nikira until the creature was out of the way. What was its weakness? How could they even get close enough to find out? She realized she still had Draaken's spectacles in her shirt pocket. Could this work?

"Alyce! Start singing!" Ellie shouted.

Without asking why, Alyce began to belt out the Song. Her clear, pure voice hampered the remaining urken's progress.

Slipping on Draaken's spectacles, Ellie now watched the battle instead of the map. She saw the glorious yet familiar vision of her crewmembers as they truly were. But she also saw their enemies. The urken looked like scrubby trees clinging to a wind-blasted plain. The crabs looked like dinner plates on spindly legs, and Nikira was as Ellie had once seen her: a hag with yellowing, cracked skin and a scaly tail, her body covered with rotting filth. Beneath her, the spider's proportions changed, making its weaknesses obvious: its unprotected eyes and soft underbelly. The crew looked around in astonishment. The spectacles had worked: for the first time, they could see the world as Ellie saw it. But there was no time to marvel.

Jariel danced in front of the spider, taunting it and trying to reach its eyes. The spider lunged forward, swiping at her with its clawed feet. Nikira, too, drove toward Jariel with her swordbreaker. Jude blocked a blow that would have struck Jariel's shoulder, but the swordbreaker caught his weapon and snapped it in two.

In the brief moment when Nikira's swordbreaker was occupied, Connor took a running dive under the spider. As Connor rolled beneath the beast, Jariel quickly thrust her sword into one of the spider's eyes. The creature screamed, and Connor thrust his knife upwards, puncturing the spider's soft underbelly. Stinking green blood splattered all over him, and he rolled away just as the spider collapsed. It gave a violent shriek, then lay still. Nikira leaped from the beast's carcass. With a poisonous glare at the Vestigians, she dashed out of the room and down a side passageway.

"We can't let her get away!" shouted Connor.

"We've got bigger problems," said Jude, pointing up.

Through the glass panel, they could see that the Vestigian fleet was losing its battle with Draaken. Corpses and floating ship debris littered the ocean's surface. New pods of urken kept rising to the surface as the tireless Genesis Engine replenished the Lagorite forces. Worst of all, Ellie could see the writhing shadow of a great black dragon. Draaken had gone out to fight the Vestigia Roi himself. If this continued much longer, the One Kingdom would be lost.

"We have to help them," said Vivian.

"How?" said Alyce. "There are only eight of us."

"And as long as the Genesis Engine is working, Draaken has a practically unlimited supply of soldiers," said Ellie. At the others' confusion, she quickly described the machine Nikira had shown her.

"Then that's what we can do to help the fleet," said Connor. "We've got to shut it down somehow."

"Do you know anything about it?" said Ellie. "You've been here a long time."

Connor shook his head. "I can't remember anything about this place. I think the Enemy did…something to my head. I feel like I just woke up from the worst night's sleep of my life."

"I saw the machine once, a few days ago, but I have no idea how to shut it off," said Ellie. "And even if I did, the urken could just turn it on again."

"An explosion shuts most things off permanently," said Owen.

"But how would we make one? We surrendered our weapons; we don't have any explosives or a power source," said Jariel.

"Do you still have that rattle of Tal's?" Owen asked Vivian.

Vivian pulled it out of her inner pocket and handed it to him. "Here. Why?"

Owen rubbed the back of his neck. "It…may or may not be explosive."

"Owen! You told me it was just scrap metal inside a capsule!"

Owen shrugged sheepishly. "Scrap metal…and a little bit of gunpowder. Don't worry though. It won't blow without a fuse."

"We still need a power source, though," said Jariel.

"Let's think about that later," said Owen. "Nikira's probably already gathering troops to guard the machine." Even as he spoke, the distant sound of tramping feet and shouts came up one of the passageways.

The crew started for the exit, but Alyce glanced over her shoulder. Beside the lectern was the huge pile of other Song Books. "Wait. What about those?"

"The Enemy was using the Song to undo things that Adona Roi has made," Ellie frowned. "If we leave them here, we let him keep that power."

"We can't carry all those, though," said Jariel, looking at the small mountain of books.

"Then we'll have to destroy them," said Connor, his mouth set in a grim line. "Cut the Enemy off from his weapon."

"Destroy Song Books?" Vivian said breathlessly. "But…they're our most sacred literature. We can't…it would be…"

"Draaken used them to destroy Rhynlyr," Ellie said quietly. "He dropped it out of the sky."

There was a moment of stunned silence. The *Legend's* crew had not heard the terrible news.

"Then this is the only way to protect the other flying islands," said Vivian.

"Besides," said Alyce, "There are other Song Books, and choir members have to have the entire thing memorized. Most Vestigians know at least some of it. *We* are the Song. We don't have to carry these books with us to keep it alive."

Connor looked at the small fire that had been used to heat the torture instruments. "I need someone's coat."

Jariel shrugged out of hers, and Connor used it to scoop up a pile of hot coals from the fire. Quickly he scattered them over the battered Song Books. With a sizzle, the pages began to smolder, then to smoke. Vivian turned her face away.

"Let's go," said Jude. With the smell of smoke building behind them, the crew raced out of the torture chamber and down the passageway.

*

Kai watched the water dragon whip around with a speed unbelievable for its great size. Doubling over its own coils, it dove straight into Trull's quarter of the fleet. A terrible sound of shattering wood and human screams came across the water. A lumena exploded in a burst of white light. The dragon let out a high-pitch shriek that sounded like an exultation of delight.

"We can't fight something so big!" cried one of Kai's sailors.

"We're doomed," wailed another.

"Courage!" said Kai. "We are not defeated yet." His one eye moved swiftly over the situation. "Raise the flag signal!"

The *Defiance* quickly ran up a yellow pennant. Immediately, Deniev's ship ran up a matching flag, and his detachment broke away to leeward. It was time to employ the original strategy. They needed to distract the dragon, divide its attention.

The *Defiance's* timbers creaked as the ship put the wind behind it. Kai ordered two crewmembers to reel in the floating lumena and put it back inside the ship. He glanced back to where the dragon was wreaking havoc on Trull's quarter of the fleet. The destruction was total. Kai wished he could sail to the admiral's rescue, but he knew he could neither reach them in time nor do anything to help. The best thing he could do was spread out the Vestigian forces, make them harder for the dragon to catch. However, he noticed Calida's quarter moving in for a direct attack on the dragon. *How brave, and how foolish,* Kai thought.

His lumena restored, Kai engaged the *Defiance's* rear propeller. His fleet quarter quickly spread out, moving away from the dragon. But Kai began to notice a change in his ship's responsiveness. The wind held steady, and the sails were full. But the helm was jerking in his hands, refusing to turn to starboard, forcing the *Defiance* to port. The deck began to rock under his feet, though the sea had been relatively calm up to now.

"Captain!" shouted the lookout. "The sea— look!"

Kai looked over the railing. Stiff waves slapped against the starboard side of the ship, though the wind was not blowing from that direction. A swift current was turning the *Defiance* to port. The ship heeled in the rising tide, and crates and barrels began to slide across the tilting deck.

"What…?" Kai left his question unfinished.

The waves were not limited to the *Defiance's* starboard side. In fact, a huge ring of waves was forming around the entire Vestigian fleet. A disabled submersible, bobbing abandoned on the waves, pulled close to the churning ring, beginning to spin in lazy circles. The waves around it grew rougher, and the submersible pitched and tossed until it was suddenly sucked underwater. It did not resurface.

"Maelstroms," Kai breathed, rubbing both hands over his hair. "A whole system of maelstroms." He glanced back up at the dragon, which was at the very center of the whirlpool ring. Having finished with Trull's decimated quarter of the fleet, it was surveying the remaining ships, the look of a prowling cat in its yellow eyes. Through his spyglass,

Kai could see that the pupils were vertical and slitted, just as Owen's had been when he had been under the *dshinn*'s power. Lowering the spyglass slowly, Kai put the pieces together. An enormous sea dragon with yellow eyes. An army of sea creatures acting as one. An unnatural ring of maelstroms surrounding the Vestigian fleet. There was only one being with the power to summon such destruction from the sea.

Draaken, the Deceiver himself, had come out to fight.

And he meant to leave no survivors.

Chapter 19
The Genesis Engine

Ellie sped down the passageways of Lagora with her crew. When they reached the ground level, they quickly retreated into the shadows. The city seemed much emptier now, doubtless because of the battle going on over their heads. A few dozen urken ran past them, headed for the Genesis Engine. Ellie pointed out the machine to the others. Heavily armed urken surrounded it, and Nikira's voice could be heard from high above, shouting orders.

"How are we going to get close enough to blow it up?" whispered Finn.

"And what are we going to use for a power source?" said Jariel.

"We could use our lumena," said Owen softly.

Jariel looked at him sharply. "But if we blow up the lumena, we can't lift the *Legend* out of the water! This close to the Edge, the current would pull us right over! We'd be goners!"

The crew watched the Genesis Engine work for a silent moment. Urken were dumping crates of the pale flowers from Lagora's gardens into a boiler at the top of the metal tower, along with what looked like assorted body parts. Ellie's stomach churned. The Enemy did not limit his harvesting to souls. Translucent tubes connected to the jellyfish-like lamp appeared to provide power, and glass pipes ran up and down the machine's length. From a chute at the bottom, fully formed urken shambled out in pairs. Their hunched backs and long arms were uniformized by the machine, and a Valsha supplied them with weapons. From there, the monstrous soldiers marched directly into pods bound for the surface. With this machine behind him, the Enemy could keep fighting forever—or at least until the Vestigian fleet was nothing more than a shattered memory.

"We have a choice to make," said Jude slowly. "It is between our lives and the future of the One Kingdom." He looked at Vivian, anguish in his eyes. "Jariel is right. If we use the *Legend*'s lumena to destroy the Genesis Engine, it is unlikely that we will escape the pull of the Edge. But if we try to escape without blowing up the machine, the Enemy will simply continue to produce more soldiers until he wins this war. As captain, I ask you to vote—and quickly. I think I know what we ought to do, but I will not do it without all of your consent."

Ellie put her arms around Connor. This war had demanded one terrible sacrifice after another. Had it come to this at last?

Vivian stepped close to Jude. "There is no choice," she whispered, her voice hoarse. "I want nothing more than to see Tal again—except for a world in which he can grow up in safety and hope. If this is the only way I can give it to him, then so be it."

Alyce bowed her head. "Little as I want to, I agree. I'm glad Aimee's not here. Then she can have that future too."

The other crewmembers nodded soberly. They knew what this choice meant, but there was no other way. Connor squeezed Ellie's hand.

"Right," Jude said softly. "How are we going to do this?"

"I'll lead a diversion force," said Connor. Ellie recognized his focused look as a strategy took shape in his mind. Free of Draaken's influence, his talent for leadership was reawakening. "We'll attack the urken, draw them away from the engine. Meanwhile, Owen and Jude, you go back to the *Legend* for the lumena and plant the bomb."

The crew split up. Connor led Ellie, Finn, Vivian, Jariel, and Alyce to a shadowy vantage point where they could see the Engine from the cover of a low building. Ellie grew more anxious every time the machine put out another pair of urken. Every wasted minute added new strength to Draaken's army.

"We need to disrupt this production line," Connor said. "Finn, can you mimic Nikira's voice? Make it sound like it's coming from somewhere else in the city?"

"Aye," said Finn.

"Good. Vivian, we need some words in the urken's language, some order Nikira would give. With Finn's voice, hopefully we can lure some of the guards away from the machine. Once that's done, we'll attack whoever's left. Hopefully that'll give Owen a chance to plant his device."

Ellie's palms were sweating, and she wiped them on her trousers. She didn't even have her usual slingshot for this battle, just an urken knife. But the Vestigian fleet needed them to succeed.

Connor nodded, and everything happened fast. Vivian said some words in the urken language. Finn repeated them in a convincing imitation of Nikira's voice that sounded like it was coming from a low building some distance to the right. The urken guards looked at each other uncomfortably, but their leader yelled something and they moved out, leaving behind only about a dozen guards.

"Their leader said to go see what Nikira wants, but to make it quick," Vivian translated. "They'll be back soon."

"Finn, keep distracting them as long as you can," said Connor. "The rest of you, follow me!"

Silently, the crew of the *Legend* snuck up on the urken guards. Taken by surprise, the sentries were not ready for Connor and Jariel's swift swords or the bladed whip Alyce had picked up. Even Ellie and Vivian, more accustomed to fighting from a distance, attacked, fighting for their friends, their fleet, and their world. Out of the corner of her eye, Ellie saw Owen and Jude heading for the base of the Engine, carrying a covered wooden bucket that leaked light through the seams.

The *Legend*'s crew was getting the upper hand over the surprised urken guards when Nikira appeared, flanked by two junior Valsha officers. With synchronized movements, all three drew their weapons. One of the Valsha carried a hooked sword, its crescent-shaped hilt designed to trap enemy weapons; the other held a double flail with two spiked heads. Nikira had a new swordbreaker and a spiked metal arm guard shaped like a scorpion. Her eyes blazed with malice and fury.

The three Valsha leaped toward the Vestigians. Connor clashed with the sword-bearing Valsha, using his own sword to keep the enemy's weapon at bay while his knife looked for an opening. Jariel took on the Valsha with the flail, slashing at its legs and nimbly dodging the swings of the spiked weapon. Jude, re-entering the battle, attacked Nikira with a fury Ellie had never seen from the gentle doctor before. But Nikira had cost them their home, their freedom, and even some of their friends. It was time to settle the score.

Ellie knew she couldn't keep up with the Valsha's speed and prowess hand-to-hand. Backing up, she found a bucket of spare parts for the Genesis Engine and threw the metal pieces at the enemies. They didn't inflict many injuries, but like stinging insects, they were an effective distraction. Vivian and Alyce found a rope and, holding it taut between them, rushed the Valsha who had the hooked sword. Connor danced out of the way, and the rope swept the Valsha's feet off the ground. It took a mere instant for the creature to get up, but in the moment of distraction, Connor plunged his knife into its back. Screaming, the Valsha twisted toward Connor, only to see his sword arcing toward its neck. The Valsha's head rolled free.

Meanwhile, Finn had crept around the back of the Valsha with the flail and threw his own knife. As the blade hurtled through the air, the Valsha dodged with supernatural speed. It was quick enough to save its neck, but Finn's blade lodged in its shoulder. The creature gave a shriek of pain and rage, swinging its flail around. Finn ducked once, but as he raised his right hand to shield his face, the heavy chains smashed into his arm. Ellie heard the sickening crunch of bone, and Finn moaned in agony.

"Hurry up, Owen!" Connor shouted. The *Legend's* crew was taking hits quickly. Jariel caught a slash from a flail spike across her cheek. Alyce took an elbow to the face that dropped her to the ground, stunned. Nikira's spiked arm guard smashed into Jude's knee, tearing flesh and bone and dropping him to the ground. Ellie glanced up at the Genesis Engine. What was taking Owen so long?

She turned back to the battle just in time to see Nikira turn away from Jude. As Connor concentrated on the Valsha with the flail, Nikira lunged toward him. The point of her swordbreaker caught Connor just below his ribs. The blade plunged into his side.

"Connor, NO!" Ellie shrieked. Connor doubled over, and Ellie ran toward him. Grabbing Connor's sword, she swung it at Nikira in blind rage. Ellie knew she was the weaker fighter and that it would only be a matter of moments before Nikira found an opening and killed her. But Ellie didn't care. She swung the sword with all her might and heard metal crash on metal. Nikira's sneer bobbed in and out of focus.

Until everything stopped.

There was a loud sucking sound, and both surviving Valsha froze in place. Ellie looked up to see a glowing spot begin its journey up a glass tube. The lumena! Owen had done it!

With shrieks of rage and despair, the Valsha suddenly whirled and ran up the passageways toward the boiler, doubtless hoping to prevent an explosion. Owen appeared from behind the Genesis Engine.

"Come on," he said. "We rigged up a bomb with the rattle and lumena. The minute it touches that hot boiler, this whole place is going to blow. We need to get out of here, fast."

"But the lumena—without it, we can't escape the Edge—" Alyce said groggily, rubbing the bruise on her forehead.

"Let's get outside first and think about that later. I'd rather not get fried in an explosion," said Owen, helping Alyce to her feet. "I'm going to open the hatch." He dashed off.

Ellie dropped to her knees beside Connor. His eyes were closed, and his shirt was quickly staining red.

"Connor...?" Ellie said, unable to keep the panic out of her voice.

"You heard...Owen," Connor grunted. He kept his eyes closed, grimacing as he pressed a hand over his wound. "Get out...first. Deal with this...later."

Slipping an arm around her brother's shoulders, Ellie tried to help him stand, but he couldn't lift his own weight. Jariel appeared on his other side, her forehead creased with silent concern, and helped lift him.

Together, the injured crew staggered toward the *Legend*. Bright daylight from the open hatch made Ellie squint as they boarded the ship. Jude, leaning on Vivian, took the helm. Ellie and Jariel laid Connor down on the deck, then helped Alyce and Owen shove the *Legend* out into the water.

A few hundred yards out, Ellie looked back. From another open hatch on Lagora, a small black shape jetted out, its top still open. Nikira sat in the fish-boat, her black cloak fluttering behind her and her face blazing with fury. She was fleeing the doomed island and heading straight for the *Legend*. Ellie tensed. How could the crew fight her now, with so many of them injured?

Suddenly Lagora exploded into a ball of flame. An intense wave of heat blasted the *Legend*, and shards of glass and debris rained down. Ellie covered her head and hunched over Connor, trying to shield both of them. When the thunderous explosion died away, Ellie dared to look up. At a distance, the flaming wreckage of Lagora floated crookedly in the water, a billow of black smoke pouring from the ruined island's top. Flakes of ash and a foul smell hung in the air.

Of Nikira and her fish-boat, only a few blasted panels of metal and a shredded black cloak remained. They floated in the water near Lagora like a skeleton picked clean. The Valsha had been too close to the island when it blew. Ellie let out a long sigh. To the last, Nikira had been bent on destruction. Yet in the end, she had been consumed by the very island that she longed to rule. She would never trouble them again.

Above the smoke was a cloud of pale vapor, the same shade as the flowers being tossed into the Genesis Engine. It looked like the trail of a campfire in the early morning. No more urken would be coming from Lagora. At long last, Draaken's stolen souls were free.

"So much for the Genesis Engine," said Owen with satisfaction.

"And for the island of Lagora," said Alyce.

"And for Nikira," Jariel nearly spat.

Finn ran his good hand over his hair. "We did it."

Ellie could not celebrate the victory, however. She was bending over Connor, gently removing his shirt. Now that they weren't in danger of being blown up or attacked by Nikira, Ellie was instantly aware of the ugly wound in Connor's side, which was bleeding all too quickly. Ellie tore a strip from her shirt and pressed it to the wound, trying to staunch the blood the way she'd seen Jude do dozens of times.

"It's deep," Jude said softly, sitting on a crate behind her. Ellie looked up at him, then back to Connor in panic. What did that mean? She'd found Connor and rescued him from the Enemy. Lagora was destroyed, and Nikira was dead. Ellie and Connor were supposed to go home now, start a new life. Not this.

"Come on, Connor," Ellie whispered, squeezing his hand. "You can do this. Hang on."

Connor half-opened his eyes. He smiled crookedly, his left cheek dimpling. "Good to see you, Ellie. I knew you'd…come for me."

Ellie's eyes swam with tears. "Of course I did. We're going to get you patched up. Everything will be fine once we get back to the Vestigia Roi."

"I don't think that's going to happen," said Jariel solemnly, looking over the ship's railing.

Though Vivian had the helm and Owen and Alyce were bravely struggling with the sails, the *Legend* was drifting irresistibly toward a giant cloud of mist filling the horizon: the Edge of the world. The oceans of Aletheia shot over it, disappearing in a cloud of spray. It looked like a waterfall running upwards. What lay beyond it? An airless, sightless void unable to sustain life? The fabled location of Adona Roi's City?

All Ellie knew was that they were heading straight toward it. The Edge was now close enough that Ellie could feel the spray of the waterfall on her face.

"Heave!" Finn shouted, wrestling a line with his good hand. "We need more speed!"

Jude, his face lined with pain, shook his head. "It's too late. This close to the Edge, the current is too strong. Even if we still had our lumena, we couldn't fight it."

Owen slowly let go of his sail line. "So…this is it, then."

Like sleepwalkers, the crew abandoned their posts and pulled together at the center of the deck. Ellie laid Connor's head in her lap. Jariel took one of her hands; Finn took the other.

Vivian slipped her hand inside Jude's. "Let's sing," she said softly.

Mutely, the *Legend*'s crew knelt down together, close enough for their knees to touch. Ellie heard all her shipmates' breathing, heard their fear. She remembered Rua, close as breath. And she was the one who began the Song with words she'd never heard before.

You were the first, there at the beginning,
you are the last, the final note of the Song.

Alyce's clear, strong voice came alongside Ellie's. The others joined in, as smoothly as if they'd heard these words a thousand times before.

You call green shoots out from ash,
You make broken coral branches whole.

The roar of the waterfall built as the current swept the *Legend* toward the Edge. Just a few hundred yards ahead of them, the broken island of Lagora shuddered, a few smaller explosions bursting out its ruined top. Then the floating city began to tip sideways. It tilted upwards, revealing the mechanical workings of its underside for a moment. Then it slipped over the Edge. Draaken's stronghold was gone for good.

But the *Legend* was not far behind. Ellie looked around with her transformed vision. Instead of the waterfall, all she saw were her friends, their pure hearts glittering like glass by firelight. This dear crew had shared so many adventures, braved each other's dangers, and become a family. She was glad to be with them now.

The ship spun like a top in the powerful current, and the waterfall's thunder drowned out the crew's voices. Still Ellie sang, sending her small voice out against the torrent.

Singer of all new mornings,
Behold! You are coming soon.

The *Legend* tipped sideways, and the crew began to slide across the deck. Ellie fought to keep her grip on the others. She cried out Ishua's name.

Then they tumbled over the Edge of the world.

Chapter 20
Victory and Defeat

K ai looked back toward the center of the ring of maelstroms, where the dragon reared its head over the ruins of Trull's fleet quarter. A ship's mast was still caught between its teeth. Much of Calida's quarter had also been decimated, and the commander herself was nowhere to be seen. The sea had grown impossibly rough, in spite of the clear skies and fair winds. The *Defiance* pitched and tossed, the sailors wrestling with the lines, the singers grabbing onto the railing to keep from being knocked overboard.

Kai narrowed his one eye. His ships might not be able to escape Draaken's unnatural maelstroms, but not even the Deceiver could stop them from putting up a fight. Kai yanked the helm to port.

"Turn back!" he shouted to his crew. "It is time to stand and fight!"

As he steered his ships back toward the dragon, Kai watched the rest of the fleet struggling against the maelstrom currents. A few ships went down, capsized or swamped as they tried to sail through the whirlpool ring. But others had turned back toward the center, following Kai's lead, intent on fighting back against the dragon. Among them were Omondi and Korrina's ships. Unfortunately, as the Vestigian ships returned, so did the pods of urken. Now that the lumena currents no longer electrified the water, the Genesis Engine could once again send out its foul creatures.

Lilia appeared at Kai's elbow.

"Any suggestions?" Kai asked, tense as a bowstring.

"This dragon is more than natural," Lilia said. "It is a physical form taken by Draaken. He has manifested his greatest might in order to destroy the Vestigia Roi."

"Yes, I'd gathered that much."

"Then know also that, whatever physical form he assumes, Draaken also takes on the weaknesses of that form."

Kai squinted up at the dragon as it let out a roar that made the *Defiance* tremble. "Eyes."

Lilia nodded. "They may be your best hope, at least to weaken him. Yet we may prove unable to defeat him nonetheless."

A muscle twitched in Kai's jaw. "Thanks for the encouragement."

Lilia nodded as if unaware of his sarcasm. Kai signaled Omondi, whose ship was nearby. The Nakuran commander came alongside the *Defiance,* then swung aboard on a rope.

"I am glad to see you still alive, my brother," said Omondi.

Kai nodded. "And you as well. Omondi—if we could get close enough, do you think you could lead a team of climbers up that dragon? Reach its head, get a stab at its eyes?"

Omondi quickly sized up the beast, his dark eyes taking in its great bulk, its snakelike speed, its barbed tail. "I do not know. But we will try."

Kai nodded once. "Then try. It may be our only chance."

Omondi returned to his ship. Clenching his jaw, Kai looked back toward the dragon.

"Keep shooting at the urken," Kai instructed his cannoneers. "As soon as we're in range, fire off a round at the dragon. Let's see what it does."

As they drew closer, the dragon looked even more terrifying than it had from a distance. It was taller than any tree or building Kai had ever seen.

"Fire!" he commanded the gunners. Many of the shots were direct hits to the dragon's body, but they bounced harmlessly off its tough hide. The volley did nothing but make the creature angry. With a high-pitched shriek, it made a dive for Kai's quarter of the fleet.

Hoping the other ships would catch on to his actions, Kai signaled Omondi to have his team ready. Omondi signaled back, a Nakuran man and woman standing by his side.

The dragon rushed up to meet them. Its open mouth gaped dark and consuming, its double rows of teeth long and sharp as swords. Its yellow eyes glowed with malice and the intent to destroy.

Just then, a volley of cannonfire sounded to starboard. Both Kai and the dragon looked up. Korrina had her detachment of ships grouped within firing range and was making a stand. Kai's heart swelled. He loved that woman.

"Lilia," he said, "can you fly up and distract the beast?"

The Alirya nodded, already gathering herself for a leap into the air.

"Keep it busy. Give Omondi and his team a chance to climb."

Lilia leaped into the air, darting behind the dragon's head.

Kai signaled Omondi.

The three Nakuran climbers dove silently into the water. The dragon was mere yards away. Lilia swooped near its head and fired a bolt of lightning. Even the shock didn't harm the beast through its thick skin, but the blinding light got the dragon's attention. With a roar, it whirled around, snapping at the air as if at a pesky insect. Kiaran flew in to help. Meanwhile, Omondi and his climbers landed, apparently without attracting the beast's notice.

"Singers!" Kai commanded.

The choir aboard the *Defiance* resumed the Song, which seemed to irritate the dragon. The beast thrashed violently, and one of the Nakuran climbers flew into the air, hitting the water some hundred yards away with a sickening smack. The Alirya continued to harry it from above.

Kai caught a glimpse of Radburne's ship, the *Fortitude*, leading the remainder of Calida's detachment around the back of the dragon. From that position, they let off a sudden volley of cannonfire. The shots did as little damage as Kai's had. But the now-enraged dragon whirled around and lunged. Its powerful tail swept through the ships like a scythe. Wood crunched and sailors screamed as masts toppled into the water. Some Vestigians were thrown overboard by force; others jumped into the sea in a panicked attempt to escape. The dragon's coils, thick and gleaming, wound around Radburne's ship, lifting it out of the water. In shock, Kai watched Radburne leap from the deck, a pair of axes gleaming in his hands. Using the force of his jump, Radburne hacked at the dragon's scales with all his might. Sparks flew at the metallic impact, but the dragon's hide still did not yield. Instead, it drew its coils even more tightly around the *Fortitude*, completely crushing the ship. Shattered timbers littered the ocean surface. Then, with a carefully articulated movement, the dragon flicked Radburne off like a parasite. The man tumbled into the cold water as the dragon dove.

"Deniev!" Kai shouted. "Go after Radburne! Save him if you can!"

The dragon resurfaced a moment later. The dive had dislodged the other Nakuran climber, leaving only Omondi. And this time, the beast was headed for Korrina's ships. Kai's chest constricted.

"Fire!" he shouted desperately to his gunners. They obeyed, but the dragon was not deterred or even distracted.

Kai hesitated for one moment. With Trull, Calida, and Ahearn likely dead and Omondi climbing toward the dragon's head, he was the only fleet commander left. Before he went after Korrina, he had to consider others' lives. But with more than half of the Vestigian ships destroyed, the urken were also focusing on Korrina's isolated detachment. If the surviving ships didn't pull together, the urken would simply separate them from each other, then destroy them.

"Full sail ahead!" Kai yelled. "Let's give that beast something to think about!"

The *Defiance* and its accompanying ships sped toward Korrina's *Venture*. As they approached, Kai shouted to his sailors.

"Courage!" he cried. "We will fight for the One Kingdom as long as we have breath! Adona Roi is still the true king, and the Deceiver can never change that. To the One Kingdom!"

Disheartened sailors, smudged dark with wounds and smoke, lifted their weapons. "To the One Kingdom!"

"May it be found!" Kai shouted back, trying to keep the uncertainty out of his voice. He saw no way for them to survive this battle, let alone win. Once the last Vestigian sailor fell, how could the One Kingdom be found?

Kai's ships were still several hundred yards away when he realized they were not going to reach Korrina's detachment in time. Her ship was fearlessly firing on the approaching urken, but the dragon was almost on top of the *Venture*. With a shout, Kai ran to one of his loaded cannons, pointed it as far up as it would go, and lit the fuse. The shot, as usual, did not affect the dragon's thick hide, but the burst of smoke did obscure its vision for a moment, halting its progress. When the smoke cleared, the dragon's head appeared again, its streamers dripping water, its yellow eyes blazing with fury.

And Omondi was right on top of it. The Nakuran climber drew a long, sharp knife. The dragon loomed over Korrina's ship, ready to dive.

Then Lilia and Kiaran released a joint bolt of lightning, blasting the dragon's nose.

And Omondi leaped at its unprotected eye.

The dragon released a roar that Kai would remember to his dying day. It was like an earthquake and a thunderstorm combined, a bellow of pain and rage. Black ooze spurted as one of the yellow eyes went dark. Korrina's ship fired off a volley, further infuriating the beast. Its powerful tail thrashed as it bucked and reared in pain, demolishing several more ships. Fifty feet above the water, Omondi clung on for dear life. But when the beast shook its head violently, the Nakuran climber lost his grip. Omondi plummeted, helpless, to smash into the water's surface. He sank and did not resurface.

Kai gripped his two knives until his knuckles were white. Omondi had wounded the creature at the price of his life, but the dragon was still very much alive. The Vestigians had no more options. Now there was nothing to do but sell their lives as dearly as possible.

Suddenly someone cried out, pointing toward the horizon. The island of Lagora had resurfaced. But now it was far away, outside the ring of maelstroms. There was a sudden explosion of light, and black smoke began to billow from the top of the island. Belatedly, a thundering *boom* floated over the water. The dragon shrieked in fury and despair. Could that have been the Genesis Engine? Kai's sailors cheered, but he whipped out his spyglass. All he could wonder was—had the *Legend's* crew been on the island when it blew?

After a moment of searching, Kai let out a long breath as he spotted sails pulling away from the island. The *Legend* had made it out. Somehow, against all odds, they had managed to not only infiltrate the Enemy's headquarters, but blow up his Genesis Engine and escape alive. *That's the crew of the* Legend *for you,* Kai thought proudly.

Then, through the spyglass, Kai saw a cloud of mist rising beyond the *Legend's* sails. His eye widened. The *Edge*? He snapped the spyglass shut and looked around in alarm. He'd known Lagora had been closer to the Edge than Vestigian ships usually sailed, but he hadn't accounted for just how far the current and the maelstroms would pull them, especially while they'd been focused on the dragon. The *Defiance* and its surrounding ships were now dangerously close—and the *Legend* was far, far closer. He had to reach them!

Kai was not the only one alarmed. Draaken took in the sight of his broken island, his destroyed machine, his battered and wounded body. His eye still oozing black blood, the dragon let out a ferocious roar. The sound vibrated through Kai and made the *Defiance's* deck shudder. Then the creature fled, diving deep into the sea. As a last act of vengeance, its mighty tail flicked into the air. It came down in the middle of Korrina's detachment, right on top of the *Venture*. There was an ear-splitting *crack*. Timbers shattered and sailors screamed.

"NO!" The shout ripped from Kai's throat. He rushed to the railing of the *Defiance* and tried to dive into the water. A sailor pulled him back before he could. Thinking better of it, he jumped into a lifeboat, shouting to his sailors to throw ropes to the sailors surfacing around the wreckage of the *Venture*.

Rowing for dear life, Kai scanned the water. Some of the *Venture's* sailors had been struck by debris and sank beneath the waves. Some had suffered broken arms or legs and struggled to tread water. Kai helped some of these reach the ropes his sailors were throwing overboard. But he did not see the face he was looking for.

Finally he found her. Korrina was unconscious and floating on her back. Blood streamed from a cut on her head. Kai rowed as if the lifeboat were made of air, then hauled Korrina in, nearly capsizing the lifeboat in the process. He let out a breath as he realized she was still breathing and the head wound was not deep. When Kai turned her on her side, she began to cough, spitting water into the bottom of the boat. He exhaled shakily.

"You're all right."

Korrina groaned and lay back, cursing under her breath. "If this is what you call all right, let me punch you and make you all right too."

"But you're not dead."

Korrina grimaced. "I have a headache and probably some broken ribs. But no, I'm not dead." She focused on Kai, her eyes still fierce and bright in spite of her pain. "You came for me."

Kai smiled, unable to account for the sudden moisture pooling in his eye. "I realized I couldn't bear to be without you. I love you, Korrina. Will you marry me?"

"Finally, you ask." Korrina's laugh turned into a cough that made her wince. "Of course I'll marry you. You must have porridge for brains if you thought I'd say no."

Kai wasn't sure whether to laugh or cry, so he did neither. He leaned forward to kiss Korrina long and soundly. Eventually she pulled away, smiling.

"Did we get the dragon?" she asked.

Kai had never felt a stranger mixture of delirious joy and despair. "No—we didn't kill the dragon. It swam off..." he looked back toward the Edge, and all humor disappeared from his face.

"Help me sit up," Korrina said. Carefully Kai propped her against him.

In the distance, the island of Lagora was tipping sideways, tilting over the Edge. Beside it was a tiny dot that must be the *Legend*. Kai's mouth felt full of sand.

For a brief moment, the island was a silhouette against the blue mist of the Edge. Then it slipped down and disappeared. A moment later, the *Legend* followed.

They were gone.

Kai's vision blurred with tears. Korrina gripped his hand.

They had fought for the One Kingdom and overcome Draaken's army against all odds. But as Kai stared at the empty screen of mist, he could almost hear the dragon laughing. Even in his defeat, Draaken had won. He had turned their moment of victory to one of despair. Their friends had gone over the Edge. They were too late.

Chapter 21
The Eternal Garden

Was this what it was like to be dead?

The crew of the *Legend*, still dressed in their battle-stained uniforms, stood in a long, white-tiled room. In the center was a pool, lined with blue tiles and encircled by slender white lamps. The water was so still that the reflections looked like a second set of lamps standing upside-down in the pool. The room held no doors, no windows, and no other people.

"We *did* just go over the Edge, right?" said Connor, leaning weakly on Ellie. "Because this isn't what I expected to find on the other side."

"We did," said Finn. "I remember that huge cloud of spray blotting out the sun."

"I remember feeling like I'd left my stomach behind when we fell," Owen added.

"So...are we dead?" Jariel asked. She touched the gash on her cheek and winced. "I don't feel dead. My cut's still bleeding."

"If we're not dead, then what is this place?" said Vivian.

"I'm not sure," said Jude, leaning on Vivian to keep the weight off his injured knee. "I can't explain why, but it looks somehow familiar."

"But there's no entrance and no exit. How did we get here if there's no way in—or out?" said Alyce.

"There's the pool," Ellie murmured, looking into the still blue water.

"That can't be an exit. We can see the bottom," Owen pointed out.

"Sort of." Ellie found that if she didn't look at them too directly, the tiles appeared to ripple slightly. "Maybe there's more to the water than we can see."

Jariel took her hand. "I trust you, Ellie."

"I'll go first," said Jude. "Make sure it's safe."

"We should all go at once," said Vivian. "We've come this far together, and that's how we ought to go on."

The crew joined hands and stood together on the edge of the pool, looking at their second selves reflected in the water.

"On the count of three," said Jude. "One…two…"

Three.

Ellie felt the momentary thrill of flight as they jumped. She felt the pool soak her boots, her trousers, her nautical coat. She felt the water close over her head.

And then it was all gone.

Ellie found herself standing somewhere entirely different. She was still clutching Vivian's hand on one side and Jariel's on the other, and behind them was a waterfall the same color as the pool tiles. But she was completely dry, and the white-tiled room had vanished. They were inside a giant glasshouse capped with a soaring dome painted every shade imaginable. Light came streaming through panes of blue, orange, green, red, yellow, and purple glass, bathing the *Legend's* crew in color. The floor was flecked with small mirrors that made the light sparkle around them. Ellie looked at her colorful friends, smiling. Then her eyes widened. Jariel's gash was gone, and she had a circlet of pearls in her hair. Connor, his wound disappeared and a healthy color back in his face, wore a shirt of mail that glittered like sunlight on a river. Finn stretched his broken arm in amazement. He somehow carried his harp, Tangwystl, though Ellie was sure it had been lost in the *Legend's* fall. Owen wore a tunic woven with tiny turtles that actually moved over the fabric. Alyce was dressed in a singer's robe that looked like it was sewn out of pages of music. Jude, the lapels of his coat embroidered with leaves and vines, balanced his weight evenly on both feet. Vivian wore a trailing white gown, printed all over with what looked like words in other languages. Only in one other place had Ellie seen such fantastical representations of her shipmates: her visions.

But now, no one was singing.

Overcome with wonder and curiosity, Ellie dared a glance into the nearest mirror in the floor. She saw a young woman wearing a blue robe, deep as a summer twilight. The cuffs, hem, and belt were gold. The girl's eyes—blue with black rings around the irises—gazed quietly back at her. Ellie knew the reflection was her own, but it did not seem real. Not so long ago, she'd looked in a cracked orphanage mirror and seen a scrawny, unwanted girl with eyes like puddles. The girl in this mirror—she looked confident, ready to face any challenge. Ellie knew her visions showed the truth about people, but…was this who she truly was? And if so, when had it happened?

Ellie and her shipmates looked up at the sound of a door opening. At the far end of the glasshouse, a tall man entered, his stride long and confident. He wore a suit of armor that caught and reflected back every color in the room. In his hands, he carried not a sword and spear, but a gardening fork and trowel.

Ellie knew him even before she was close enough to see his face. She started to run.

He met her halfway and caught her up in an embrace she knew so well. She felt herself twirled around in a pair of strong arms. His beard was scratchy against her cheek, and he smelled of fresh grass clippings. When he finally set her down, he knelt so she could look into his face. His dark eyes still twinkled with their joyful secret. Only now Ellie knew what the secret was: it was this. This moment.

"Ishua," she breathed.

He grinned. "Ellie." It was like a new line of the Song, hearing him say her name. This was no dream.

Remembering herself, Ellie glanced over her shoulder at her crew. "Ishua, these are my friends, the crew of the *Legend*."

Ishua stood and strode toward them. "I know you. Welcome, Jude and Vivian. Connor, I'm glad to see you. Welcome, Jariel, Finn, Alyce. Owen, where is Sunny?"

"I left him behind...Ishua, sir," Owen explained. "I wanted to keep him safe."

"Well done. Please, follow me."

"Ishua—" Ellie began, trotting after him to the doors of the glasshouse. "Where...where *are* we?"

"My friends," Ishua said, pausing a moment before the great doors. "Welcome to the Eternal Garden."

He flung open the doors, and Ellie stepped into a garden that she would never fully be able to describe. It was a beautiful spring day outside, though it had been deep winter when she'd left Dhar. Bordered by a tall, thick hedge, the garden was completely filled with plants. They were more or less grouped into beds with flagstone paths winding between them, but some of the borders were uneven, some of the grasses grew long, and some of the flagstones had little sprouts springing up between them. The whole place looked more like a gently guided wilderness than a regimented formal garden. Ellie loved it. Every leaf, every flower, burst in such sharp definition, such saturation of color, that she struggled to take it all in, yet she was hungry to absorb it all without missing a single sight.

"May we go explore?" Jariel begged.

"Of course," said Ishua with a smile. "Refreshments will be ready for you in a little while."

"Come on, Ellie!"

Laughing, Ellie let Jariel grab her hand and drag her down a winding path, the rest of the crew close behind them. Bursts of color flashed by, and Ellie recognized blue cornflowers, yellow daisies, orange lilies, purple foxgloves. But most of the plants were completely unknown to her. Jude marveled at a clump of hard, shiny blue spikes twice as tall as he was. Vivian stopped to smell a vine of fragrant, cascading purple flowers the size of her face. There were ball-shaped plants that squished when Finn poked them. Some of the plants yielded blackberries, strawberries, and grapes, none smaller than Owen's fist, though that did not stop him from sampling. Alyce stood in an orchard of fruit trees, their snowy pink-and-white petals drifting down into her hair.

Jariel saw a silver squirrel and ran off to chase it through a mossy sunken garden. Ellie hung back, watching a little waterfall that flowed past a patch of rushes into a reflecting pond.

"Look," said Finn softly from behind her. Ellie followed his finger to see a large moth alight on the petal of a purple water lily. She would have missed it if Finn hadn't pointed it out—its wings were clear as glass.

Following the music of songbirds and the grumble of their stomachs, the crew eventually found their way to a round lawn at the center of the garden. In the middle stood a huge tree, its trunk thick and gnarled. But instead of leaves, the tree had a canopy of what looked like glass flowers, flat and round as dinner plates and easily three times as big as Ellie's head. Their colors were breathtaking: emerald and aquamarine and cinnabar, violet and crimson and gold, and some colors Ellie didn't have names for. Under their richly colored light rested a low picnic table surrounded by cushions. Six winged Alirya stood ready with silver trays and bowls.

Ishua smiled. "Lunch is ready."

Barely able to contain their wonder, the crew joined hands with Ishua and listened to him sing the blessing.

To you, our Father King
Our voices do we bring
For food and love and light our thanks we give.
With you, for you, we may truly live.

The blessing was like the one usually sung over Vestigian meals, and yet it was slightly different. *Like hearing a whole song when you used to know only one part*, Ellie thought.

The Alirya, their fingers and the hems of their robes transparent as glass, served a feast. Ellie couldn't even remember the last time she'd eaten a square meal, let alone a banquet like this. The produce of the magnificent garden was on display: a heaped salad with crisp cucumbers and juicy tomatoes, a creamy vegetable soup, an assortment of ripe fruits with the shapes of birds and flowers etched into their peels. There were loaves of warm, fresh bread and at least ten different kinds of cheese. And best of all, for dessert there were giant strawberries and delicate flaky pastries that squirted out blackberry jam or chocolate cream when you bit into them. Ellie could see Connor trying to figure out how to bake them.

When the crew had eaten as much as they could, the dishes turned to clouds and vanished in a passing breeze. The attending Alirya retreated, leaving the crew alone with Ishua.

Now that she'd had time to think, Ellie's mind was troubled with a question. "Ishua…you said this place is called the Eternal Garden, and it's beautiful. But I was wondering…if we're here…are we dead?"

Ishua cocked his head, gazing up at the glass flowers overhead. "Not exactly."

Connor frowned. "I thought you were either dead or you weren't."

Ishua pointed at the high hedge surrounding the garden. Its branches were so tightly woven that nothing could be seen of the other side.

"Beyond that hedge is the road that leads to the city of my father, Adona Roi. It is a place that surpasses beauty. Its white walls stand on a mountain above the clouds, surrounded by the pure blue sky. Rua's flame gives the city constant light, and those who live there enjoy true peace, fearing nothing. And the gardens there—this one is but a few dry leaves in comparison."

Jude made a small moan of rapture at that thought.

"But," Ishua continued, "those who leave this garden and take the road to that high country do not return."

"So...the people there are dead?" said Connor.

"You might say that. But death...is something that really only makes sense from the other side," said Ishua. "I've heard people in the City say that they number the days of their lives from their arrival there. That while they'd had tastes and glimpses of life in Aletheia, only in the City did they truly begin to live it."

"So...even here in this garden, we're not truly...alive," murmured Ellie, looking at the hedge.

"This garden is closer than most get, short of actually taking the journey," said Ishua. "But it cannot compare with the splendor of the City."

"So, when do we get going?" said Jariel, rubbing her hands together. "I can't wait to see this place."

Ishua shook his head. "We're not going there—not today, at least."

"But Ishua—" Jariel's face fell. "I want to begin living! And after all, we fell over the Edge—"

Ishua rumpled her red hair with a thoughtful smile. "There will be plenty of time for the City in your future, little one. You will never run out of time there. But your work in Aletheia is not yet complete—none of yours is," he said, looking around the group. "Indeed, you sailed over the Edge, and most who come this way do not return. But the fulfillment of the One Kingdom is drawing near, and each of you has been given a gift that will help it rejoin. Its coming is very close, and so I am sending you back to finish the work set before you."

"What kind of work, Ishua?" said Finn. "What are we to do?"

Ishua looked kindly into his gray eyes. "Listen to the song that is in your heart, my boy," he said. "Then watch for places where the world needs music."

Finn looked down at Tangwystl. With a smile, he plucked a swift, joyful chord from the harp.

Owen looked around the garden and sighed. "I guess going back is the right thing. But I'll miss this place. Even if it isn't Adona Roi's City, I could stay here a long, long time."

"You may stay a bit longer, at least," said Ishua. "I have something to show Ellie."

"Me?" Ellie squeaked as everyone's eyes turned to her.

"You," Ishua smiled. "Because of your gift."

Chapter 22
A New Vision

As the crew of the *Legend* dispersed to enjoy a few more moments in the garden, Ishua led Ellie around the side of the glasshouse. There, a small door opened onto a simple winding staircase, and Ellie followed Ishua up. At the top was a small room inside the dome of the glasshouse, its ceiling just high enough for Ishua to stand up in the center. The floor was solid, but the curved walls and ceiling were made of airy wooden latticework. The holes in the lattice glittered like a sky full of stars. Ishua lit several candles, and his armor reflected their light. Ellie saw a locked glass case containing an enormous hourglass, its top half nearly empty. In the center of the room was a stone pedestal on which sat a green copper bowl with handles, half full of water.

"What are you going to show me, Ishua?" Ellie asked.

Ishua looked at her thoughtfully. "Not so very long ago, I gave you a gift of Sight. You have used that gift to speak the truth and bring hope to others. You have helped inspire and guide the Vestigia Roi when they wandered. You have shown great courage."

Ellie looked at the floor, scuffing at it with her shoe. "I don't think so, Ishua. I've always been so full of fear. I ran away from the

Vestigia Roi—I was even willing to work with Draaken to save my brother. If I ever did anything brave, it was only because it needed doing and there was no one else to do it."

"That is exactly what courage means," said Ishua, his expression full of compassion. "Though you may have made wrong choices sometimes, you were still willing to put yourself at risk for the sake of others—the very love and sacrifice that have defined the greatest Vestigian heroes. And for that reason, I am going to show you a new vision. The One Kingdom is coming soon, but it has not yet arrived. In the days to come, you must continue to use your Sight to give the Vestigia Roi courage—to hold out hope for them when they cannot hope for themselves." Ishua gestured to the copper bowl. "Take hold of the handles."

Ellie did. The well-worn metal felt cool and smooth in her hands, and the water in the green basin was as still as glass. Then a low murmur began to rise from the rim of the bowl. Gradually it grew to a rich golden hum. When the pitch reached the first glowing note of the Song, the water began to ripple. Then it disappeared. Ellie felt herself falling.

When she stopped, she found herself suspended in empty, black space. Bowl, pedestal, candles, and Ishua were all gone. She was alone in the dark.

Then, slowly, stars came into view. Ellie looked around. She was floating, somehow, in the night sky. In the distance, a small boat appeared. As it came nearer, Ellie saw that no one was rowing it, but it was filled with shining glass shapes in brilliant colors. In each one, Ellie began to see oceans, continents, cities—each shape was a world. The boat finally reached Ellie, bumping against her leg, and she picked up a delicate glass cone. Its flat surface was deep blue, dotted with green islands. *Aletheia.*

Then the light blinked out, and stars, boat, worlds all vanished. When she could see again, Ellie saw a vision of a continent breaking into many islands. Could that be Verana, the ancient land mass that had given way to the islands of Aletheia? A man in glittering armor clashed with a giant black water dragon, then a fleet of flying ships and islands appeared.

As the images flashed faster and faster, Ellie realized she was seeing the history of Aletheia. Many scenes went by that she did not recognize. Then she saw a man and a blue-eyed woman climbing down a ladder to an island that looked like Freith. *My parents!* A little boy and girl sat on a sled in a muddy play yard. *Connor and me,* Ellie realized. Then a carriage pulled up to a gray, weathered building. A family got out—two adults and a boy, pushing a girl in a brown coat before them. *Miss Sylvia's orphanage.* Ellie watched as the events of the last year played out before her—her first glimpse of the Academy's spires, the firestars falling on Rhynlyr. The Vestigian fleet emerged from the caves of Mharra, branching out in every direction like rays of light. Rhynlyr fell from the sky. The *Legend* tipped over the Edge.

And then the vision continued.

With wonder, Ellie watched as the *Legend*, whole again, sailed back over the Edge into Aletheia. The black dragon, wounded and put to flight, swam back underwater, disappearing into the deeps. Ellie saw the Vestigia Roi gathered together on a flying island—not Rhynlyr, but one that showed signs of peace and cultivation. Jude and Vivian embarked on a ship with two baby girls and Tal, now a toddling little boy. Wherever they sailed, light flared up and islands grew roots and began to fuse together again—the great rejoining, the One Kingdom coming.

And the vision went on. Ellie saw her friends grown up—Owen, his glasses perched on his nose, wore the green cloak of an Academy professor and blew up a vial of chemicals before an admiring group of students. Sunny sat beside him, wagging his tail. Alyce, wearing a sky-blue robe, sang as the leader of the First Choir. Aimee rode the bow of a ship, looking forward as the falcon Zira circled overhead. There was Meggie, wearing a gold councilmember's pin and giving a speech to a huge crowd. Kai and Korrina stood together at the helm of a ship. Katha read a story to a group of little children. Surprises kept coming, though: Ellie saw a couple angled away from her, the dark-haired man's arm around the red-haired woman's shoulders. As they turned, Ellie recognized Connor and Jariel. Both wore wedding rings. Ellie almost laughed aloud.

And then she saw herself—her older self. She noticed that the irises of her eyes were completely clear. She wore a white robe and sat on a high stool against a sloped desk, carefully applying gold ink to the pages of an open Song Book with a quill pen. Brother Reinholdt stood behind her, pointing out her mistakes.

Then someone else was behind her too: a tall young man with lanky limbs and flaming red hair. He wore a woven Innish poncho and carried a harp. Ellie saw her older self turn and smile up into his eyes as the young man gently ran his fingers through her hair. Ellie's face scorched and she couldn't catch her breath. What…?

Then the vision pulled away again, and Ellie saw a last great duel in the sky between the black dragon and Ishua, his armor all aflame with stars. The Captain of Winged Armies wielded a long sword that burned like white fire, and at last he pierced the dragon and it fell from the sky. When its body hit the ocean surface, a giant plume of steam rose to the heavens, but it dissolved harmlessly and made way for a cloudless sky. On the ocean surface, the last of the islands fused back together, as if Verana had returned in even greater glory. And thousands and thousands of Alirya crowded the sky, glittering like an illuminated manuscript, filling the air with harmonies of the Song more beautiful than any Ellie had ever heard.

> *To the Good King, to Adona Roi*
> *To Ishua, vanquisher of monsters*
> *And to Rua, flame eternal*
> *Be might and splendor and wholeness and hope!*

One section of the sky sang, "Forever!" And another section answered it: "Forever!" until the whole sky rang with the music—the sound of the One Kingdom come, and come to stay.

At last, the music and colors faded. Ellie was pulled back through blackness until she stood staring into the copper bowl, the starry lights of the latticed room twinkling around her. She let out a shaky breath and looked up to see Ishua leaning against the wall, watching her quietly.

She could only manage one word: "When?"

Ishua glanced at the giant hourglass in the case. "Soon," he murmured. "The Time-Glass is almost empty."

They spoke no more. Ellie silently followed Ishua back down the staircase, her mind reeling from all she had seen. When they reemerged into the garden, Ellie's eyes watered in the bright light.

Jariel was the first to come bounding up. Connor was right behind her. Both were red in the face and breathing hard.

"I...told you I could run around the garden...faster than you," Jariel panted.

Connor bumped her arm. "That's only because...you said *go* after you started running," he panted back.

"What did you see, Ellie?" said Alyce, turning the corner.

"What happened to your eyes?" said Finn.

"My eyes?" Ellie turned to see her reflection in the side of the glasshouse. Her irises were clear, like panes of washed glass—just as she'd seen them in the vision. It was already coming true. She raised her eyebrows and looked at Ishua.

"You have been changed by seeing," he said softly.

The others arrived, all remarking on Ellie's surprising change of eye color and asking what Ishua had shown her. Ellie looked from one face to another, images flashing behind her eyes of a boat full of planets and the dragon crashing into the sea and a host of Alirya singing forever and ever. She saw each person's future as she looked at them, blushing when she met Finn's eyes. And yet she couldn't seem to find a way to say any of it—as if the words she needed simply didn't exist yet. Her throat was empty, though her heart was full. Finally she answered:

"All will be well."

And, while it didn't even begin to describe all that she'd seen, it was enough.

At least for now.

Ellie and the crew of the *Legend* turned to go back inside the glasshouse. They were reluctant to leave the garden, but knew they must return to the work awaiting them in Aletheia. But Ishua stopped them.

"Wait," he said. "There is one more thing."

He led them past the tree with the glass flowers, all the way up to the hedge separating them from Adona Roi's City.

"I am about to pass through the hedge and bring you something from the other side," he explained. "You may not go with me, but you may look through."

Ellie could hardly breathe as Ishua placed his hand on a branch of the hedge. A note of music came from deep inside him, and as he sang a few lines from the Song, the branches of the hedge unwove themselves as easily as the tumblers of a lock responding to a key. A space like an arched doorway formed in the hedge.

And through it, they saw Forever.

A road wound through meadows whose colors Ellie could not name. She could say only that every blade of grass was as brilliant as a candle, and the flowers were stars. Under a clear blue sky, the road climbed a mountain towering in the distance, its slopes lush with forests and glinting with hidden waterfalls. At the very top of the mountain, so bright that Ellie could not look at it directly, was a point of light that sang out like the rising sun.

Ishua stepped through the hedge and strode off through the bright meadows, the brilliance of his armor making them look dim by comparison. Traveling faster than seemed possible, he walked far away to a huge, white-flowering tree at the foot of the mountain.

And as he returned, he was not alone.

Behind him was a group of people. As they drew nearer, the crew murmured in shock and crowded close to the hedge. Ellie cried out, covering her mouth.

She knew them.

There was Captain Daevin, wearing a white nautical coat embroidered in gold.

There was Navir Zarifah, robed in white, wearing her secretive smile.

There was Estir Kellar, her gentle hands reaching out to them.

There was Councilman Tobin, standing tall and straight-backed, his blue eyes shining.

There was a curly-haired sailor whom Jude seemed to recognize.

There were the councilmembers Trull, Calida, Ahearn, and Omondi, along with the Alirya Hoyan, all offering the Vestigian salute.

And there, standing at the front, were a sandy-haired man and a woman with blue eyes, their arms around each other.

Gavin and Kiria Reid.

They were standing in the meadow, looking young and healthy. Their eyes held so much love, the kind of love Ellie had spent all her life looking for. Her family.

Ellie lurched forward, unable to hold herself back. She reached out for them.

Her hands struck something hard. Though she could see nothing, it was as if a glass wall filled the archway in the hedge, preventing her from passing through. Ellie beat on it with her fists and sank down to her knees, sobbing.

"Mother...Father..."

Connor was beside her, his arm around her shoulders. He was crying too. They watched as Ishua crossed the meadow, leaving the group of people behind him.

As Ishua passed through the hedge, the people waved. Ellie saw her father smile, noticed the dimple like Connor's in his cheek. Her mother blew a kiss, looking right at Ellie.

And then the branches in the hedge wove themselves back together. Ellie pressed against them, devouring every moment of the vision until the meadow, the mountain, and the people disappeared completely from sight. When she could see them no longer, Ellie bent to the ground, huddled before Ishua's feet.

"Why, Ishua? Why did you show us that? Please let me stay. I want to go to them."

Gentle, callused fingers touched her chin. Dark brown eyes gazed into hers, so gentle.

"Because, even though the time is not now, I wanted you to know that you *will* be with them again. Because I knew you would need strength to fight for the One Kingdom, just as your parents did. When you are finished with your life's work—and only then—they will be waiting for you."

Ellie turned her face into Connor's shoulder, unable to stop her tears. She knew why, she understood. But her heart still ached with longing for what she had seen. For forever with her family.

"Before you go, I have something for you all," said Ishua. "A gift to bring hope to the Vestigia Roi."

As Ellie looked up, she saw what looked like a lustrous pearl in the palm of Ishua's hand.

"The islands will not need caris powder to rescue them anymore, not with the gift young Talmai carries. But take this stellaria seed as a reminder of the coming Kingdom, and of the City you have seen."

None of the group moved to accept the gift, until finally Ellie stood and held out her hand. The seed felt weightless, so insubstantial to carry such power. But she put it carefully in her pocket for safekeeping.

Then Ishua led the crew back inside the glasshouse. Ellie noticed that the patches of colored light had not moved at all. Did time not pass in this place?

Before them stood the waterfall they had come through.

"Farewell for now," said Ishua, looking at each of them in turn. His eyes lingered on Ellie. "I am coming soon, and the dragon's days are numbered. Remember the sands in the Time-Glass."

Ishua smiled, and for the first time Ellie noticed just how deep his smile was. His eyes held all the sadness, anger, and fear of the history she had seen in the basin, but the other emotions were all somehow wrapped up in joy—just as everything would be, at the end of ends.

"All will be well," he said.

Ellie nodded, too full of impressions to have any room for words.

Ishua held out his hand toward the waterfall. "Pass through, my friends."

Connor tapped two fingers to his left shoulder, then to his forehead, in the Vestigian salute.

"To the One Kingdom," he said.

"It is coming, it is here," said Ishua.

With those words ringing in her ears, Ellie clasped hands with her friends. Together they stepped through the waterfall.

The crew of the *Legend* stood in the ship's Oratory. Ellie looked around. There was no sign of the glasshouse or the white-tiled room they had come through earlier. There were just the familiar floorboards and colored lights of the *Legend*. Around Ellie, her friends looked normal again, though their uniforms were clean and their wounds healed. They stared at each other in bewilderment.

"Did I just...dream that?" said Jariel.

Owen patted his coat. "We're not wet from the waterfall."

Finn looked at Ellie. "Ellie's eyes are still clear, though."

Ellie reached into her pocket. "And I still have this." She drew out the stellaria seed, its pearly surface reflecting the colorful lights of the Oratory.

"So it wasn't a dream." Connor leaned against the wall. "I'll never forget that as long as I live."

"Nor I," said Jude.

"Since we've been given a second chance at life in Aletheia, though, I think we ought to set sail for Freith," said Vivian. "Who knows how much time went by while we were gone? And I, for one, have someone I'm anxious to see."

"I second that," said Jude.

"Me too," said Alyce.

The crew explored the ship, knowing they had left it at the Edge without a lumena. But when they went up on deck, they realized they were surrounded by air and clouds. The ship was flying, and the sails, lines, and navigational equipment were all in perfect working order. The lumena hummed away happily. The *Legend* had never been readier to sail.

"Well, that saved us a jolly lot of ship repairs," Owen commented.

"Would you do the honors, Captain?" said Jude to Connor. "We're glad to have you back."

Connor hesitated a moment, then stepped up to the helm, touching the polished wood lovingly. Ellie smiled. Now that the crew was together again, things could finally start going back to normal. Whatever *normal* looked like after seeing the Eternal Garden.

"Well, what are we waiting for? Hoist sails!" Connor shouted. The crew scrambled to the lines, and the *Legend's* sails filled, carrying them home.

Chapter 23
Reunions

When the *Legend* made a water landing three days later, the Freith harbor was already full of Vestigian ships. Swarms of sailors were busily mending sails or swabbing decks. Ellie did not see Kai's *Defiance* or Korrina's *Venture*, though. As the *Legend* landed, heads turned and sailors stopped to stare, their mouths hanging open.

"It's like we've come back from the dead," chuckled Jariel.

"Well…we kind of have," said Ellie.

A few inquiries told them that the orphanage was now doubling as Vestigian headquarters. The rest of the fleet was either staying aboard their ships or occupying Governor Hirx's former mansion. The crew of the *Legend* set out for the Sketpoole Home for Boys and Girls, retracing their steps from the night of the attack. Ellie noticed how different the city already looked. Trash had been cleaned from the streets, sagging structures had been reinforced, and some homes and shops sported new coats of bright paint. A few even had homemade VR banners hanging in their windows.

The orphanage, too, looked different. A trim picket fence now bordered the yard, where a new crop of grass was coming up, and other green shoots hinted at spring flowers. The walls had been painted a cheery yellow, and the shutters hung straight and even. All except one, that is.

A boy came around the corner of the building, whistling and carrying a stack of boards on his shoulder. Ellie stopped in shock. The boy's face had already lost some of its pasty whiteness and baby fat, and his nose was more crooked than she remembered, but she would still know Ewart Cooley anywhere.

"Ewart?"

Ewart gave Ellie one glance, then his eyes darted to Finn just behind her. He dropped his boards and fell to the ground, covering his head.

"Don't hurt me! Don't hurt me!" he wailed at the top of his voice.

At the racket, Miss Sylvia came running out. When she saw the *Legend's* crew, surprise burst over her face, followed by a huge smile. "Well!" she exclaimed. "If this isn't the gladdest sight! When they told me…what had happened, I thought I'd never see you again."

"Where's Tal?" Vivian asked anxiously.

"He's just inside. Won't he be happy to see you," Miss Sylvia beamed. "Ewart, you can get up now."

Ewart lifted his head. "Don't let that boy punch me again."

Ellie looked at Finn in shock. "You punched Ewart?"

Jariel crossed her arms. "I wanted to, but Finn got there first."

Finn shrugged. "He needed it. Shook some brains into his head." He approached the cowering boy and offered his hand. "Come on, old chap. Let's put the past behind us. Be civil to Ellie, and you can keep your nose where it is from now on."

Sylvia smiled. "I think you'll find that this is not the same Ewart you once knew. With a little help from Kyuler, he's become quite an accomplished carpenter. All our tidy new shutters are his work."

"Really? Well done, Ewart," said Ellie.

Ewart shoved his hands into his pockets and looked at the ground.

"Where are your parents?" Ellie asked.

"Gone," said Ewart.

"They worked off their debt," said Sylvia, looking as if she'd tasted something spoiled. "Then they decided to move on—doubtless to some new scheme for easy profit."

"And you stayed behind?" Ellie said to Ewart.

"They told me to come with them. But I—I found out I like building things," Ewart said with a shyness Ellie had never heard from him. "I never knew that before. My mum and dad—they never built anything, only took it from others. I didn't want that life—not anymore." He dug into the dirt with the toe of his shoe. "Don't know where I belong now. Once these shutters are done, I dunno where I'm going to go."

"The Vestigia Roi is home for all sorts of people who don't belong anywhere else," said Ellie gently. "Trust me. I should know."

Ewart looked up. His eyes were clear in his thinner, more serious face. "I'm sorry, Ellie. For all we—I—did. To you."

Ellie nodded. "Thank you." She extended her hand. "Welcome to the Vestigia Roi, Ewart."

He accepted her hand and shook it.

"Wonders abound," said Miss Sylvia. "Come in! Everyone will be glad to see you!"

Inside, the old orphanage bustled with life. Half a dozen cooks banged pots and pans in the kitchen. In the dining room, Meggie looked up from a huge stack of papers.

"Ellie! You're alive!" cried Meggie, running up to hug her. "All of you are alive! Whatever happened to you? The sailors who came back from the battle said you...you went over the Edge," Meggie ended in a whisper.

"We...um...we did," said Ellie. "But it's a very long story. Maybe later tonight?" She looked around. "Where's Katha?"

"And Tal," said Vivian.

"And Aimee," said Alyce.

"In there." Meggie pointed to the back room where first Connor, then the *Legend's* crew had been held captive. They quietly filed in.

Katha was sitting in a chair at the far end of the room, reading dramatically from a colorful storybook. A group of children crowded close to her, hanging on her every word. It reminded Ellie of the evening when Miss Sylvia had told the story of Ishua—the story that had changed the direction of Ellie's life. Chinelle sat in a rocking chair, cradling a gurgling Tal. Vivian uttered a low cry, and all the children turned to look at her.

"Liss!" shouted Aimee, running to hug her sister. Sunny was right behind her. He jumped up on Owen and licked his face.

"I expect you'll be wanting this one," said Chinelle, passing Tal into Vivian's eager arms. Vivian covered the baby with kisses as he giggled in delight. Jude put his arms around both of them, looking as if he'd swallowed the sun.

"Don't let us interrupt your story," Ellie said to Katha. "Go on."

That evening, there were even more joyful reunions. Kai and Korrina arrived with the Alirya and a detachment of other ship captains, including Deniev. With them, to Ellie's great shock, was the former Consul Radburne, who had one arm in a sling.

The returning captains brought news that Ilorin had at last been fully cleansed of urken traces. They were amazed and delighted to see the crew of the *Legend* alive, and Kai slapped Connor on the back and immediately apologized to Ellie for driving her away at their last Council meeting. Ellie hugged him.

"I'm sorry I ran away. I know you were just trying to look out for me. Friends?"

Kai smiled. "Friends."

At first Ellie was suspicious of Radburne, with whom she'd once worked on the Council. Hadn't everything they'd suffered been his fault, directly or indirectly? What, then, was he doing back here? But as Radburne told his story, Ellie's thoughts began to shift. Kai, Korrina, and Deniev described his bravery and loyalty in the battle they had fought with Draaken. And Radburne himself was greatly changed. The arrogance and bravado of the former consul had disappeared, replaced with new quietness and humility. His transformation had been hard-won from the sounds of it, but Ellie liked the new version of the man much better.

The Vestigians spent all of suppertime sharing the stories of their adventures: the Freith rescue mission, the infiltration of Lagora, the great dragon's defeat. Eventually the conversation turned to the other side of the Edge.

"What was it like?" Meggie asked curiously.

The *Legend*'s crew shared a look filled with meaning, but found themselves strangely tongue-tied.

"It was…beautiful," Alyce attempted.

"Full of splendor," said Vivian.

"Animals," said Owen.

"Plants," said Jude.

"Food," said Jariel.

"Lots of light," said Finn.

Ellie knew that all of the words were true, but none of them even came close to expressing what the Eternal Garden was like. So she did not try to describe it. She just placed the stellaria seed on the table and exchanged a glance with Connor. Only those who had been there could really understand—until the Vestigia Roi were all united there together.

"We should plant this wherever the Vestigia Roi finds a new home," Ellie said simply.

The pearl-like seed passed from hand to hand. Kai fingered it thoughtfully. "I think, strange as it sounds, that Ilorin may be that home," he mused. "It seems ironic to start the new Vestigian headquarters on the site of a prison for traitors. But those who were once traitors have fought bravely on our side and redeemed themselves. And the island has everything necessary for a settlement—a temperate climate, plenty of land, and even a number of surviving buildings. Besides," he said, looking at Radburne with a smile, "it seems fitting that the island should be given a second chance."

"We could restart the Academy there," said Vivian excitedly.

"We'll need some new classes now—A History of Rua, Resisting Invisible Creatures, Beast Speaking..." said Owen, scratching Sunny's head.

"I'll help!" said Aimee. Zira squawked agreement. Alyce hugged them both.

"And we can finally hold proper elections for the Council again," said Meggie. "I'm awfully sorry about the fallen councilmembers, especially Admiral Trull. I'll miss him, and I've been keeping up the Council paperwork in his honor. Once we have a new home, though, I'm thinking of running officially for the Administrative House seat. I've even got my notes to restart Council records."

Radburne patted her hand. "A fine councilwoman you'd be."

"I may run as well—though not against you, Meggie," said Deniev, bouncing Gresha on his knee.

Laralyn looked at him. "Well, someone has to represent Occupational House in Councilman Tobin's stead."

"What about you?" Katha asked Sylvia. "Will you stay here to keep the orphanage going?"

Sylvia shook her head. "Age is quickly catching up with me, especially after several nights of captivity and the threat of execution. I think I'd like to settle down on Ilorin, spend my twilight years in peace there. But—" her eyes twinkled—"I would stay on a bit longer if I had someone to train—someone young, with a love for children and a knack for reading aloud..." She gave Katha a pointed look.

Katha blushed. "I've loved helping out here. For the first time in my life, I feel like I have a purpose. I'd like very much to stay, if you'll have me." She perked up. "Maybe we can finally paint the upstairs dormitories! I think a nice lilac would be lovely, don't you? Maybe with pink trim?"

Sylvia smiled. "With Ewart's extra help, I'm sure it will all work out."

Korrina made a harrumphing sound and raised her eyebrows at Kai. "Tell them our news."

Kai's ears turned red. He cleared his throat and placed his hand over Korrina's on the table.

"Er...hm, there's something else. Korrina...er, I...we—"

"We got married," Korrina blurted out. She grinned at Kai, looking pleased as a cat in the cream.

"Er—yes. After the battle, we...we decided we didn't want to waste any more time." Kai looked into Korrina's eyes, smiled, and stopped stammering. "One of the other ship captains came aboard the *Defiance* to perform the ceremony. Once the Vestigia Roi is settled, we'd like to submit to the Council our petition for joint captaincy."

"And if I'm elected, I promise you'll have it," said Meggie, barely containing the laugh shining in her eyes.

Epilogue
Sailing On

"How do I look?" Meggie asked nervously, turning from side to side in front of the tall mirror.

"Perfect, Councilwoman Radburne," Ellie smiled, straightening her friend's gold pin with its ten-pointed Administrative star.

"You're lucky you have me," muttered Katha, tugging down her sister's fitted waistcoat and straightening the creamy collar of her blouse. "On your own, you'd probably still be wearing your mucky old uniform. *I* hope to wear only dresses for the whole rest of my life." Katha happily smoothed the fluffy pink skirt of the one she was wearing.

Meggie laughed and hugged Katha and Ellie. "Remember when all three of us were on the Council together? Deniev's clever and the other elected members are all right too, but meetings won't be as much fun without you two."

Katha made a disgusted sound. "Meetings. I'd rather change a thousand diapers than sit through another one of those."

Ellie laughed. "Be careful what you wish for! But you're the one who's gifted at governing, Meggie. This is yours to do, and you're going to amaze today's crowd with your speech. Now, I have to go find my seat. The others are waiting for me."

Ellie slipped out of the dressing room and left the building by a side exit. Hundreds of Vestigians were seated in what had been the parade ground of the Ilorin Reformatory. When they'd arrived three months ago it had been a dull and severe place, but now it was transformed into an outdoor amphitheater. The flagstones had been scrubbed to a shine and the stage was decked with flowers. A huge crowd had turned out, wearing their best attire, to hear the acceptance speeches of the newly elected councilmembers. The Vestigia Roi were finally sending down roots in their new home.

Ellie slid into a row of chairs and sat down next to Connor. Her brother had been officially restored to his post as captain of the *Legend* and sported a shiny new medal on his coat for his bravery as a prisoner of war. Connor said he didn't care about pieces of metal, but Ellie caught him polishing it every chance he got.

On Ellie's other side was Vivian, holding a bouncing Tal on her lap. Kiaran sat watchfully a few chairs down, having taken over Hoyan's role as Tal's bodyguard. The baby cooed and gurgled with oblivious happiness. At almost seven months old, he was growing a fine sheen of sandy hair and learned new skills every day—already he could roll over and make an extensive variety of noises. And supernaturally heal coral, of course.

"Everything all right backstage?" Jariel whispered.

"Yes. Meggie was just a little nervous," Ellie explained.

The crowd hushed as the First Choir, dressed in their sky-blue robes, mounted the stage. At their head, Alyce gave a small bow to the audience. She had helped select and train new singers, many of them orphaned children, to replace those who had been lost in the battle. The choir had become a new family for them, and the harmonies they created as they began the Song were truly angelic.

You were the first, there at the beginning,
you are the last, the final note of the Song.
You call green shoots out from ash,
You make broken coral branches whole.
Singer of all new mornings,
Behold! You are coming soon.

They sang from memory, without the aid of a Song Book, though Vivian had carefully catalogued all surviving copies of the Book and recommended a filing system to the new Academy librarian. The First Choir's gesture was symbolic, reminding the Vestigians that *they* were the Song, and that new music could surprise them at any time.

After the singing, the new councilmembers gave their speeches. Lady Lilia, continuing her role as Alirya advisor, sat with them on the stage. Meggie was the last councilmember to speak. If she was still nervous, no one could tell. She took the stage with an air of complete confidence.

"Brothers and sisters, fellow Vestigians," she said, her clear voice ringing across the courtyard. "We are here today, not only to commission new councilmembers, but to celebrate a new beginning in the history of the Vestigia Roi—the Fourth Age. We remember those who courageously gave their lives to make this possible. Let us honor them with a moment of silence."

Though the courtyard was packed with people, the air went absolutely still. Everyone knew someone who had fallen in the battle against the dragon. Ellie thought of Hoyan and the brave fleet commanders, grateful for the sacrifice they had made.

After a long moment, Meggie continued.

"May this be the time when the ancient Vestigian prophecy is fulfilled:

When all the islands rejoin
and Aletheia again is One Kingdom,
The Captain of Winged Armies
Will return to rule his own.

Already it is coming into being!"

Meggie signaled a pair of attendants. They brought forward a large, beautifully tiled garden pot. From the dirt inside it sprouted a slender, vibrant stalk of green.

"The new stellaria tree of the Vestigia Roi!"

A cheer went up from the crowd.

"As this tree grows and flowers, so may the Vestigia Roi also grow and flower. May we work, and wait, and hope, in expectation of that day." Meggie saluted the crowd. "To the One Kingdom!"

The crowd returned the salute with the new response: "It is coming, it is here!"

Ellie clapped and cheered along with the rest of the assembly. At the end of their row, she saw Radburne wipe his eyes. She guessed what he might be feeling. Though he had once been a traitor, today he was sitting here watching his daughter be elected to a position of honor and responsibility. In her own way, Ellie felt the same. She had disobeyed the Council, run away from the Vestigia Roi, and placed her friends in danger. By rights, neither she nor Radburne belonged in this assembly. And yet, like drifting islands given new coral roots, here they were, welcomed back to watch the Vestigia Roi bloom. They, too, were a part of the One Kingdom, which made room even for traitors and runaways. It was coming, but it was also already here.

After the celebration, the *Legend's* crew gathered for a farewell supper in Jude, Vivian, and Tal's rooms. The space was almost empty of furniture, though of course a few books were still stacked here and there. Tomorrow the *Legend* would be setting out on its journey around Aletheia. It was time for Tal to begin his work of rejoining the islands. Jude, Vivian, and Kiaran were, of course, going with him, along with Connor as captain and Jariel as navigator of the *Legend*. But not all the old crewmembers would be joining them.

"Remember when we had a party like this at Jude and Vivian's flat on Rhynlyr?" Jariel asked, slurping a spoonful of stew. "It was your birthday, Ellie. Well, yours too, Connor."

"I remember making that cake," sighed Connor dreamily. "Maybe I can get back to baking once we're aboard the *Legend* again. I want to try making those pastries that we had in the…the garden."

"Don't have all the fun without me," said Ellie, poking him teasingly in the ribs. "I want to try some."

"Me too!" said Owen. "You know how Academy food is."

"Maybe it'll be better now that Meggie's on the Council," said Alyce. "She'll put in a good word for us."

"There's still time for you all to change your minds and join us on the voyage," said Finn.

Aimee huffed dramatically, startling Zira on her shoulder. "I wish I was going. I don't want to go to school."

"You'll like it once you get started, Aim," said Alyce. "We'll always love sailing, but our places are here for now. Besides, once Academy classes get started, I'm sure you'll be too busy to be sad."

"Yeah," Owen echoed. "With so few professors left, you might even get asked to be a class aide. Not too many people can teach beast speaking, after all." He patted Sunny's head. Aimee reached over to scratch the dog's belly, and he thumped his tail on the floor.

"I finally got a response to my letter to Brother Reinholdt today," said Ellie, holding up an envelope. "Now that the Council doesn't need me, he says I can come to Amalpura right away to begin training as an illuminator. I'm leaving in the morning aboard Captain Radburne's ship, the *Fortitude*. I can't wait, but Brother Reinholdt warned me that it's going to be a lot of work."

"Sounds difficult. Much better to run away aboard the *Legend*," Finn said with a wink, strumming a few chords on his harp.

Ellie smiled and shook her head. "I'm not afraid of hard work, and I'm excited for what I'm going to learn. But I'll miss you all very much. Anyway, who are you to lecture me about leaving, Mr. Innish Bard? The *Legend* is dropping you off in the Orkent Isles to teach people more about the One Kingdom and the Song."

Finn shrugged one shoulder with an impish smile. "It was worth a try."

"Speaking of letters and messages, I almost forgot," Vivian said, pulling a small roll of paper from her pocket. Tal tried to put it in his mouth, but Vivian whisked it out of reach just in time. "This arrived from Kai and Korrina aboard the *Defiance*. They wish us all safe journeys and say they're sorry not to be able to see us off in person. But their mission to recapture the other Havens is going well. Dhar and Amalpura were safe to begin with, and Ilorin is safe now, but they've managed to liberate Gwalior and Sylt, which means there are just two left. Korrina says that now the urken just seem to give up when they see Vestigians coming. With Draaken in hiding at the bottom of the ocean, his headquarters and Genesis Engine destroyed, I can imagine the urken are terrified."

"With Kai and Korrina working as a team, how could they not be?" said Connor. "The Enemy's remaining soldiers don't stand a chance."

"The Kingdom is coming," murmured Jude.

"I can't wait for the day Draaken is defeated forever," said Ellie.

In the morning, Ellie and her friends gathered at the docks. It was time for them to say their goodbyes and set out on their new voyages. Owen, Alyce, Aimee, and Meggie were staying on Ilorin, but the rest were dressed in their nautical uniforms—all except for Katha, who would be traveling with Ellie as far as Freith and wearing a frilly dress the whole way.

Ellie hugged her friends one by one. Sunny licked her hand, and Tal gurgled and waved his arms. Meggie sniffled. "We'll miss you, Ellie."

"*I* miss you already." Jariel squeezed Ellie's ribs in a bone-crushing hug.

"Voyaging on the *Legend* won't be the same without you," said Connor, his voice low and tight.

Ellie hugged her brother. "Neither will Amalpura without you. Though," she sniffled, "it will definitely be quieter."

"Hey!" Connor bumped Jariel's shoulder. "She's the loud one, not me."

"Be nice to her, Connor," said Ellie. "You might be…spending more time together in the future."

"Huh? Like aboard the *Legend?* It's not like we can avoid each other," said Connor, wrinkling his nose.

Ellie shrugged, a smile peeking through her tears. "Who knows? Just be nice. You might thank me one day. And…take care of yourself."

Connor ruffled her hair. "You too."

"We made you something, "said Jude, pulling a parcel from behind his back. "To take with you."

Curiously, Ellie pulled away the cloth wrapping.

Inside was a beautiful new sketchbook. It was covered in fine leather, with careful stitches binding the pages together. Ellie stared at it in amazement.

"Open it!" squealed Jariel.

The first pages of the book were already filled with notes and sketches. "Smooth sailing!" wrote Alyce. "Bring me back some bugs to classify!" said Owen.

"The rest of the pages are for you to fill," said Vivian. "With your new adventures and illuminations."

"I will," said Ellie, blinking back the tears brimming in her eyes. "I'll draw in it every day until I see you all again."

Finally it was time to go. Owen, Alyce, Aimee, and Meggie stood waving on the pier while Katha joined Radburne on the *Fortitude* and Connor led his crew aboard the *Legend*. But Finn hung back with Ellie. He flipped to the second page of the sketchbook.

"That one's mine," he said, pointing to a tiny but incredibly detailed Innish knot, painstakingly drawn in green ink. "It took me two hours. Those knots are more complicated than they look."

"Most things are," said Ellie, looking up into his face. "Thank you, Finn."

"You're welcome." He shifted awkwardly from foot to foot. "Don't stay away forever, Ellie. I…I'll miss you."

Warmth bloomed inside Ellie. "No," she said softly. "I won't stay away forever—only until I've learned to use the gift I've been given." She grinned. "And you can come visit me, you know."

Finn smiled. "Hey, that's a pretty good idea. Maybe I will."

Then it was time for Ellie to board the *Fortitude*. As the ship sailed west, she looked back and watched the *Legend*, carrying so many of her dearest ones, shrink to a small speck in the bright morning sky. Ellie hugged her new sketchbook. How she would miss her crew. But, as she'd promised Finn, she knew they wouldn't stay apart forever.

Ellie crossed the deck to stand at the bow of the *Fortitude*. As she looked forward with her clear eyes, a fresh wind rose and stirred her hair. This might be the end of her voyages aboard the *Legend*, at least for now. But it was not the end of her sailing. There were still journeys to take, illuminations to draw, and a Kingdom, both coming and already here, to reunite. And as Ellie began to hum the music of the Song that was in her heart, her vision changed so she could almost see it.

Glossary

A

Academy, the: School on <u>Rhynlyr</u>, comprised of <u>Administrative</u>, <u>Scholastic</u>, <u>Nautical</u>, and <u>Occupational</u> Houses, that trains future members of the <u>Vestigia Roi</u>.

Administrative House: <u>Academy</u> House focusing on <u>Vestigian</u> business, political leadership, and diplomacy. Its emblem is a ten-pointed star.

Adona Roi (uh-DOE-nah roh-EE): "The Good King"; the immortal and supernatural ruler of <u>The One Kingdom</u>.

Ahearn (AH-hern): Chieftain of the <u>Innish</u>; commander in the <u>Vestigia Roi</u>.

Aimee Kellar (KELL-ahr): Six-year-old sister of <u>Alyce Kellar</u>, gifted with the ability to communicate with animals.

Aletheia (ah-LEE-thee-ah): The known world, home to the <u>Four Archipelagos</u>. Its surface is covered with ocean and dotted with islands.

Alirya (ull-EER-yah): Supernatural winged beings, servants and messengers of <u>Ishua</u>, <u>Rua</u>, and <u>Adona Roi</u>.

Alyce Kellar (AL-iss KELL-ahr): A twelve-year-old <u>Scholastic</u> student with an exceptional singing voice. Accompanist to <u>Ellie,</u> daughter of <u>Estir Kellar</u>, older sister of <u>Aimee Kellar</u>.

Amalpura (ah-mall-PUR-ah): Southernmost of the <u>Vestigian Havens.</u>

Anadyr (ANN-ah-deer): <u>Newdonian</u> island; <u>Jude Sterlen</u>'s home island.

Arcvon (ARK-vonn): A <u>Lagorite</u> agent and servant of <u>Draaken</u>.

Arjun Mador (ARR-jen mah-DORE): One of the Four <u>Archipelagos</u>.

Asthmenos (ASTH-men-ows): A poison deadly to island-supporting coral. Its only antidote is <u>caris</u> powder.

Aton (AH-tawn): Fever-reducing plant.

B

Basilean (bah-sill-AY-en): Term of contempt for a member of the Vestigia Roi, most commonly used in Newdonia.

Black borrage root (BLACK BORE-udge ROOT): Antidote for helkath poison.

Bramborough: A Newdonian island.

C

Calida (CAL-i-duh): A Newdonian commander in the Vestigia Roi.

Caris (CARE-iss): Powder made from the leaves of the stellaria tree, used to feed and restore coral sickened by asthmenos poison.

Cloud trout: A type of fish native to clouds; common food source for flying Vestigian ship crews.

Connor Reid: Fourteen-year-old captain of the *Legend*, twin brother to Ellie.

Cooley, Horaffe, Loretha, and Ewart Horaffe Theodemir (YOO-art HOR-aff thee-AWE-deh-meer COO-lee): Ellie's former adoptive family.

Council, The: The highest human authority over Rhynlyr and the Vestigia Roi. Made up of four elected members, one from each House, plus an Alirya adviser.

Cygnera (sig-NER-ah): Swan-like bird; figurehead of the *Legend*.

D

Daevin Blenrudd (DAY-vinn BLEN-rudd): Deceased Vestigian sailor and former captain of the *Legend*.

Defiance: A Vestigian ship under the command of Kai.

Deniev (DEN-ee-ev): Vestigian sailor; husband to Laralyn and father of Gresha.

Dhar (DAR): Vestigian Haven being used as a safe base and staging ground for the attack on Rhynlyr.

Draaken (DRAY-ken): "The Deceiver," the supernatural being served by believers in Khum Lagor. Occasionally takes physical form as a great sea serpent.

Dshinn (JINN): A powerful servant of Draaken that inhabits a human's mind and communicates what it learns to its master.

Œ

Edge, the: The boundary of Aletheia and the ultimate fate of islands that break free from their coral trees. None who go over it have ever returned.

Elbarra Cluster (ell-BAR-ah): The fifth archipelago of Aletheia, believed to have been destroyed by asthmenos during Thelipsa's Rebellion. See Lost Archipelago.

E'liahnea (eh-lee-AH-nyah): Innish word meaning *light*.

Ellianea Reid (ell-ee-an-AY-ah REED): A fourteen-year-old girl with the gifts of a seer and an illuminator. Daughter to Kiria Reid and Gavin Reid, sister to Connor Reid. Her name means *light*.

Ellie Altess (ALL-tess): See Ellianea Reid.

Estir Kellar: Late mother of Alyce and Aimee Kellar.

Eyret (EYE-ret): Heron-like messenger bird used by the Vestigia Roi.

ℑ

Finn: Fifteen-year-old Innish orphan and shanachai, now a sailor aboard the *Legend*.

Firestars: Missiles that fall, blazing bright trails, then explode on impact.

Fortitude: Ship captained by Errol Radburne.

Four Archipelagos, The (ARK-i-PELL-ah-go): Groups of islands connected to a single coral tree. Aletheia's four surviving archipelagos are Newdonia, the Orkent Isles, Arjun Mador, and the Numed Archipelago. The Fifth or Lost Archipelago was called the Elbarra Cluster.

Freith (FREETH): Newdonian island; Ellie's home island.

G

Gresha: Daughter to Deniev and Laralyn.

ℌ

Hakara/hakaran (HAH-kah-rah): Literally, "fire mountain"; Numbani for *volcano*.

Hasheya (ha-SHAY-ah): Nakuran leader, mother of Omondi.

Havens: Vestigian flying islands; outposts of refuge and sources of lumenai for the One Kingdom.

Helkath (HELL-kath): Butterfly-like creatures of Draaken whose bites cause a loss of hope in their victims.

Hoyan (ho-YAHN): One of the Alirya; a winged messenger of Ishua, Rua, and Adona Roi.

I

Ilorin Reformatory: A flying island prison for violent or traitorous Vestigian criminals. Rehabilitation is encouraged, but some prisoners remain on the island for life.

Innish: An island in the Orkent Isles. The word is also used as an adjective for the island's inhabitants.

Intrepid: A Vestigian ship commanded by Vice Admiral Trull.

Ishua (ISH-oo-ah): Son of Adona Roi, Commander of the Winged Armies, bringer of caris to the islands, and founder of the Vestigia Roi.

Ithrom Jaron (ITH-rum JARE-un): A regent in the Second Age who first began to record the Song.

J

Janaki (jah-NAH-kee): An island in the Numed Archipelago, formerly the home island of Makundo and Korrina. Also an adjective used for residents of the island.

Jariel Kirke (jare-ee-ELL KIRK): Spunky thirteen-year-old girl with an interest in navigation; Ellie's best friend.

Jude Sterlen (JOOD STIR-lenn): Vestigian doctor and second mate aboard the *Legend*, husband to Vivian Edrei.

K

Kai: Vestigian commander and captain of the *Defiance*, formerly bodyguard to Ellianea Reid.

Kaspar (KASS-par): Early Lagorite, servant of Draaken, deceiver of Thelipsa, and first known source of asthmenos.

Katha Radburne: Elder daughter of Errol Radburne.

Kentish: A family of dialects spoken in the Orkent Isles.

Khum Lagor (KOOM la-GORE): The ultimate goal of all Lagorites: to subjugate or destroy all land-walkers until the whole world serves Draaken.

Kiaran (kee-ARR-un): One of the Alirya; a winged messenger of Ishua, Rua, and Adona Roi.

Kingdom Bridge: An iconic Rhynlyr monument formed from the living roots of the original stellaria tree, reportedly planted by Ishua himself.

Knerusse (neh-ROOS): A long-dead language of Aletheia, original language of lyrics to the Song.

Korrina (corr-INN-ah): A Janaki warrior; captain of the *Venture*.

ℒ

Lagora (LAH-gor-ah): Moveable underwater island, headquarters of Draaken.

Lagorites (LAH-gore-ites): Followers of Draaken and believers in Khum Lagor.

Laralyn (LEH-rah-linn): Wife to Deniev and mother of Gresha.

Legend: A Vestigian ship.

Lilia, Lady (LILL-ee-ah): One of the Alirya; a winged messenger of Ishua, Rua, and Adona Roi.

Lost Archipelago, The: Modern name for the Elbarra Cluster, believed to have been destroyed during Thelipsa's Rebellion.

Lumena, lumenai (LOO-men-ah, LOO-men-eye): Water ferns whose fronds carry electrical current. Cultivated at Havens, they power Vestigian flying ships and islands.

ℳ

Makundo (mah-KOON-doe): A Janaki warrior.

Mapepo: Literally, "demon spawn." Janaki word for *urken*.

Markos (MAR-kose): Former lookout and navigator aboard the *Legend*.

Meggie Radburne: Younger daughter of Errol Radburne.

Melkyr Mountains: (MELL-keer): A mountain range on Rhynlyr.

Mharra (MAR-ah): A volcanic island in the Numed Archipelago, former hideout of the Vestigia Roi.

Moby: A Mundarvan bluestripe ribbon snake owned by Owen Mardel.

Mor Nathar (MORE nah-THAR): "The Great Serpent," Innish manifestation of Draaken worshiped as a deity.

Mordaz (MORE-dazz): A powerful dshinn.

Mundarva (mun-DARR-vuh): An island, now destroyed, from the south of Newdonia; a renowned center of learning and home of the Mundarva Library.

N

Nakuru (nah-KOO-roo): A desert island in the Numed Archipelago known for its skilled cliff climbers.

Nautical House: Academy House focusing on training members of the Vestigian fleet. Its symbol is a four-pronged propeller.

Navir (nah-VEER): Suor term of respect meaning *teacher*.

Newdonia (noo-DOE-nee-ah): One of the Four Archipelagos.

Nikira (ni-KEER-ah): Draaken's highest-ranking Valsha.

Numbani: A family of dialects spoken in the Numed Archipelago; also an adjective used for residents of that archipelago.

Numed Archipelago (NOO-med): One of the Four Archipelagos.

O

Occupational House: Academy House focusing on teaching skilled trades. Its emblem is a wheel.

Omondi (oh-MOAN-dee): Nakuran cliff climber, son of Hasheya. Now a commander in the Vestigia Roi.

One Kingdom, the: The original state of Aletheia; all the archipelagos unified under the governance of Adona Roi. Its restoration is the goal of the Vestigia Roi.

Orkent Isles (OR-kent): One of the Four Archipelagos.

Oron Talmai (OR-on TAL-mye): A historical Vestigian seer and warrior whose military victory ended Lagorite violence for three hundred years.

Owen Mardel (MAR-dell): A ten-year-old boy with an interest in animals and science.

P

Phylla (FILL-ah): Former acting councilwoman for the Vestigia Roi.

Pinta: Miniature tortoise owned by Owen Mardel.

R

Radburne, Errol: Former Administrative member of the Council on Rhynlyr and father to Katha and Meggie Radburne. After he betrayed the Vestigia Roi to Draaken, he disappeared.

Regents: Caretakers of the islands appointed by Adona Roi during the Second Age. Some became hungry for more power, leading to revolts like Thelipsa's Rebellion.

Reid, Gavin and Kiria: Vestigian agents, late parents of Ellie and Connor Reid.

Reinholdt, Brother (RINE-holt): Head illuminator at the Vestigian Haven at Amalpura.

Rhynlyr (RINN-leer): Historical headquarters of the Vestigia Roi; the largest and most central flying island.

Rilia (RILL-ee-ah): Plants commonly known as "falling stars." Its berries are used for relief of stomach pain.

Rua (ROO-ah): A supernatural presence equal to Adona Roi and Ishua. Invisible and mysterious, it offers Vestigians a source of power, guidance, and inspiration.

S

Sai (SIGH): Long, slender daggers.

Saklos Mountain (SACK-lows): A mountain on Dhar containing the Vestigian fortress of Vellir.

Scholastic House: Academy House focusing on the three branches of academics: the languages, the sciences, and the arts. Its emblem is a triskele.

Scorpionflies: Creatures of Draaken whose stings cause temporary, localized paralysis.

Serle (SURL): Former acting councilman for the Vestigia Roi.

Shanachai (SHAHN-ah-hai): Innish for *bard* or *storyteller*.

Sketpoole (SKET-pool): A coastal city on Freith.

Song of Ishua, The: The powerful, continuously developing melody used by Adona Roi to create life and sustain the universe. Also the anthem of the Vestigia Roi and the basis of Ellie's visions.

Stellaria (stell-AH-ree-ah): Tree native to the City of Adona Roi, transplanted to Rhynlyr by Ishua. Later clippings were planted on other Havens. Stellaria leaves are used to make caris powder.

Sunny: A shaggy golden dog belonging to Owen Mardel.

Suor (soo-OR): An island, now destroyed, in the south of Arjun Mador.

Sylvia Galen (GAY-len): A Vestigian agent and keeper of the Sketpoole Home for Boys and Girls.

T

Talmai Sterlen (TAL-mye STIR-lenn): Infant son of Jude and Vivian Sterlen, gifted with the ability to heal broken coral branches.

Tangwystl (tang-GWI-stul): Finn's harp.

Tehber (teh-BARE): A dead language of Aletheia.

Thelipsa (thell-IPS-uh): Regent and later queen of Vansuil, instigator of Thelipsa's Rebellion, and destroyer of the Elbarra Cluster.

Thelipsa's Rebellion: The first large-scale show of disloyalty to the One Kingdom. Thelipsa followed Lagorite advice and used asthmenos to break up the Elbarra Cluster, leading to the eventual poisoning of Aletheia's other islands.

Tobin, Councilman (TOE-binn): Former Occupational member of the Council on Rhynlyr.

Triskele (TRISS-kell): A design made up of three intersecting spirals. The emblem of Scholastic House.

Trull, Admiral: Head of the Vestigian Council.

Twyrild (TWEER-illd): A Newdonian island; Owen Mardel's home island.

𝔘

Ulfurssh (ULL-fursh): Contemptuous <u>Lagorite</u> term for the <u>Vestigia Roi</u>.

Ujuba (oo-JOO-bah): Waxy berries whose oil burns slowly and is suitable for use in lanterns.

Urken (URR-ken): Cruel and brutal creatures of <u>Draaken</u>; souls plundered from falling islands and attached to deformed bodies.

𝔙

Vahye (VA-yay): An island in <u>Arjun Mador</u>; <u>Vivian Sterlen's</u> home island.

Valsha (VAL-shuh): Former <u>Alirya</u>, now <u>Draaken's</u> captains and most powerful servants.

Vansuil (VAHN-soo-ill): Island governed by <u>Thelipsa</u> in the lost <u>Elbarra Cluster.</u>

Vellir (vell-EAR): <u>Vestigian</u> fortress on <u>Dhar</u>.

Venture: A <u>Vestigian</u> ship commanded by <u>Korrina</u>.

Verana (vehr-AH-nah): The original <u>Aletheian</u> continent, which later broke into the Five <u>Archipelagos</u>.

Vestigia Roi (ves-TI-jee-ah roh-EE): A secret organization following <u>Ishua</u>, <u>Adona Roi</u>, and <u>Rua</u>, whose goal is to restore the <u>One Kingdom</u>. They use land-based agents as well as flying ships and islands to counter the effects of <u>asthmenos</u> with <u>caris</u> powder and rescue people from falling islands. Members are known as <u>Vestigians</u>, but are sometimes called <u>Basileans</u> as a term of contempt.

Vestigian (ves-TI-jee-an): A member of the <u>Vestigia Roi</u>.

Vivian Sterlen (STIR-lenn): <u>Vestigian</u> scholar and linguist, wife to <u>Jude Sterlen</u> and mother of <u>Talmai Sterlen.</u>

𝔷

Zarifah (zarr-EE-fah): A blind seer from the island of <u>Suor</u>, late mentor to <u>Ellianea Reid</u>.

Zelfmyr (ZELF-meer): A leaf that purportedly cures bruises.

Zira (ZEER-ah): Falcon belonging to <u>Aimee Kellar.</u>

Discussion Questions

1. Why does Ellie disobey the Council's orders to stay on Dhar? (29-30)

2. Why does Ellie first agree to cooperate with Draaken? What changes her mind later? (116, 151)

3. At first Meggie doesn't want to allow her father back into the Vestigia Roi—or her life. Why does she decide to give him a second chance? (123)

4. Why does Radburne risk returning to the Vestigia Roi? (143)

5. Why does the Vestigian fleet decide to attack Draaken in his lair, even though they know they may not win? (147)

6. Why does the crew of the Legend decide to use their lumena to blow up the Genesis Engine, even though it means they will likely not survive? (193)

7. Ishua advises the crew, "Listen to the song that is in your heart...then watch for places where the world needs music" (220). What do you think he means?

8. Ellie feels like a traitor for cooperating with Draaken. Yet Ishua later tells her, "You have shown great courage" (221). What does he mean?

9. Why do you think those who have seen the Eternal Garden are unable to describe it to others? (238)

10. Though Ellie at first despises Radburne for his treachery, how are the two of them alike? How does Ellie view Radburne differently by the end of the story? (244)

11. Radburne gets a second chance to be part of the Vestigia Roi. Who else gets a second chance in this story?

12. What do you think it means that the One Kingdom is both coming and already here?

Project Ideas

1. At the beginning of the story, Finn composes a poem in tribute to Connor (19). Compose your own poem in honor of one of your friends.

2. For the feast on Vellir, Katha, Hoyan, and the youngest Vestigians create table centerpieces out of pinecones (18). Try creating a table centerpiece out of materials collected from around your home.

3. Connor tries to figure out how to re-create the delicious pastries in the Eternal Garden (218). Find your own recipe for sweet pastries. Then try baking them with help from an adult!

4. When the Vestigia Roi establish a new home on Ilorin, they plant Ishua's stellaria seed and wait for it to grow into a tree (244). Plant some seeds in a garden pot and watch them sprout!

5. When the crew of the *Legend* returns to Freith, they are welcomed by banners decorated with the VR symbol (233). Make your own VR banner and hang it up in a window.

Acknowledgments

What a journey this book series has been! Over the last nine years of conceptualizing, writing, revising, and publishing, the *Legend* has certainly taken me on some exciting voyages, and in many ways Ellie and I have grown up together. While I am excited for my next writing project, I will also miss living in this magical world of ocean and islands.

So many people have been part of these adventures that it is impossible to name them all here. But here are a few without whom this final book would not have been possible.

Mama: You've faithfully attended book events, uncoiled me from the fetal position more than once, and kept me from homelessness and insanity throughout the process. Thank you not only for proofreading, but also for reminding me to eat, go outside, and even have fun sometimes. Most of all, thank you for your steadfast and loyal cheerleading all along the way.

Daniel: Thank you to my bloodthirsty war correspondent for making sure my tacticians actually used tactics and that people didn't walk into too many obvious traps. I hope you enjoyed getting to harpoon a shark!

Hamlet: My sweet puppy, you sat with me (sometimes on me) through many long hours of writing/revising. Thank you for your unconditional love and for reminding Mom to get out of her chair and cuddle you sometimes. I love you even when you walk all over my manuscript pages!

Whitney: Thanks for getting me thinking about water dragons! More than that, thank you for always being supportive and interested in what's going on in my imaginary world.

Jenny Zemanek of Seedlings Design Studio: Your artwork, once again, blows me away. This fourth cover was a challenge, but thank you so much for your incredible patience and creativity along the way! I'm so happy with the final product!

Angela Wallace: Thank you for formatting my entire series of lovely e-books!

I'd like to thank Dale Chihuly and the late Julia Morgan for the inspiration their art and architecture gave me.

This book would not have been possible without coffee beans. I offer them my sincerest appreciation.

Thank you to my amazing test readers: Evgenia A., Amy and Sarah B., Tom, Tammy, and Michael C., Colin G., Robbie R., and Daniel S. Your diverse and insightful perspectives helped me spot and fix problems I didn't even know were there! Thanks for your enthusiasm and for making this a better book for everyone!

Finally, to everyone who will pick up this book and read it: thank you. You encourage me to keep on sharing stories.

About The Author

Alina Sayre began her literary career chewing on board books and has been in love with words ever since. Now she is the award-winning author of *The Voyages of the Legend* fantasy series as well as an educator, editor, and speaker. Her first novel, *The Illuminator's Gift*, won a silver medal in the Moonbeam Children's Book Awards and was a finalist in the Shelf Unbound Best Indie Book competition and a semifinalist for the BookLife Prize in Fiction. All four *Voyages of the Legend* books have received 4- or 5-star reviews from Readers' Favorite. When she's not writing, Alina enjoys hiking, crazy socks, and reading under blankets. She does not enjoy algebra or wasabi. When she grows up, she would like to live in a castle with a large library.

If you enjoyed this book, please help spread the word by sharing a review on Amazon.com!

Connect with Alina online!

Website: alinasayre.com

E-mail: alinasayreauthor@gmail.com

Facebook: www.facebook.com/alinasayreauthor

Twitter: @AlinaSayre